JENNIFER S. ALDERSON

Rituals of the Dead

An Artifact Mystery

First published by Traveling Life Press 2019

Second edition

ISBN: 978-9-083001-12-8

This book was professionally typeset on Reedsy.
Find out more at reedsy.com

Contents

Dedication

To my darling son—for putting up with another book.

Author's Note

Life is often stranger than fiction, and the coincidences that occur are sometimes extraordinary. In 2008, I worked on an exhibition of Asmat bis poles in the Tropenmuseum, two of which were collected by Michael Rockefeller in 1961. I also witnessed the opening of several crates of Asmat artifacts that had been lying in the depot of Rotterdam's Wereldmuseum (World Museum) for more than fifty years. Because a paradigm shift occurred while these objects were on a ship destined for the Netherlands, they were moved from the freighter to the depot and forgotten about. During my internship, the Tropenmuseum (Museum of the Tropics) was also wrestling with an extensive collection of human remains, many of which were collected in the 1930s through the 1960s in Dutch New Guinea.

Because the chapters set in the Asmat region take place in 1962, I refer to historical events as taking place in "Dutch New Guinea." Nowadays, this region is part of the Indonesian providence of Papua. This is why I also refer to the government of Papua when alluding to contemporary events in the region.

These facts provided the context, and several actual museums the settings, for my artifact mystery. The resulting story, all of the characters involved, and the restitution cases discussed in this novel are figments of my imagination.

How to Survive on Land and Sea

August 17, 1962

"Dip, scoop, pour. Dip, scoop, pour. Dip, scoop, pour." Nick Mayfield's dry lips cracked open as he repeated his mantra. Just a few more inches, then she'll float as the survival guide had explained. He leaned against the T-shirt and bits of plank filling the gashes in the sides of the canoe, willing the stream of seawater to stop pouring in faster than he could scoop it out.

The sun was slowly descending, growing in size as it neared the horizon. Bands of pink and orange streaked across the sky, intensifying in color by the second. The new moon was barely a sliver. In an hour's time, he would be plunged into darkness.

Nick squinted to orient himself, thankful he could see an emerald belt of jungle rising in the distance. He must be in Flamingo Bay, he reckoned, and not too far from land. Still, the expanse of blue-green water between him and the shore was vast. A strong wind tried to push him seabound. Only the weight of the water and a few crates of barter goods still filling its hull kept the canoe in sight of land. Nick sighed. He was in for a long paddle back once his boat was seaworthy again.

Nick stopped scooping to reposition the jeans tied to his head, arranging the legs so that they covered most of his sunburned back. His thoughts turned to the eight rowers who had jumped overboard hours ago. Had they already made it to shore? Nick wondered for the hundredth time if he should have abandoned ship and swum back

3

with them. Though his faith in his survival guide was unwavering, the water was rushing in extremely fast. The holes were too large to plug completely.

Nick gazed again toward the shoreline. He was a strong swimmer. He knew he could still make it to land if he had to, but he wouldn't leave his boat unless there were no other options. His guide made it clear you should never abandon ship until all attempts to save it have failed. It was the captain's code. Okay, the real captain had jumped overboard hours ago, but still. It was Nick's collection trip that went amiss and his supplies now bobbing in the waves close to his crippled watercraft.

Nick shook his head in disdain, certain the locals had given up too quickly. They all sprang into the water and began swimming as soon as they had discovered the first leak. If only they hadn't moved that bag of beads, then the water wouldn't have filled the hull so quickly. Nick bashed his coffee tin onto the bottom of the canoe as he scooped, his irritation manifesting itself as Albert Schenk entered his mind. *That Dutchman should be here helping me,* Nick thought. His fever couldn't have come at a worse moment.

A few feet away, a gurgling noise made him jump. The second canoe finally took on more water than it could handle. As soon as the holes in both were found, he'd cut it loose along with the makeshift platform connecting them together like a catamaran. Nick's face paled as he watched its stern slowly rise until the canoe was perpendicular to the water's surface. The platform hung off it like a starched flag. Nick watched in fascination as it stood stock-still, seemingly frozen in space and time, before suddenly disappearing into the sea. Several large air bubbles broke on the surface, the only sign the boat ever existed.

Nick gazed down into the dark water and redoubled his efforts.

Inexplicably, a can of tobacco soon rose from where the canoe had gone under, and it bobbed next to him. *Its airtight container would make a useful flotation device,* Nick thought, resolving to keep it in sight. Almost all of his supplies had gone under as soon as he cut the second canoe loose. The rest he had thrown into the sea in hopes of making his boat light enough that the two holes in the stern would rise above the water's surface. Not that he had to worry about wasting supplies. He had plenty more stored in Agats. Losing these trading goods was a minor delay, not a setback.

Nick laughed, splitting his lip further. Blood dripped down his chin as his thin bray drifted across the waves. *Just as capsizing and sinking was a minor irritation,* he thought, giggling again despite the pain.

Cracks of lightning tore across the broad sky. Thunder rumbled seconds later. The storm was closing in fast, Nick realized. He hadn't taken into consideration the storms that frequently whipped across the jungle. If the rain started soon, he would never be able to get the boat floating enough to paddle back. Especially with only one oar to help—the rest had floated away in the ensuing panic when his rowers discovered the gashes in both boats' sterns.

As a second streak lit up the sky, Nick cleared his mind and focused on nothing but his coffee can. *Dip, scoop, pour. Dip, scoop, pour.* He had to survive—he was a Mayfield. It was his destiny to do great things, not die in the open ocean. *Dip, scoop, pour. Dip, scoop, pour.* And as every Mayfield knew, he had his destiny in his own hands.

Human Remains project

May 1, 2017

The bones spread out on the table before her were a creamy white. In contrast to the first batch they'd viewed, these were clean of any bodily tissues and the overpowering smell of decay. Even so, Zelda Richardson had to stifle her gag reflex constantly to remain in the room.

Bert Reiger followed her gaze down toward the skeletal remains. "She was a native of the Asmat region in Southwest Papua," the curator and head of the Human Remains project stated. "Shall we begin today's session, or do you have to throw up again?" he added rather irritated, clearly eager to get the workday started.

Zelda tore her eyes away from the fifty-year-old bones on the table in front of her and gazed across the vast hall. Spread out before her were twenty rollaway tables containing a variety of femurs, ribs, hips, vertebrae, and skulls. These were the remains of men, women, and children transported halfway around the world in the name of science. A few of the beds held a complete skeleton, though most missed crucial pieces. They reminded Zelda of half-completed puzzles waiting for a patient curator and his two assistants to solve.

Even though these skeletal remains had been sterilized long ago, Zelda pinched the skin between her thumb and index finger as a distraction, preferring to draw blood than to puke on the medical slabs and mess up months of research. Death was not something she enjoyed contemplating, and this room reeked of it, literally. She'd barely made it to the toilet last time, and chances were she wouldn't be so lucky again.

"Thanks to the mishap at the Academic Medical Center, the contents of several crates were mixed together. Though we cannot assume the skeletons were crated up with all their parts when they left the islands..." The curator rattled on, immune to the visions of carnage dancing in Zelda's head. She'd read many newspaper articles about the Academic Medical Center's macabre findings two years earlier. A series of water leaks led to the discovery of sixty-five crates of human remains stored in the hospital's long unused atomic bomb shelter. They'd been sitting there for thirty-odd years, a forgotten 'gift' left to the medical center when a Dutch anatomical museum closed its doors. While reading those articles, Zelda never imagined she would be working for the project group tasked with sorting through them all.

Bert moved casually through the long rows as he continued the tour of his team's workspace. Zelda followed closely behind, watching his feet rather than the grisly assemblages. The impromptu lab was set up in the Tropenmuseum's external storage facilities, built several feet below the museum's parking lot. The fluorescent lights and windowless rooms reminded Zelda of a morgue, even without the body parts. Bert led them out of one hall and into another filled with giant papier-mâché dolls. Their bright colors and strange grins made her think of the figures she'd seen during Mardi Gras festivals on television.

"We bought these for the *Carnaval* exhibition five years ago," Bert explained, referring to the Netherlands' version of the Catholic celebration. The happy smiles and exuberant colors of the figures contrasted sharply with the remains in the adjoining space.

They passed through another door and were in the museum's archives. Rows of archival cabinets set on rollers filled one side. Empty reading tables lined the other. At the far end sat the Tropenmuseum's only archivist.

"Hi, Yvonne," Bert called out. "Let me introduce you," he said to Zelda, veering off toward Yvonne's desk.

The archivist's eyes remained on her computer until they were standing next to her. "This is my new intern, Zelda." He let them shake hands then asked, "I thought you were working topside."

"A researcher is coming by in a few minutes, and I needed to pull some files first. When are you going to be done, Bert?" Her irritation made it clear she was not thrilled the Human Remains lab had been set up on her turf.

Bert chuckled. "Not soon enough, apparently—for you or Victor Nalong."

Zelda knew Nalong, as the official representative of the government of Papua, had submitted a claim on the bones of his Asmat ancestors. The Tropenmuseum wasn't willing to release them until they'd completed their research, which was why they had assigned her to assist the team with data entry. At least, that's what her mentor told her. She still wasn't certain what her specific tasks would be. Zelda fervently hoped it didn't involve having to touch the remains.

"It's creepy enough down here without all those bones filling the spare rooms"—Yvonne sniffed—"not to mention the smells."

"We should be done in a few months."

Yvonne blanched then turned back to her computer with a huff.

"We'll leave you to work," Bert said, saluting the archivist as he led Zelda into another long hall filled with more skeletons on rollaway tables. This room smelled even mustier than the first one. In one corner, Bert's assistants were unpacking the last crate, gently laying the pieces stored in the foot-tall wooden box onto a rollaway table. Zelda blushed as her new boss waved at his staff. Jacob and Angela briefly looked up to establish eye contact and wave back before continuing with their work.

Zelda and Jacob had only been on a few dates since meeting at the Tropenmuseum's staff party last month, and his presence still made her stomach flip-flop with joy.

Bert, oblivious to his new intern's blossoming cheeks, walked to the closest table and picked up the clipboard hanging from the end of it. He positioned himself so Zelda could easily read along.

"These are the notes our researchers have made for each skeleton." He slowly flipped through several pages of illegible scribbles, stopping at one with a simple drawing of a naked man. It was a skeletal diagram, reminiscent of high school biology, with Roman numerals assigned to each bone.

On this sheet, several bones had been colored in lightly with blue, red, and green pencil so the numbers were still visible. "These colors tell us which bones have been found and the condition they are in. Blue is complete and undamaged. Green means chipped or fractured. Red is broken or incomplete. The anthropologists responsible for packing these crates up didn't always keep the bones of one corpse together. After they'd prepared them for shipment, many chose to pack up the remains in the most economical way. Because physical anthropologists were documenting an ethnic group—not individuals—they weren't concerned with keeping the skeletons complete, only the measurements of each bone. We've found several skeletons spread across two or even three crates. We've also had to discard some of the bones because they'd already succumbed to rot. That tells us the anthropologists who collected them didn't clean them properly before crating them up," Bert said, clearly not impressed by his predecessors' handling of these remains.

"How did they clean the bones?" Zelda asked, not really sure she wanted to hear the answer.

"The Asmat would place the body on a platform built high in the trees, which allowed insects and scavengers to strip it clean before the Asmat retrieved some of the bones—in particular, the skull and jawbone. Of course, there was always the risk that parts of their loved ones would be taken by larger predators, which is why they sometimes removed the head first."

Zelda covered her mouth and coughed hard. It reminded her of the way Tibetan monks disposed of their dead, chopping them up and laying them out for vultures to pick off the flesh. She understood why it happened in a rocky, mountainous region where there was little topsoil to dig a grave, but in a jungle, surely there was a way to bury the dead?

"Physical anthropologists boiled the bones in a mixture of bleach or barium. That was the most effective way of removing any residual muscle tissue and flesh. After the bones were clean, they would boil them in an alcohol bath to remove the oils, then allow them to air dry. The whole process took a day or two. Most physical anthropologists adhered by these rules, though some were careless and didn't boil them long enough, skipped the alcohol bath, or didn't allow them to dry completely before packing them up. Those remains often rotted before they made it back to the Netherlands."

Zelda tried hard not to visualize that process. She was sure her stomach wouldn't be able to handle the sights and smells of such a lengthy and gruesome procedure.

"This batch of crates is particularly sloppy. The man responsible for packing these up was an old Nazi who robbed graves. Van den Hof was his name, but we've nicknamed him the Vulture. He fled Europe after the war and set up a new life working in Dutch New Guinea as a physical anthropologist. We've had to throw away several crates he'd collected due to rot."

"A Nazi grave robber? Why would the museum buy objects from someone like that?" Zelda asked, incredulous.

"Grave robbers were useful allies of ethnographic museums back then. They were active everywhere physical anthropologists were working. The shape and size of a skull were important to the field of study while the rest of the body was secondary. And it didn't take a university degree to measure a bone. Several gravesites in Dutch New Guinea were robbed, as these crates attest. Colonial administrators, surveyors working for mining companies, explorers, and the like were all encouraged to send specimens to European museums. They

10

paid fairly well, which attracted all sorts."

Zelda had to force her jaw to close, surprised by what Bert was telling her.

Noticing her shock, the curator continued in a conspiratorial voice. "This mandate by Western museums to collect bones from their colonies meant most weren't worried about getting caught or punished for stealing human remains. For example, our friend the Vulture included notes in his crates recording the names of the villages whose graveyards he plundered and the dates he collected his samples. Between 1950 and 1963, he collected thirty-five crates full of remains, often only taking the skull. We've also found documents proving he took more than a thousand bones from a single gravesite. His notes make it possible to return those remains to the village they came from, a luxury we don't have in most cases."

"If you have documentation proving where they came from, why not return the crates to the villages he robbed?" Zelda asked.

"The crates contain remains collected in Dutch New Guinea, Borneo, Fiji, and Indonesia. After the flood at the Academic Medical Center, the bones got mixed together. We have to first reconstruct these skeletons and determine their ethnicity before we can give them back to their communities," he explained.

Bert's standpoint seemed logical enough, though Zelda knew Victor Nalong strongly disagreed. Marijke Torenbouwer had already told her about the controversy surrounding these remains. Well, most of the story. She'd said nothing about the grave robbers or the Nazi connection. Zelda knew Victor Nalong was breathing down the museum's neck to give them all of the crates and let their researchers reconstruct the skeletons. For Bert, Marijke, and the rest of the Tropenmuseum, it had become a point of pride to finish what they'd started. After all, Bert's team had already spent eighteen months sorting through everything and were days away from reconstructing all of the skeletons. The major holdup was the data entry, which was where Zelda came in. The faster the bones' measurements were entered into the museum's collection database, the happier the entire board of directors and Victor Nalong would be.

Bert tapped the clipboard. "So these notations and measurements correspond to bone numbers"—he flipped back through the hand-written notes—"and need to be entered into our database. If you aren't sure what one of the notes says, highlight it with a marker. I don't want you guessing. We need to enter this information exactly, or it will be worthless to our researchers. Oh, and the measurements are in centimeters, so don't forget that." Bert rubbed in the fact that she was American—again.

Zelda sighed inwardly, sensing this was going to be a long day. Bert had already interrogated her before coming down to the lab, certain her Dutch wouldn't withstand his tests. When she proved him wrong, he grudgingly invited her to join him for a tour. She was glad it was only twice a week, and it was nice to see Jacob at work. She hoped they could sneak away for coffee and a kiss later.

At least she had her train trip to Rotterdam and the opening of the Asmat crates tomorrow to look forward to. The Bis Poles exhibition was why she wanted to intern at the Tropenmuseum in the first place. The Asmat ancestor poles fascinated her as few ethnographic objects did. And the recent discovery of seven poles in the Wereldmuseum's depot, unopened since being shipped over from Dutch New Guinea in 1962, made the exhibition even more interesting. She only hoped the poles hadn't already succumbed to rot.

Asmat bis poles

May 2, 2017

"Watch out!"

Zelda automatically apologized and took a step forward off the foot of the older woman behind her. The bright camera flashes and video lights momentarily blinded her. The noise of the impatient crowd echoed off the high ceilings of the hangar-sized room. Hundreds of open racks were set up in the wall-less space, filled with cultural and artistic treasures collected from all corners of the globe. As one of the oldest ethnographic museums in the Netherlands, the Rotterdam's Wereldmuseum collection was so sizeable, they could only display about twenty percent of it in the museum's exhibition halls.

Zelda recognized most of the logos gracing the sides of the video cameras, though not all. She hadn't realized or expected so much press coverage. Obviously, all three of the museums' public relations departments had done their best to interest the local and national press. Then again, the story itself deserved their attention. There weren't many crates left unopened for fifty years in a museum depot, especially ones that contained such a monumental collection of artifacts.

The seven crates were time capsules, Zelda realized as she listened to Albert Schenk, the director of Wereldmuseum, eloquently describe the bis poles they were about to see. "These cultural treasures reached our shores at the same time indigenous communities were rightfully demanding equal rights and representation. This shift in political and cultural thought rendered these artifacts—collected for their association with headhunting—a shameful reminder of colonial attitudes," he lectured.

"These crates were pushed to the back of our depot and forgotten. If it were not for our upcoming exhibition, who knows how long they would have remained there. We still don't know what condition the poles are in." Albert looked out across the cameras, his stern gaze belying the twinkle in his eye. "Though, for the sake of our exhibition, we do hope they are still whole." He chuckled, and his remark received polite laughter in response.

Albert rattled on for another thirty minutes. His posture reminded Zelda of a red-breasted robin puffing up his chest. Just as she was starting to lose interest, Albert motioned for the co-creators of the upcoming exhibition to join him. Jaap Meulendijk and Karin Bakker, directors of the National Museum of Ethnology in Leiden and Tropenmuseum respectively, emerged from the crowd to stand next to Albert.

After introductions were complete, he signaled to his staff to open the first of the seven crates set up in a long line to the right of the crowd. The only text visible on them was 'Museum for Geography and Ethnology Rotterdam'. Zelda knew from her initial research that this was the Wereldmuseum's original name. The fact that the boxes were not marked 'bis pole' didn't matter. Their length gave their contents away.

First up was a crate approximately twelve feet tall. After several attempts, two burly depot staff members managed to squeeze their crowbars under the top and pried it open. As the heavy lid rose, the smell of rotting straw wafted out. Zelda wriggled her nose, attempting to rid her body of the heavy, musty scent. From where she was standing, only a moldy layer of dried palm leaves and thin reeds were visible.

A team of five collection assistants, wearing white lab coats and long yellow rubber gloves, descended upon the crate. They swiftly removed the natural packaging, laying clumps of decaying vegetation onto a black tarp spread out on the floor next to them. Overseeing the team was the head curator of the bis poles project and Zelda's boss, Johan Dijkhuizen. Several members of the press stepped forward. Their cameras' flashes and red record lights visibly distracted the team members, but they all pushed on with their delicate task. Slowly, the contour of a long wooden totem pole emerged. After removing most of the debris, an assistant cleaned the artifact off with a soft-tipped brush.

Johan stepped forward and gazed into the crate, a wide smile forming on his lined face. "Well, well. This is a fine example of Asmat art. Let's get this tarp out of here, shall we?"

Four assistants picked up the black sheet, now overflowing with organic packing material, and carried it away.

Aware the cameras were already pointed at them, the three directors quickly glanced inside, their delight also evident.

"Janna?" Karin Bakker asked, signaling for the Tropenmuseum's staff photographer to join her.

Janna Kolen rushed over to take pictures of the pole before Albert Schenk waved members of the media over to the crate. Zelda wanted to push forward but didn't want to embarrass herself in front of her new boss, either. Resigned to waiting a bit longer, she watched as the press corps snapped photos and videos of the object, wondering if the pole would remain whole once removed from its crate.

Albert Schenk allowed the press to take some pictures before saying, "Now, if everyone could step back, we will attempt to remove the pole."

Someone rolled over a gurney similar to those used in a hospital yet significantly longer. Zelda wondered if it was custom built. Six museum workers gently worked long canvas strips under the pole. On each side was a hole cut into the fabric. Once the entire artifact rested on the canvas hammocks, the depot workers stood on one side and hoisted it about a foot higher than the crate. The men's arms were visibly shaking. The room went silent as everyone watched one of the assistants quickly roll the crate away as another replaced it with the gurney.

Once the pole rested on the gurney, the assistants slid the canvas strips out from under it and stepped back, allowing the room to view it in all its glory. Zelda couldn't help but wonder if it was the ugliest thing she'd ever seen. She'd grown up with totem poles in the Pacific Northwest and knew they were often meant to scare off ghosts or serve as a territorial marker, warning other tribes of their presence. Yet this seemed evil.

Three life-sized carvings of men standing on each other's shoulders made up the bulk of the pole. Their faces were carved into grimaces, and their menacing expressions and sharp, black teeth made her shiver. White and red stripes decorated the bodies, while their well-defined genitalia confirmed their masculinity. Palm frond tassels adorned two men's ears. Protruding from the belly of the topmost figure was a lattice-carved wing with a bird and small child worked into the intricate pattern.

Full of enthusiasm, Johan Dijkhuizen stepped forward and cleared his throat loudly to get the press's attention. "Here we have a spectacular Asmat bis pole, carved from a wild nutmeg tree. A bis pole, also called an ancestor or spirit pole, is a way of making the spirits of the recently departed visible." Johan spoke slowly, enunciating his words to ensure the journalists and cameras understood his introduction to Asmat art.

"They were carved during a bis ceremony, which is in effect a six-week-long party honoring the dead. They would prepare special meals, play music, and carve new objects, which all incorporated the image of their loved one. Because the Asmat didn't believe an adult could simply die, there was always an enemy to blame, usually a neighboring village. To restore the spiritual balance in their community, the ceremony concluded with a headhunting raid."

Johan paused for a moment to allow his words to sink in. Zelda

16

gazed across the press corps and saw the journalists were doing their best to write down all he said while the camera crews and photographers were using his momentary silence to get close-ups of the pole.

As soon as most of the reporters looked up at him expectantly, Johan gestured toward the figure at the top of the pole. "Here we see the man who has recently passed literally standing on the shoulders of his forefathers. Note the designs painted on his arms and legs. He would have received these scar tattoos during the men's brutal initiation ceremony. Generally, two or three figures—or generations—were depicted on one pole. This is a way of summoning their ancestors' spirits and asking them to help ensure the success of the upcoming headhunting raid."

He laid his hand on the large protrusion jutting out of the pole. "This wing is actually the root of the nutmeg tree. To create the bis pole, they turned the tree upside down and carved so the wide plank root protruded out of the topmost figure's abdomen. The Asmat call it the *tsjemen*, which means both 'projection' and 'penis.' Though, if you look carefully, you will see this figure also has genitalia." Zelda couldn't help but stand on her toes and look for it.

Despite the feeling of dread they incited in her, she was in awe of the Asmat's artistry. Native American totem poles were solid tree trunks carved in relief. Yet these figures were three-dimensional humans, whose appendages were fully formed, which meant the carver had to remove a significant portion of the tree without breaking off the arms, facial features, genitalia, or legs. Zelda marveled at what they were able to achieve with the tools they had available.

"In Asmat culture, headhunters see themselves as the siblings of animals that eat fruit, such as flying foxes, hornbills, or black king cockatoos. Here we can see the stylized head of a hornbill worked into the tip of the *tsjemen*. The small boy carved close to the base represents the children this man left behind. Women were sometimes depicted at the bottom of the pole, closest to the earth. They represent the continuation of life. The dugout canoe at the bottom is meant to carry this person's spirit to the realm of the dead." Johan walked slowly from one end of the gurney to the other, pointing out the different shapes on the long pole as he spoke. The press was eating it up, their silence only broken by the clicks and flashes of their cameras.

"Bis poles are carved by other villages in the region, but those created by the Asmat are considered to be the most exquisite. As you will learn during our upcoming exhibition, they were desired by ethnographic museums as well as art collectors. And not just those in Europe. Several poles were even collected for Harvard's Peabody Museum of Archeology and Ethnology in the 1960s. Two of which were later donated to the National Ethnography Museum because of the Dutch government's assistance with the search for—"

A brief round of applause stopped Johan short. The clapper, Albert Schenk, chuckled as he said, "Thank you for your fascinating introduction to Asmat art, Johan. You are clearly the right curator to lead the exhibition team. Now, why don't we open the second crate? I can't wait to see what we find next." Schenk shifted the media's attention a few feet to the right.

The second crate was even easier to open. After removing the packing material and taking more photos, the pole was gently lifted out of its crate. Before the assistant could roll it away, the tip of the wing snapped off and fell back inside the wooden box.

The press gasped in unison and began snapping photos as Johan Dijkhuizen simply shrugged. "We were concerned all of the poles would be rotten. It's quite extraordinary that these two are in such good condition."

Once the pole was secure on the gurney, Johan turned his attention to the crate. "I'll get the tip." He pulled out a large piece of lattice-carved wood and laid it next to the pole. "Hmm, it looks like it fragmented. Let's see what else is in here." He stuck his hand in the crate again. "Ow!" he yelled, springing back as he cradled one hand in the other. Blood streamed out of two fingertips. An assistant brought him a towel to wrap his hand in while another began pushing the leaves and reeds to one side to see what was inside the crate.

Whatever the assistant saw next stopped her in her tracks. She inhaled sharply and looked up at Johan as she pulled out a bundle of spears almost as long as she was. "How did they get in here?" she asked.

"Excellent question," Johan murmured as he took ahold of them, slowly turning them in his good hand. The room exploded in a cacophony of flashes and noise as the press corps descended upon the curator simultaneously. Johan held up his palms, signaling for silence. "I don't know how or why these spears ended up in this crate. They were not on the inventory list we have on file," he said in a strong voice. Johan glanced over at Albert Schenk as he spoke, but the director was resolutely ignoring him. The curator opened his mouth—to ask a question, Zelda thought—when Albert intervened again.

He grabbed the bundle out of Johan's hand and held them up high for the photographers. "What an exciting day! Until we have a chance to consult our archives, we cannot explain how these objects came to be in this crate. However, they are in excellent condition." He grinned at the spears in his hand, which were long sticks with sharpened stones and birds' talons attached to their tips by a thick twine. "Now, shall we set these aside for now and see what other treasures the rest of these crates contain?"

His smile was infectious as he placed the spears down alongside the second pole before drawing everyone's attention to the next unopened crate. Zelda was surprised Albert was so nonchalant about this discovery. However, she quickly realized they had five more crates to open today. Apparently, there wasn't time to stop and reflect on the spears' unexpected presence.

The museum professionals worked methodically, slowly releasing four more poles from their crates. Three were unscathed. Only one showed visible signs of insect infestation. Tiny wormholes dotted the uppermost man's chest. The media's initial excitement tempered as the afternoon dragged on. Oddly enough, more spears and a small ancestor statue of an Asmat woman holding a child were found.

By the time the last crate was about to be opened, most of the press had stopped snapping photos, content to watch as the museum professionals worked. Zelda had taken a seat at the back of the room, her attention also waning. Being inside this windowless hanger all day was taking a toll. She wondered if the sun was shining and how much longer this would take.

When they opened the lid to the seventh pole, Zelda stood back up and moved closer, glad to see the last one was also in good shape. After the crate was rolled away, the bottom of the pole, shaped into a boat, broke off and shattered into splinters, which spread across the depot's concrete floor. A gasp of horror reverberated through the hall. Zelda, like everyone else in the room, instinctively moved closer. In among the rotten shards was a leather-bound journal. As Zelda's mind registered its existence, Albert Schenk sprang forward to pick it up, but Jaap Meulendijk reached it first. The cameras came to life once again, their spotlights and flashes illuminating the room as if it were a crime scene. As Jaap examined the book, a murmur of speculation and wonder filled the room. What was a journal doing inside a bis pole?

Jaap opened the clasp holding the thick book shut and gasped. The other directors and curators leaned in closer to see why. Karin Bakker exclaimed, "Does that actually say property of Nicholas Mayfield?"

As soon as his name was spoken aloud, a roar went up from the press corps as reporters shouted questions for their audiences back home. The museum professionals ignored them—instead, turning to the crate and carefully checking the rest of the box. Hidden among the remaining packaging material was a large belt buckle.

"How did this get in here? Could it be Mayfield's?" Jaap Meulendijk wondered aloud, turning the buckle over in his hands. It was a gaudy gold piece shaped in a chunky oval. From her position at the back of the small crowd, Zelda could tell there was a pattern etched into it but didn't recognize it.

The press continued hurling questions about Mayfield at the curators and directors. Unable to answer them, the museum professionals huddled into an increasingly tighter circle around the crate, searching each other's faces for answers—to no avail.

Finally, Hermina de Jong, the Tropenmuseum's public relations director, turned to the hungry crowd. "Ladies and gentlemen, you are a witness to history." She held up the journal and belt buckle. "Obviously, we cannot yet explain how these objects got into this crate, but we are going to do our utmost to find out."

She laid them on the gurney next to the shattered bis pole. "Please, take photographs, and share them with your readers and viewers. They may recognize the belt buckle. We will keep you abreast of our investigation into how Nick Mayfield's journal came to be inside this bis pole's crate. I thank you all for coming."

As the photographers and camera crews took turns getting close-ups for their audiences, Zelda looked at the throng of museum professionals standing together a few feet away. Karin Bakker and Jaap Meulendijk stepped forward to help Hermina field questions, but Albert Schenk and the rest remained well away. *Schenk looks less than pleased*, Zelda thought. Yet, at the beginning of the press conference, he was practically preening. She was surprised to see he didn't take this chance to bask in the limelight again. Instead, he stood at the back of the group, far away from the cameras. Intrigued by his change in attitude, Zelda studied him, wondering why he ignored questions from the press and his staff. Instead, he stood stock-still, staring at Nicholas Mayfield's journal with a ferocious intensity.

Hermina called out loudly, "Albert, you were both in Dutch New Guinea working as anthropologists in 1962, correct? Did you know Mayfield personally?"

Albert's focus snapped, and he seemed flustered. Hermina and the journalist interviewing her walked toward him, a microphone already pointed in his direction.

Before they could reach him, Albert strode out of the hall and quickly disappeared behind a door marked 'Staff Only.' Hermina merely shrugged and steered the reporter back toward the gurney.

Why was Albert Schenk acting so strangely, and what was his connection to Nick Mayfield? Zelda wondered as the door shut behind him.

We don't do sensationalism

May 2, 2017

After the last member of the press was ushered away, Zelda looked around for Johan Dijkhuizen, wondering if she could leave yet. It was a one-and-half-hour ride back to Amsterdam, and she was eager to get to the train station. *What a day*, she thought, scanning the group for her boss. Technically, she was only here as an observer, but she still felt strange about leaving without checking in with Johan first. She wandered along the rows of Nigerian drums, Mexican masks, and Brazilian flutes laid out on open racks filling the vast hall, scanning the faces of the museum assistants milling about.

When she was certain Johan wasn't in the depot, she dared to enter the door Albert Schenk had gone through. As she slowly walked down the long corridor of closed office doors, she checked the names, hoping to find a familiar one to knock on.

Halfway down the hallway, raised voices attracted her attention. She quickly ascertained they were coming from the last door on her right, the only one that was partially open. She wanted to say goodbye to Johan but didn't want to interrupt a heated discussion to do so. She was about to turn around when a shout reverberated down the corridor, startling her.

"I don't want to hear his name mentioned again!" Zelda was almost certain it was Albert Schenk bellowing. "There is no reason for us to hang on to this thing. It is clearly his property, and we should arrange to have it sent to his family's lawyer straightaway."

"Hold on a second. This is a gift from the gods, delivered straight into our laps. We have to copy it first. He may have written about villages he bought artifacts from or the artists who carved them," Jaap Meulendijk countered, his deep voice booming.

Curiosity won over, so Zelda slowly crept closer until she was standing right outside the door marked 'Hermina de Jong.' Zelda shook her head. She should have known the head of public relations would be involved.

"I agree with Jaap. We should copy Mayfield's journal before returning it to his family. If we don't, we will all regret it later. Why don't I arrange an official handover? We can invite his family to fly over and present them Nicholas's journal in Leiden. We can frame the shot so the poles he collected are in the background. If we plan it right, we'll have enough time to make a copy of it first," Hermina piped up, her shrill voice a dead giveaway.

"By including excerpts from Mayfield's journal, we will link the exhibition to his disappearance. And that is exactly the kind of publicity I want to avoid!" Schenk exploded. "This exhibition is about Dutch collection policies and the Asmat culture—not Nick Mayfield! You know it was a prerequisite of our museum's participation that Mayfield, dubious conspiracy theories, and Nazi bone collectors were not to be discussed in the displays."

"Of course, Asmat artifacts and our collection policies are the focus," Hermina soothed, "but we would be fools to ignore his presence in New Guinea, especially now that his journal has been found in one of the poles we will be displaying. Mayfield was there conducting anthropological research when he disappeared, so it will be easy enough to justify his inclusion in the exhibition. Besides, you saw how the press went crazy. Collection policy is fascinating to a few, but Nick Mayfield and the mystery surrounding his death will draw far bigger crowds. I'm sure the discovery of his journal will lead the articles and reports about today's event."

Zelda admired Hermina's ability to turn every situation into a marketing opportunity.

"Those types shouldn't come to the exhibition. We don't do sensationalism. They will be sorely disappointed," Albert countered. "And I disagree—Mayfield is not a part of this. His research has nothing to do with our collections or the Asmat. Do you realize what a terrible anthropologist he was? Including information about his research is an insult to those of us who worked there. I wouldn't trust anything you read in his journal. The man was more interested in starting tribal wars than learning about the Asmat culture or people."

"That is exactly what I mean. Albert, you just told us you were his assistant. How can you say he had nothing to do with your time in New Guinea?" Hermina countered.

"His translator, not an assistant." Albert snarled.

Zelda couldn't believe it—Albert worked for Mayfield in Dutch New Guinea? *They must not have gotten along,* Zelda thought. *He clearly thinks poorly of the millionaire's missing son.*

"If we include a display about the two poles Mayfield collected, it will fit within the parameters of the exhibition," Jaap Meulendijk said, his tone resolute, "especially considering they were gifts from his family to thank our government for their help in searching for him. A small display containing a few photos and journal excerpts will suffice. Harvard's Peabody Museum houses a large collection of photos Mayfield took while in Papua. I have a contact there. I'm sure they would be interested in collaborating—"

"No! If you go through with this plan, I will pull our poles out of the exhibition," Albert responded firmly.

"You know it's too late for that. Information about this exhibition will be all over the newspapers and internet by this afternoon, and the Wereldmuseum is listed as one of the three lead organizers," Karin Bakker said, ever the voice of reason, "but let's all step back and take a moment to think. We're getting ahead of ourselves. I agree we need to make a copy of this journal. Any information about the artists who carved the poles we are displaying would be a nice addition to our exhibition and keep the focus on the artwork. Of course, we will first need to ask the family's permission to include any excerpts from it."

"If there's anything relevant in it…" Albert began again, clearly unwilling to give in.

Karin calmly interrupted, "Let's shelf the Mayfield display idea for now and concentrate on contacting his family and informing them about the journal. I'm certain some eager reporter has already called them. I can imagine they will want it back as soon as possible."

"It would take about a week to photograph all of the pages," Janna Kolen, the Tropenmuseum's photographer, chimed in. "The pages are far too delicate to photocopy or scan. I'm afraid I might rip or crease them in the process."

"I see nothing significant coming out of that insolent boy's journal," Albert Schenk replied with obvious disdain. Zelda couldn't believe her ears. Did Albert really just refer to Nicholas Mayfield as 'that insolent boy'?

Silence told Zelda the others ignored him.

"If we could arrange a handover in ten days, that should give Janna plenty of time to photograph it. I'll look up their lawyer's name as soon as I get back to Leiden," Jaap Meulendijk said. His tone indicated their course of action was already set.

"Okay, that's settled then. Janna will take it back to the Tropen-museum for now," Karin Bakker said, pride in her voice. The other two directors could only mutter sullenly in agreement. Their own photography departments had already closed, victims of subsidy cuts, leaving the Tropenmuseum the only one with its own in-house photographer and studio.

Albert Schenk's anger was palpable even to Zelda in the hallway. "Enough! I've said from the start Nicholas Mayfield is not to be a part of this. If you pursue this path, I will have no choice but to pull our objects out of the exhibition regardless of how it looks to the outside world. I refuse to see the Asmat culture sidelined for conspiracy theories and the ramblings of a poorly trained anthropologist, regardless of who his father is," Albert said before striding out of the office and right into Zelda.

"What are you doing here?" he roared.

Zelda shrank down, trying to disappear into the floor. "Looking for Johan Dijkhuizen."

Albert jerked his head toward the office. "He's all yours," he said before turning on his heels and walking toward the exit.

Diary of a missing anthropologist

May 3, 2017

"So I push this button once to take the picture?" Zelda asked, her finger hovering over a trigger connected to the camera via a long cable.

"Yeah, that's it." Janna nodded encouragingly as she admired her lighting setup. The Tropenmuseum's photographer had constructed a cube made of steel tubes upon which a plethora of small spotlights was attached. A camera hung in the middle of the open construction and pointed down onto the white tabletop, which was softly lit from eight small spots shining down on it from oblique angles.

"Then I change the lighting setup by flipping this switch before taking another?"

Janna nodded. Now twelve tiny lamps shone almost parallel to the tabletop.

Still a bit flustered by her difficulty in finding the photography studio this morning, Zelda was determined not to screw this assignment up. How could she have been expected to know it was tucked up under the eaves of the museum's west wing and only accessible via the service staircase?

"Don't forget to place the glass before you shoot anything." Janna laid a plate of thin glass down on the open pages, heavy enough to flatten the delicate sheets gently without cracking or creasing them. She shifted the journal under the camera lens while watching the computer monitor hooked up to the viewfinder, adjusting its position

28

until she was satisfied. Using masking tape, Janna made an outline around the journal, making it easy for Zelda to place it correctly.

"Make sure you take two shots—one with each lighting scheme. We'll combine them in Photoshop later. Check the focus in the monitor first, but the camera should find the best focal point automatically. Otherwise, you can adjust it here." Janna turned a ring on the camera's lens to demonstrate. "Once you are sure both shots are clear and sharp, lift the glass off with your gloves, and gently flip the page. Even if there's no visible writing, we want to take photos of every sheet for our documentation. Don't forget to wear gloves. We don't want the oils from your fingers getting onto the pages or glass."

Janna raised her eyebrows and held Zelda's gaze until she nodded diligently.

"There are eighty pages, and we have ten days to photograph them all. That should be plenty of time, so work slowly and accurately. Any questions?"

"Nope, clear as a summer's day," Zelda said in English, blushing when Janna looked at her quizzically. "Perfectly clear," Zelda added in Dutch for clarification, reminding herself to stop using American expressions here in Holland. Her hard work had paid off as she was now fluent in this guttural language—well, almost. There were still times when she had to resort to an English word or phrase because she wasn't sure of the Dutch equivalent. Thankfully, those moments were becoming less frequent.

"Okay, go ahead and get started," Janna said, breaking Zelda's train of thought. "I've got to get ready for a photo shoot. I'll be in the corner if you need me." She nodded toward the back of the room where a standing spotlight shone brightly onto a gray backdrop.

In between shots, Zelda watched with fascination as Janna arranged ladders, tables, and crates in front of the gray screen. She couldn't help but notice the plethora of tattoos covering both of the older woman's arms. *Sleeves*, she thought, *that's what they call those kinds of tattoos*. Janna having tattoos didn't bother Zelda. It was their poor quality and choice of designs that surprised her. The roughly drawn skulls, jokers, and dice almost looked like prison tatts, something that didn't seem to rhyme with the photographer's spunky personality and artistic nature.

Zelda wondered what the attraction could be. She had heard the photographer was into karate, judo, and other martial arts. Maybe the tiny redhead's love of Asian fighting sports somehow related to the tattoos. Janna's life outside of the Tropenmuseum was a well-guarded secret, and therefore, it was a favorite topic of speculation among several staff members. Zelda thought back to all of the lunches, coffee breaks, and chitchat sessions she'd had with her co-workers, realizing even the gossip hounds revealed little of their private lives. Who really knew their co-workers?

"Why do you think Albert Schenk is so against including any information about Nicholas Mayfield in the exhibition, Janna? From his comments yesterday, it sounds like he knew Mayfield quite well." Zelda said, still curious about the connection between the two men.

"Oh, yes, you were listening at the door, weren't you?" Janna said with a laugh. Zelda grew quiet as her face turned crimson. "Rumor has it he and Mayfield didn't get along. As you may have noticed, Albert is quite bullheaded. If Mayfield acted like a spoiled rich kid, Albert wouldn't have tolerated it. Not that I know what happened between them, specifically. He's probably worried Mayfield's story will overshadow the displays about collection policies or the bis poles' role in Asmat culture. He knows as well as the marketing department that including Nicholas Mayfield in the exhibition would attract larger audiences," Janna said dismissively, her attention focused on moving tables and lamps around until the lighting was perfect.

The photographer had worked at the Tropenmuseum for twenty years and knew most of curators and researchers working in the many museums of the Netherlands. And considering Hermina de Jong was her good friend, Zelda figured she wasn't passing any old gossip on.

"And as much as it pains me to agree with Albert, including Mayfield in the exhibition would draw a larger crowd but one more interested in conspiracy theories than Asmat culture."

"So they never found his body?" Zelda had read up on Mayfield's mysterious disappearance last night after getting home from the museum depot. There were all sorts of theories about how he had died—crocodiles, cannibals, drowned, or even a shark. Others claimed to have seen him walking around the island's inner forests, living like a king deep in the rainforest.

"Nope, to this day, no one knows how he died, where his body ended up, or if he is even dead. Some conspiracy theorists believe he disappeared to escape the pressures placed on him by his family. Personally, I'd have chosen a New York penthouse over a jungle in New Guinea, but that's just me," Janna said, laughing.

"Me, too," Zelda replied. Wouldn't most people choose luxury? "Do you think the curators will use excerpts from his journal in the exhibition? Albert seemed dead set against it."

The photographer grinned. "High visitor numbers are crucial to obtaining subsidies and grants as well as interesting donors in becoming a 'friend' of the museum. This exhibition is our summer blockbuster and needs to pull in an exorbitant amount of visitors. Hermina has a way with words. Give her time. She'll probably be able to find a convincing reason to explain why a display about Mayfield will elevate the exhibition to a whole other level. I bet she'll make it seem like it will be doomed publicity-wise if they don't, whether Albert likes it or not."

Returning to Dutch New Guinea

May 1, 1962

Nick sat cross-legged in the opening of his hut built on stilts, surveying the world before him. Small brown children cavorted in the dark water of the swampy, mangrove-filled morass below. The slow-moving Asewetsj River was full of standing men rowing long, thin canoes upriver, their blades dipping in and out of the water in perfect unison.

Coming back here was the right decision, he thought. In contrast to his pampered life in New York, he was in control here, responsible for his every action and his own well-being. Being master of his own destiny was more freeing than he could have ever imagined.

His stomach grumbled. He pulled a roasted sago ball out of the bag next to him and popped one in his mouth, ignoring the chalky texture as he chewed. *Tom was a fool for leaving*, he thought, though a twinge of concern flitted across his conscience. His friend had been admitted to the intensive care in Darwin straightaway. Perhaps he was right to seek medical attention in a more Western land. Why Tom thought it was all right to eat raw fish from a local market stall and wash it down with tap water was beyond him. He should have known better, but he was a born and bred New Yorker. Tom simply didn't think about the possible consequences in spite of Nick's warnings on the plane and boat rides to stay away from raw products and unfiltered water.

Still, Nick was glad he hadn't changed his plans to accommodate his friend's possible return. If he recovered rapidly enough, Tom could always join them later. Waiting in Hollandia, twiddling his thumbs, hoping his friend recovered enough to accompany them to Kopi wasn't his style. After he had finished his business in Hollandia, there was no reason to wait around for Tom.

The Dutch capital of New Guinea turned out to be a modern, thriving metropolis, and not the backwater town he'd been expecting. Organizing the storage of his trading supplies—complete with round-the-clock security—and reserving space on a container ship for his trip back to America in five months had been easier than he'd anticipated. The container was larger than he figured he would need, though the taller bis poles he'd seen in the Netherlands were easily twelve to fourteen feet tall. Depending on how productive his trip was and how quickly the local carvers worked, he might need the extra space after all. *It was better to be safe than sorry,* he thought, recalling one of his father's favorite sayings, especially when one had enough funds to cover any expenses.

Nick shut his eyes and recalled the spectacular views over the dense jungle-encrusted hills of the interior he and Roger had enjoyed on their flight from Hollandia to Agats last week. A grin pulled his lips upwards. In a few short hours, he and Roger would be on their way to the heart of Asmat territory. Kopi was a short five-hour paddle across Flamingo Bay and up the Lorentz River.

He could hardly believe he managed to get back to Asmat territory so quickly. Only eight months ago, he'd flown back to New York after completing his first collection trip on the island, knowing he needed to return as soon as possible yet unsure how he would manage it.

Harvard was quite receptive to his idea of expanding the Peabody Museum's Asmat collection. It hadn't taken long to arrange the trip back, not once he'd convinced his father of the Asmat's artistic worth—esthetically and financially. His family regularly supported their alma mater. A pittance was all the Asmat were expecting for their glorious artwork and hand-carved beauties he couldn't find anywhere else in the world. Especially when compared to the price tag of a single modern painting.

Once he received the blessings of both Harvard and his father, it was only a question of getting his crew together. Nick eyed the third ticket on top of his backpack. If only Professor Carroll had agreed to the prerequisites his father had made, he would be here traveling with them. *A pity his ego could not accept the official role of assistant,* Nick thought, chuckling. It was too bad about Tom and Professor Carroll, but between Roger and the Dutch anthropologist who was to accompany them on their journey, he should be able to collect and ship back everything he desired.

Nick wondered what kind of character the anthropologist would be. Everyone he'd met so far was a cowboy, survivalist, or misplaced colonial patsy. All he knew was that Albert Schenk was Dutch, spoke several Asmat dialects, and had been collecting objects from villages in the region for several years. Nick guessed he would be the cowboy type.

The American Embassy in the Netherlands recommended him to his father, so he must be okay, Nick figured. Five of the bis poles he'd seen in Rotterdam were collected by Albert. The Dutchman clearly knew which villages to visit and who to negotiate with. He'd also seen photos of Schenk with decorated skulls in his hand, another item Nick hoped to collect this time around. He was certain the ample supply of bartering goods he'd shipped over from New York would convince the villagers to work with him. Once this anthropologist got him in front of the right people, his wares would do the rest.

Roger clambered up the ladder leading into his hut, breaking his train of thought. His friend stuck his head inside the door opening and smiled broadly. "Quite a place, eh, Nick?"

His grin faded as he swatted at the flies and mosquitoes swarming around him, smacking at his arms and legs so often it sounded like he was drumming. "I can't quite get used to all of the insects, I'm afraid." As Roger entered his hut, Nick noticed his friend's face was already red and puffy from numerous bites.

Nick smiled. There were no biting flies in their New York penthouses. He should have known Roger wouldn't have bothered to read up on how to minimalize insect bites. That was why Nick wore long pants and a long-sleeved shirt at all times, despite the suffocating humidity. One of the deadliest strains of malaria was present here, and he wanted to do everything in his power to limit his chances of contracting such a debilitating disease. He'd already covered himself in DEET, as his survival guide recommended. *Roger should have read his copy more carefully*, Nick thought. He hoped his friend was cut out for this adventure. The first leech and he was probably gone. *I may be hard of hearing, but I can still fend for myself better than most of my friends, military service or not,* Nick thought smugly.

"Do you want to slosh on some DEET?" Nick asked.

Roger scrunched up his nose, shaking his head. "I can't stand the smell of that stuff. Although it might be preferable to being eaten alive." He looked down at his arms, new welts already rising on his patchy skin. "Yeah, why not?"

After Roger applied the insect repellant, Nick offered him a sago ball. Roger waved his offer away with a grimace. "I'm not sure about the food here, especially after what happened to Tom." Instead, he pulled a nutrition bar out of his backpack, one of the many rations he'd brought along from home.

Nick said nothing, yet again wondering if he'd made the right choice. He'd purposefully asked two close friends, instead of fellow anthropology students, to accompany him. After what had happened with Professor Carroll, he didn't want to deal with another anthropologist trying to upstage him. Of course, he made the right decision. All Roger had to do was to help carry objects and watch his back, Nick told himself. He would handle the negotiations himself.

"Are you ready to go?" Nick asked.

Roger nodded. "Yep. Let me get my sleeping bag, and we can head out."

"Excellent." Nick gazed once again out at the Asewetsj River and the thick swash of green visible on the opposite banks. From here, the rainforest seemed ominous and impenetrable. A smile spread across his face. He couldn't wait to see what adventures lay ahead.

New job prospects

May 8, 2017

"So, Zelda"—her mentor turned away from her computer screen and gazed over her reading glasses at her intern—"according to your agenda, you've been working with Janna for three days now. How are you getting on? Are the photographs turning out as she expected?"

"They look good. Janna created two lighting systems that work well together. When I combine the scans in the computer, almost all of the text is legible, and the few words that are missing can easily be filled in thanks to the context." Zelda tried to sound upbeat when describing the work. It was the most boring assignment she'd had so far. Two clicks, review the photos on the screen, and then save them according to Janna's naming system. Carefully flip the page, adjust the glass, and repeat.

Because the paper was so brittle, Zelda held her breath each time she turned the journal's fragile pages or adjusted the glass's position, certain it would rip. Mold present on several pages smeared the glass, meaning she was forced to clean it more frequently than Janna expected. Waiting for it to dry completely before daring to place it on the journal again took more time than taking the photographs. Still, it was important to remain patient. She didn't want to be the one responsible for damaging the pages of this controversial little book.

At her current rate, Zelda figured she had four days of photo taking ahead of her. At least she could listen to music while she worked. Janna was a good conversationalist, but Zelda knew she would be out of the studio for the rest of the week, busy documenting the new displays of the recently renovated Africa wing for the marketing department.

Zelda was actually sorry she wouldn't be able to help at the bones lab tomorrow. Though her sorrow had more to do with missing a day with Jacob than the bones or database entry work, she realized, blushing as she thought of the young PhD student who had captured her interests as of late.

"Good. I know the Human Remains project was supposed to be your priority, but the journal supersedes it. Theodore Mayfield, Nicholas's youngest brother, will be flying in sometime next week to pick it up. Apparently, he's negotiating with a French company about a take-over and will 'drop by' whenever he is finished." Marijke rolled her eyes as she spoke, clearly not impressed by the man's arrogance. "Once they get the journal back, I doubt the family will let it out of their sight again," she said.

Zelda's mentor didn't need to reiterate that this was their only chance. Janna had already drilled that into her head.

Marijke Torenbouwer was quiet a moment as if she weren't sure how to broach the next subject. "Janna and I met with our IT department last Friday to discuss the quality of the photos you are taking. Karin Bakker wants Mayfield's journal transcribed straightaway. There may be information in it we can use in our exhibition. Unfortunately, the handwriting is not clear enough for our OCR scanners to recognize all of the words."

Marijke paused again, making eye contact with Zelda before continuing. "Karin asked if you would be interested in transcribing the journal for us. It will be an arduous task, I know. The handwriting is difficult to read, the ink is faded in spots, and mold has blurred some of the pages. Seeing as you are a native speaker, we figure it will be easier for you to decipher the text than it would be for any of our staff secretaries."

Zelda felt simultaneously honored to be asked and irritated her mentor considered transcribing the journal work for the secretaries.

"We are willing to pay you," Marijke quickly added, "but do ask that you not discuss the transcription with other researchers or curators just yet. If we find passages we wish to use, we would still need the Mayfield's permission to include them in our displays. To avoid any uncomfortable conversations, perhaps you'd be willing to work on it in the library? I have reserved a computer station for you, starting next week."

Zelda nodded gratefully. She recalled Albert's reaction to the possible inclusion of a display about Mayfield and instantly understood her mentor's request for discretion. There was no way she would be able to hide her work from the eight other staff members working in their shared office. Considering how tight-knit the Dutch museum community was, someone was bound to tell Albert Schenk about it.

She wanted to read the journal, and if the museum was willing to pay her to transcribe it, then it didn't matter if they used any passages from it or not. This internship included a monthly stipend of four hundred euro a month, which was barely enough to pay for groceries. It was a difficult year financially. Interning here full time for six months meant she'd had to give up her job at the English Bookstore. She'd been living off her savings for two months, and her resources were dwindling faster than she'd expected.

She was thrilled to be working in this museum. The eighteen months of university lectures in museum studies, cultural identity, art history, and exhibition design had flown by. Though art history still fascinated her, exhibition presentation, collection research, and project management intrigued her more. It was going to be difficult to choose one path, she feared.

Zelda wasn't sure if an ethnography museum would be her first choice as an employer. Her previous internship at the Amsterdam Museum had been a better fit, even though the work hadn't been as challenging as she had hoped. Well, the official work wasn't in any case, Zelda recollected as memories of the recent past invaded her brain and soured her thoughts. Either way, she was glad to have landed this internship at this renowned museum. And in a month's time, she'd already developed a deeper respect for ethnographic art and artifacts. Objects she would normally pass by now tickled her imagination. Some of the masks, statues, and dancing costumes she'd seen in this museum were as intricate and impressive as any painted masterpiece. *Who knows*, she thought. Perhaps after the six months were over, she would want to apply for a job here.

"Yes, of course. I understand the journal is a sore subject in Rotterdam. I will do my best to ensure no one knows what I'm working on."

"Excellent." Marijke said, smiling broadly. "Before I forget, I have to cancel our meeting next week. Karin and I have another appointment with Victor Nalong. He's going to be taking up quite a bit of my time in the coming weeks. Since Steyl denied his restitution request, he's bound and determined to get the remains of his people back."

"Oh, okay." Zelda's shoulders sagged. Their weekly meetings were her favorite hour of the week. Marijke always treated her like a colleague instead of the intern and student she was. Plus, she'd learned a lot about museum politics and the dynamics of working within a project group from her. Though she'd originally wanted to be a curator, Zelda was beginning to see how interesting a project manager's role could be. *Perhaps I should focus my energies on obtaining such a position*, she thought. For now, she was content to study her mentor's every move.

"The Human Remains project will keep you busy for two days a week, but we don't want this to be your only task. I have another assignment ready for you that will involve collection research."

Zelda sat up straighter and leaned forward, thrilled to know she wouldn't be relegated to data entry for the remaining five months.

Marijke picked up a thick pile of paperwork off her desk and handed it to her. "We want to include several photographs and films in the Bis Poles exhibition. Here are printouts of the photographs in our collection that we are planning to use. However, we don't have enough to visualize all of the themes. Several important photographic and film collections are held in other Dutch archives and private collections. We can use them to supplement our displays."

Zelda nodded eagerly, already excited about the project.

"You will be searching for images which visualize both the collection practices of Dutch museums and the Asmat culture between the 1930s and 1960s. We have smaller displays dedicated to the types of Western explorers who collected Asmat artifacts—missionaries, colonial administrators, surveyors, anthropologists, and adventure-seekers. We also want to show films and photos of Asmat rites and rituals being performed—dancing, carving sessions, initiation ceremonies, and the like."

Zelda's eyes widened as she took in what Marijke said. Most interns didn't have the chance to work independently on a research project. A smile spread across her face. "This assignment sounds fascinating," she said, puffing up with pride.

Marijke rummaged around her desk, and when she finally found the sheet of paper she was looking for, she handed it to Zelda. "Here are the names of the archives. You will be visiting them as a representative of the museum, which means they should extend you every courtesy that they would me. At the bottom is a list of keywords. Use these to search for images, and compile a list of the inventory numbers you deem suitable. To expedite the selection process, be sure to obtain either the digital file or a photocopy. The exhibition project team will make the final selection next month so we can begin the official loan process."

Zelda still couldn't believe they were giving her this chance. She shook her head a little and started to ask why, when her mentor added, "You've been so flexible about helping out in the Human Remains lab and with the journal, so you deserve to be our researcher. Besides, this will round out your internship." Marijke glanced away before adding hesitantly as if she were afraid to mention it, "And I know about the work you did for the Amsterdam Museum last year."

Zelda blushed. Her internship at the Amsterdam Museum had been a life-changing experience in so many ways. Most importantly, her research into Arjan van Heemsvliet's collection got her into the museum studies master's program, though it had taken months before the more harrowing memories stopped haunting her dreams. She shuddered a little, thinking of how close she'd come to being murdered over those missing masterpieces.

Marijke noticed Zelda had turned inward and pressed on. "This assignment will also be a good way for you to learn more about working with archivists and private collectors. Both are an extraordinarily passionate bunch, though they can be quite eccentric. I'm going to let you decide the order of visits so long as you get to all seven before the end of the month. We will reimburse your travel expenses. Just keep your receipts and print off a record of your train tickets at the end of the month."

"I can't thank you enough," Zelda gushed.

A smile passed over Marijke's lips. "Three weeks isn't a lot of time, I know. In light of your other duties, it will be a challenge but a rewarding one, I suspect. I recommend you contact the archivists first and inquire as to their procedures. I know the Missionary Museum in Steyl, Museum Bronbeek, and Beeld en Geluid in Hilversum all require you to submit an official request before they will grant you access. Give me a call if you need help."

Marijke noticed Zelda's face lit up when she mentioned Steyl. "You've heard about Steyl's restitution case?"

Zelda nodded. "Of course." How could she not? For the last two weeks, the court case had dominated every Dutch newspaper, radio talk show, and television news report. The Mission Museum of Steyl housed one of the finest collections of Asmat carvings in the world. Because the colonial government and missions did everything in their power to ban headhunting, similar ceremonial artifacts and Asmat carvings were now rare in Papua.

Though the Papuan government demanded the artifacts be returned to the island, a Dutch court of law determined they belonged to the priest who'd brought them back to the Netherlands in the 1950s and 60s. The priest in question, Father Kees Terpstra, remained steadfast in his assertion they were gifts given to him by appreciative locals he met while working as a missionary in the Asmat region. And, as such, they were his property.

Ultimately, the courts agreed with Father Terpstra and Steyl's curatorial staff. They rejected the Papuan's claim that the objects in questions were too significant—culturally and historically—to have been allowed out of the country in the first place.

Most Western museums watched with bated breath, waiting to see which way the courts would rule. Their decision sent shockwaves of astonishment and relief throughout the international museum world. Though the Papuan government vowed to fight the decision in a European courtroom, no official documents had been filed.

"Steyl's collection of Asmat artifacts is exquisite. Now that the court case has resolved any question of ownership, we hope to include several of their pieces in our exhibition," her mentor added.

Zelda was fascinated by the case and collection. As she walked back to the photography studio to continue copying Mayfield's journal, she decided she would block out an entire day for her visit to the archive and museum.

An unexpected discovery

May 10, 2017

Zelda smiled as she switched on the lighting scheme, happy to see there were only a few more pages to go. Then she would have a complete photographic record of Nicholas Mayfield's entire journal.

She couldn't wait to get this task behind her and begin with the archival research. Her heart rejoiced just thinking about it. This morning, she'd come in early and sent emails to all of the archives and collectors on her list. She was ecstatic the curator at Steyl's Mission Museum responded immediately, scheduling their appointment for May 22. Their collection was the one she wanted to visit most.

Two hours later, Zelda flipped to the last page, thrilled to know she was finished. "Woohoo! I'm done photographing the journal, Janna."

The Tropenmuseum's photographer looked up from her keyboard, her concentrated frown softening when Zelda's announcement sank in. Janna whooped in delight. "That's wonderful news. And with a day to spare. Good job." Zelda knew the photographer was as happy as she was to be done with this project. The daily calls from the museum director to check on their progress was getting on Janna's nerves as much as her own.

Zelda removed the thin glass and gingerly picked up the journal. The leather cover slid out of her gloved hands and hit the table hard. Zelda looked to Janna, expecting to be yelled at, but the photographer was so focused on cropping and editing images of the African wing, she hadn't even noticed.

Gently, Zelda picked up the book and checked it for torn pages or a broken spine. A soft sigh of relief escaped her lips when she realized it was intact. She started to close the journal when a flash of white sticking out of the cover caught her eye. "Oh, shit," she muttered. A page had ripped after all. Only when she tilted the book's edge toward her did she realize something was sticking out of the slit between the leather and the journal's hard cover. Being open flat on the table for a week, in combination with her dropping it, must have jarred the paper loose.

"Janna?" she called out.

"Yes?" the photographer responded without looking away from her screen.

"I think you need to see this."

Janna glared at Zelda before pushing back from her desk. "What is it? I thought you were finished."

Zelda held the journal up. "It looks like there's a piece of paper stuck inside."

"That's odd." Janna pulled on gloves and took the book out of Zelda's hands. Using tweezers from her tool drawer, she tugged on the mystery object.

A folded sheet of paper slid out. A slight bulge showed there was something inside. Janna lay the page down and pulled it open. Staring back up at them was Nicholas Mayfield—smiling, happy, and clearly at home in his environment. He leaned against a bis pole twice his length, attached to a bamboo scaffolding with twine. The arms of his long-sleeved shirt were rolled up, as were his pant legs. The exposed skin was decorated with a transfixing pattern of stripes and dots. Behind him were palm trees, huts built on stilts, and a wide river.

Standing next to Nicholas were two white men, somewhat less jovial. On his left was a tall, thin man smiling toward the camera as if he knew happiness was required. His arms and legs were devoid of decoration, as were the extremities of the man standing on Nicholas's right. He was shorter than the other two, a scowl adorning his face.

He pulled away from the others as if he was an unwilling participant in this photograph. His face seemed familiar, though Zelda couldn't place him.

Janna turned the photo over and read the faded text aloud, "Albert, Kees, and me." She flipped it over and held it close, examining it intently. "I'll be damned—that's Albert Schenk!" His thick black hair was long gone, and his waistline had grown substantially since the photograph had been taken. "We have to scan this in," she said, giggling as she added, "I wonder if this is why he didn't want us to copy the journal. He was afraid we were going to find this photograph and include it in the exhibition."

Janna hopped over to her computer and quickly scanned it in. "It's saved as page eighty-one. We can take this up to Marijke Torenbouwer in a minute. I know it will make her laugh. Let's scan in that sheet and the other photographs before we do anything else."

Zelda glanced at the page as she handed it to Janna. It seemed to be a letter with writing on both sides. As tempting as it was to read it, Zelda was more interested in the four photographs in her gloved hand. They weren't of people but of handwritten lists. She squinted to decipher the tiny words. They were the types of artifacts one would collect in Asmat: shields, spears, bis poles, headdresses, ancestor sculptures, and stone hatchets.

She quickly counted eighty-seven objects listed in the first photograph. As she skimmed the other three, she realized there were more than three hundred objects recorded. Next to each object was a column of numbers that appeared to be dates, starting in 1956 and going through to August 1962. And the final column contained names of villages. Zelda recognized several from her preliminary research into the Asmat region.

Was this Mayfield's own inventory list? It couldn't be, Zelda suddenly realized. He didn't visit New Guinea until 1961. Upon closer examination, she noted there were gaps between the years. It looked as if only a fraction of the inventory had been photographed.

But if this wasn't Mayfield's collection, whose was it?

"Check this out. It looks like someone's inventory list. But it can't be Mayfield's—see these dates here?" Zelda pointed to the first photograph, comprised entirely of objects collected in the 1950s.

"Perhaps the dates refer to when they were carved?" Janna offered while examining the photographs. "I wonder why these pages are so special," Janna asked as if she were reading Zelda's thoughts.

She laid a photograph on the scanner bed and picked up the phone. "Marijke? Do you have a moment to stop by? We've found something in Nicholas Mayfield's journal you'll want to see." She was quiet for a moment, listening. "Great." Janna dropped the receiver back onto the hook and started her scanner.

"Marijke may know what this list means. She and Johan have done the most research into Mayfield's collection. Though I can't imagine he collected all of these objects. I recall her saying there were only a handful of pieces at Harvard."

As Janna scanned in the last of the photos, Marijke knocked on the door. "Hello, ladies. What do you have for me?"

Marijke's roar of laughter filled the room when Janna showed her the photograph of Albert. "No, he'd never allow its inclusion, but it is tempting to add it to a display anyway," she said as she wiped away her tears of merriment. When enlarged on the monitor, even more detail was visible. Zelda wondered if this was the village Nicholas had used as a home base or if the bis pole in the photograph was one of those to be displayed in the upcoming exhibition.

Marijke's laughter subsided when Janna clicked to the first image of the inventory list. She silently studied the list, her brow creasing in bewilderment. "This collection is incredible, though I don't understand how it ended up in Mayfield's journal." Marijke used her finger to point at the dates visible on the monitor. "This says 1957, doesn't it, Zelda?"

The text was so small that some of the numbers were difficult to read. Zelda leaned forward. "Yes, I'm certain that's what it says. This page starts on July 30, 1956, and stops on May 15, 1957."

"Oh, for a moment, I thought this might be his missing collection," Marijke mumbled before standing up, disappointment evident in her voice. "I know Mayfield acquired several objects during his first acquisition trip in 1961, but it was a small collection. That's why he asked for a translator the second time, in the hope of picking up more pieces. If I recall correctly, he was collecting for a Dutch art gallery as well as Harvard. Though I doubt he acquired as many pieces as are listed here. And if these numbers are indeed dates, then they don't correspond to either of his trips."

Marijke sat down before the monitor and clicked through the scanned photographs again, studying the entries intently. "Janna, would you email these photos to Johan? He may be able to tell us more about them. Though if we don't include Mayfield in the exhibition, then there will be no reason to puzzle out whose list it is."

Computer problems

May 11, 2017

"Work, damn it," Janna growled as she slapped her monitor again. Zelda glanced up from the printed pages she was sorting and was surprised the cables were still connected to the screen.

"That's it—I've had it!" Janna picked up her phone and began dialing. "What now?" she said, moaning in exasperation. She held the horn away from her ear. Even from across the room, Zelda could hear the irritating beep-beep-beep tone reserved for disconnected telephone lines.

"Did Karin forget to pay the bills? Or did the government cut our subsidies again?" Janna joked half-heartedly. The never-ending rounds of subsidy cuts had forced the museum—and most other cultural institutions in the country—to lay off members of its scientific staff to hire more marketing types able to wrangle up enough private funds, monies and sponsorships to keep the lights on and the doors open. Even the Netherlands oldest museums were not spared.

"Try your extension, will you?" Janna asked, motioning toward the telephone next to Zelda's elbow.

"Sure." She picked up and dialed the front desk, only to get the same grating beeps.

"First, the network stops responding, and now the phones." The photographer pinched her nose. "The marketing department is going to throw a fit if I don't get these photos of the African exhibition displays uploaded to the server today. Could you do me a favor, Zelda? Would you run down to the IT department and ask them to send a technician up? Let them know I can't connect to the network. While you do that, I can finish storing my gear. If I'm not out the door by four o'clock, my sister is going to kill me." Janna pushed back from the computer. "Why she scheduled her wedding's dress rehearsal at five p.m. on a Thursday is beyond me. Everyone she's expecting to be there works for a living. And the wedding isn't until Sunday," Janna grumbled.

She'd been complaining about it all week. Zelda figured it was because her sister was making her bridesmaids wear fluffy pink dresses. Janna was not a fluffy pink dress kind of girl—more like leather and straps. Zelda couldn't wait to see the pictures.

"No problem. I'm just about done here. Let me get these papers out of your way." Zelda hurriedly sorted through the last few pages and divided them into two stacks, doing her best to position herself so the photographer couldn't get a good look at the printouts. She'd spent the day combining the two photos of each page and manipulating them in Photoshop until the text was legible. Luckily, the whole mind-numbing process went quickly. The resulting printouts were so easy to read, Zelda decided to print off an extra set for herself. This second copy would make her transcription work so much easier.

Since the Tropenmuseum's director had promised the Mayfields that Nick's journal would not be shared with anyone outside of the museum—lest it was to fall into the hands of the media—Zelda's copy was in fact contraband. She knew she should have been satisfied with the electronic files, but the printouts were so clear, she couldn't help but break the rules.

Zelda rushed to snap rubber bands around the two stacks of paper, quickly double-checking that the copies of the photographs and the mysterious letter were included in each pile. They still baffled her mentor and Johan Dijkhuizen, but Zelda figured they were an important part of the journal, and she didn't want to forget them. As

Janna rose from her chair, Zelda slipped her copy into her backpack as nonchalantly as she could.

Moments later, Janna approached the long workbench Zelda had been using to sort the pages and picked up one of two camera bodies lying on the other end. A dozen lenses of different lengths spread out on a smaller table were positioned next to the two safes Janna used to store her gear.

Thanks to a break-in a few years ago, Janna was now required by the museum's insurance provider to lock up her equipment every night. That was the same reason all of the desktop computers were bolted to employees' desks.

"Okay, here it is, all eighty-five pages of the journal, ready for the safe."

Janna opened the smallest safe. She placed the thick pile of paper inside, next to the journal and a stack of DVDs Zelda had already burned of her photographs, before closing the door and spinning the lock. "Great, now the Mayfield's wishes have been fulfilled. The scans of his journal on our servers are password protected, and all of our physical copies are now secure. There's no way anyone can get ahold of Nick's precious journal. Everybody's happy," Janna finished sarcastically. She knew if the media somehow got their hands on it, she would be held responsible.

"I'll go get a technician for you," Zelda said, slipping her backpack over her shoulder.

"Do you have your mobile with you?"

"Yep."

"I'll give you a call if I regain access to the network before you get back, okay?" Janna added.

"Please do," Zelda said, one hand on the doorknob.

"Toodle-loo," Janna called out as she picked up another lens.

Zelda set off down the staff-only staircase, toward the ground floor where an underground corridor connected it to the Colonial Institute for the Tropics next door.

The Anti-Colonial Brigade

May 11, 2017

Visiting the IT department was like stepping back in time for Zelda. Three short years ago, she had given up her job as a multimedia developer at Microsoft to come to Amsterdam and study art history. Though she didn't miss her old job one bit, she did miss her co-workers, the majority of them odd ducks with a sense of humor unique to those who preferred to interact with computers instead of people. She'd become fond of those geeky types during her days in Redmond.

Zelda bounced down the last of three stone-carved staircases to the subterranean passage connecting the museum to the Colonial Institute. The *Koninklijk Instituut voor de Tropen*, better known as KIT, was established in 1910 as a center of expertise in a wide range of subjects relating to Dutch colonialism. The current Tropenmuseum began as the *Colonial Museum*, a space KIT used to educate, inform and promote the benefits of having colonies to the Dutch people.

She rounded the last bend and felt the floor rising as she approached the KIT building. The IT department was the first office on her left. Zelda knocked loudly on the diffused glass door and waited patiently for one of the IT staff members to open it. She'd quickly learned you must be invited inside. Otherwise, everyone ignored you completely. Besides, it gave whoever was smoking a moment to put out their butt and throw away the evidence. She knew most of the large windows were propped open all year round to keep the servers cool and purify the air of the IT department's hard-to-break smoking habit.

As she waited, Zelda chuckled to herself as she thought back to her old colleagues and their many idiosyncrasies. After ten minutes, her patience was rewarded. Lynne threw open the door and ran back to her terminal, ignoring Zelda's cheery greeting. She was puzzled. Lynne was usually the friendliest of the bunch. Zelda stepped inside. A chorus of mobile phones was chirping and chiming out of rhythm, creating a chaotic symphony of noise, yet all were resolutely ignored. Every geek in the room was glued to their keyboard.

"What's going on?" Zelda asked. No one responded. She walked over to Lynne and repeated her question.

"We've been hacked, and ransomware has infected our networks," she said flatly without taking her eyes off the screen. Lynne's fingers flew across the keyboard, yet all Zelda could see was a string of meaningless code appearing and reappearing, the orange text glowing on the black background. No matter what Lynne typed in, the screen did not change.

Zelda glanced over her co-worker's shoulder to see the same coded message on their monitor. Next to her was an unmanned terminal with KIT's website open on the screen. Zelda watched as animated colonial figures danced around a boiling pot of water, full of dark-skinned cutouts wearing sarongs. Zelda assumed these were meant to be Indonesian. Anti-colonial messages rolled across the screen like a ticker tape interspersed with the message "Give Back What Is Not Yours" every sixty seconds. Zelda knew KIT was a frequent target of hate mail, but this was the first virtual attack she'd heard of.

She watched as another obscene message referencing the Tropen-museum's colonial past rolled by. Each snippet of text was signed *Brought to You by the Anti-Colonial Brigade*.

"What is the Anti-Colonial Brigade?" Zelda asked.

It took a few seconds before Lynne tore her eyes away from her screen and answered Zelda. "We don't know. This is a new organization for us. Some of us think the Papuans are behind this attack, but their government is not officially associated with any protest group. Besides, the figures seem to be Indonesian, not Papuan. So far, I've yet to find any mention of the Anti-Colonial Brigade. Not online or in our Crazy Fuckers file," she said, referring to a folder full of death threats and crazy demands held at KIT's reception desk for reference. The colonial history of the institution, the origins of the museum's collection and even the decorations on the building sparked quite a bit of hate from indigenous groups. The recent publicity around the Human Remains project and the restitution case at the Mission Museum only increased the amount sent their way.

"Did they take down the phones, too? Or is that a coincidence?" Zelda asked.

"The website, internet, intranet, phone lines, and keypads to our storage facilities are all down. Guards are clearing the museum right now. God knows if someone is trying to rob the place," Lynne said, her face showing the strain of the day. She turned back to her keyboard and began to type when she suddenly stopped. "Why did you come down here?"

"Janna couldn't log on to the network or use the phones, so she sent me down to enlist your help."

Lynne snorted. "She's going to have to get in line. Until we figure out who this hacker is and get them out of our system, we're shutting everything down. It looks like most of our network's files and programs have already been corrupted. Even if management decides to pay three million bitcoins to unlock the system, we have no way of knowing what kind of bugs, Trojan horses, or other fun surprises they've left behind."

Zelda nodded, sure Janna would go through the roof. Even in their short time together, Zelda noticed she hated being late for an appointment, fluffy dress or no. Though if the whole network were down, the marketing department wouldn't be sending any press releases out today, anyway.

"Well, I'll go tell Janna the bad news."

Lynne grunted in acknowledgment. Zelda showed herself out.

Bad news

Zelda knocked loudly on the photography studio door before opening it. She knew Janna didn't like to be surprised and was often so engrossed in her work that she wouldn't notice the door's loud click. On her way back up, she'd been thinking about how upset Janna would be by these turn of events. If by some miracle the IT department got the network back online before five p.m., she could make a DVD of Janna's images and deliver them to the marketing department for her.

"Bad news, I'm afraid, Janna," Zelda called out as she walked inside. "The networks are down and are going to stay that way for a while." She stopped short, suddenly realizing the lights were off. Did Janna get tired of waiting and go to the marketing department to discuss a solution with them? *Strange that she didn't lock the door,* Zelda thought, especially considering how fanatical she was about her expensive gear and the insurance policy.

Zelda stepped back toward the door and felt for the switch. As she flipped on the light, fright pushed her against the wall, taking her breath away.

Janna lay on the floor, her neck at a strange angle, her legs flailed out. Blood was pooling around her head and shoulders. From her glassy stare, Zelda knew instantly she was dead.

Zelda felt faint as flashbacks of the last time she was confronted with so much blood filled her mind. She grabbed the table's edge for support. Anger, fear, and rage poured out of her as an endless scream.

Seconds later, collection researchers working in the office next door were at her side. "What's going on?"

Her cry turned to sobs as she pointed at the body.

"No!" One of the researchers ran to check Janna's pulse as another dialed security. Zelda couldn't tear her eyes away from the photographer's face frozen in shock. Zelda only hoped Janna hadn't suffered and was truly surprised by the violence that had ended her life.

Someone put their hands on her shoulders and tried to lead her away, but Zelda couldn't leave Janna like this. Blood still seeped out of the triangular-shaped wound on her forehead. Zelda had to suppress an overwhelming urge to stroke Janna's hair and comfort her spirit.

The wound on her head corresponded with the swash of red on the workbench's corner. *Janna was so strong, how could this have happened?* she wondered. Zelda knew Janna was a brown belt in karate, a blue belt in judo, and had recently started kickboxing. Just yesterday, Janna told her proudly how she'd knocked out a classmate—a man twice her size—during her first lesson. From her body's position, she'd obviously fought her attacker. Whoever did this was either exceptionally strong or had caught her by surprise. *But why her?* The photographer was so full of life. How could someone take it so callously? Was she even the target of this attack or simply at the wrong place at the wrong time?

Zelda glanced around the room, finally registering that Janna's usually pristine desk was a ravaged mess. Worse yet, both safes were open and empty. The camera gear, DVDs, printouts, and Mayfield's journal were gone. The rest of the room was as bad as Janna's desk, loose sheets of paper and office supplies strewn across the floor. Were those pages the printout of the journal? Somehow, Zelda doubted it. Through the shock of Janna's death, she barely registered what their absence meant for the museum and Mayfield's family.

She looked again to the empty safe. Where were Janna's camera bodies and lenses? Those safes usually contained thousands of dollars' worth of gear. *Janna would be furious,* Zelda fumed. She crumpled a little at the thought, realizing the photographer couldn't care, not anymore.

The researcher squeezed her shoulder. "We shouldn't be here. Let's wait for the police next door, shall we?"

Zelda nodded, tears splashing on her t-shirt as she did. Despite her desire to comfort Janna's soul, she couldn't bring herself to step any closer to her lifeless body. And the room was a crime scene, she realized as sobs racked her body once again.

Tropenmuseum in upheaval

May 17, 2017

"How could you have let this happen?" Theodore Mayfield screamed. "If you had given it to the United States Embassy immediately—as we'd requested—this never would have occurred. Why didn't you? Thanks to your incompetence, we may never get the journal back." His words echoed across the Tropenmuseum's Light Hall and ricocheted throughout the exhibition halls.

Zelda was on the second floor, officially surveying the Asmat artifacts in preparation for her new assignment. She'd spent so much time studying it already, she knew the Oceania collection almost as well as the head curator did. In reality, she was killing time, waiting for her supervisor to be done with her weekly staff meeting. Seeing as this was the first day the museum was open since Janna's death six days earlier, Zelda figured the meeting would be a long one.

The museum's director and Nick Mayfield's brother were directly below her. Following closely behind them were a gaggle of men in matching suits, closely monitoring their conversation. Zelda blushed, thinking how embarrassed Karin Bakker must feel by Theodore Mayfield's dressing down in front of the museum's board of directors. Zelda stepped closer to the railing, hoping to catch the rest of their conversation.

"Our incompetence?" Karin retorted with the same ferocity. "Our computer and security systems were hacked and our photographer murdered. It is not as if we left the journal on the library's reading table and allowed it to be stolen. It was in a locked safe located inside one of our offices. We had it in our possession because your lawyers in New York gave us permission to take digital photographs of it for research purposes. We had completed photographing the journal the day before Janna was murdered. As soon as we get our network back online, we will be able to get you the files," Karin said.

"We don't want a digital copy of it—we want his actual journal. Don't you understand its significance to his brothers, cousins, and aunts? The police have been informed and are aware of the importance of finding it."

"I know they already arrested a suspect in Janna's killing. If he stole Nick's journal, the police will have it back in no time," Karin said quietly yet firmly. Zelda leaned in closer to hear her. Karin glanced up at the changing shadow. "Let us discuss this further in my office. Please follow me."

The museum's director walked away without waiting for a response, effectively shutting down the conversation. After a moment's hesitation, Nick Mayfield's brother and their entourage followed.

Zelda had heard Janna Kolen's ex-boyfriend was the prime suspect in her murder. According to the police, he was a known heroin junkie with multiple arrests for violent assault. Zelda could hardly believe a levelheaded woman such as Janna could get mixed up with someone like that. Marijke Torenbouwer told her they'd met at a boxing class ten years ago and had an on-again, off-again relationship since. More staff gossip revealed that Janna had kicked him out last week, going as far as to throw all of his clothes and CDs in a dumpster before changing the locks. He'd tried to kick in the door and was arrested after neighbors called the cops. Apparently, Janna wasn't home, but her boyfriend was too high to notice.

No wonder she was so into self-defense courses, Zelda thought.

But why would he have taken the journal? The camera gear could easily be sold at a pawnshop, but Nick Mayfield's journal wasn't an object many would value—though Janna was one of the few people on this planet who had access to it. Even if the boyfriend knew about it, would he dare to steal the journal and try to extort money out of Mayfield's family for its return?

An acquisition trip to Ow

May 23, 1962

Nick sucked in the warm, musty air and smiled in delight. In the shafts of amber light struggling to break through the dense foliage, he could see butterflies the size of dinner plates wafting by. A few feet in front of his boat, a cockatoo dipped down, pulled a tiny fish from the water, and then swooped back up into the air, all in one swift motion.

Floating on this muddy, palm-fringed river was paradise. Here he didn't have to worry about impressing anyone or doing what was expected of him. In New York, he was a Mayfield, and he was required to act accordingly. Here in this far-flung jungle, he was simply another anthropologist on an acquisition trip. The locals had no idea who his family was, nor would they care. Money meant nothing to them, only what they could obtain through barter or trade. Those who did recognize his name, like that snotty Dutch anthropologist assigned to guide him, were his subordinates. Their opinions were meaningless.

His boat turned into a narrow tributary. As the catamaran slowly made the turn, Nick chuckled as he pushed low-lying palm leaves and branches out of his way. Gliding along like this, so close to the water, was an unusual experience. Speedboats and yachts were the norms back home. He couldn't recall ever sailing in a boat without a motor before.

Nick folded his arms behind his head and leaned back against the stern, reveling in the sounds of nature. White-tailed cockatoos screeched as they shook the branches of a Pandanus pine above, jostling for position. In the underbrush along the river's banks, he heard snorts from a wild boar snuffling for food. These strange noises brought joy to his heart—as if the water's surface amplified every sound, compensating for his damaged ear in a way he'd never experienced before. He couldn't recall a time when he could hear normally, though he should have been able to. Scarlet fever robbed him of one ear when he was eleven years old, yet his mind had wiped that sensory memory away. Here in this boat, he felt complete again.

His canoes rocked violently as one of the rower's thin oars got stuck in a mangrove tree's gnarly roots. The men were having trouble navigating the narrowing waterway in the makeshift catamaran, which was wider than any boat the Asmat typically made.

His transportation was unusual for these waters yet well suited for his needs. He'd paid the villagers to strap together the two longest canoes in the village and attach a series of planks across the middle. On top of that, they'd secured two large crates to hold supplies and artifacts, as per his instructions. The illustration accompanying his survival guide's description of how to make such a craft made it easier for the Asmat men to understand what he wanted to accomplish. Tarps brought from home were stretched across the crates' tops to protect the tobacco, knives, iron axes, fishhooks, and steel pans from the rain.

Unfortunately, when fully loaded, the weight of his barter goods pushed the boat down deep into the river. Water regularly lapped in, meaning Nick kept himself busy scooping the bottom with an old coffee tin. In the boat next to him, his friend Roger was the designated scooper. Albert preferred to take notes as they sailed. Nick wiped the sweat from his brow with a handkerchief, grinning across at Roger as he did. His friend tried to return the smile but grimaced instead.

The weight also made it difficult for the Asmat rowers. Even with eight in each canoe, they were struggling to push the catamaran upstream. They'd been rowing for most of the day yet still hadn't reached the first village on his list. With a motor, they would have arrived and already begun the complex negotiation process. As the men grunted with exertion, Nick called out, "Albert, where can I buy an outboard motor?"

The Dutch anthropologist laughed callously, refusing to look up from his notebook as he yelled back, "Father Terpstra may be able to help you."

Nick knew Albert disapproved of his boat, certain the makeshift catamaran would be too heavy. Despite his protests, Nick felt he had no choice. The boat was so fully loaded because so many villagers expressed interest in trading with him. Ten axes per skull or shield was turning out to be a lucrative offer. Despite the lack of roads, word traveled fast through this dense, waterlogged jungle.

"When do you expect him to come back to Kopi?" Nick responded evenly.

"Next week. He usually returns once a month to pick up more trading supplies before going back and doing the rounds again."

"What kind of supplies?"

"Steel hatchets, fishing line and hooks, same as you." Albert kept his eyes on his notebook.

"How many villages does he serve?" Nick was raised Catholic and had learned early on to respect its clergy, although the bishops and priests he'd known wouldn't be tough enough to survive out here, he reckoned. The Dutch ambassador credited Father Terpstra with being the first to connect with these savagely shy Asmat. Nick was looking forward to meeting this priest and finding out more about his work.

"Forty-seven at last count, though he's always on the lookout for new souls." Albert said, chuckling. "He's converted most villages in this region, including Ow. I know he's been traveling further down the coast, searching for new ones."

"What does he do exactly?"

Albert finally made eye contact, his irritation shining through. "What you would expect a Catholic priest to do—baptisms, marriages, funerals, church services, and training new priests to help serve his growing community. He's also introducing Catholic iconography as a way of saving the Asmat's carving tradition. As an anthropologist, it is quite interesting to witness this transference firsthand. Though this Christian influence is only making their traditional designs more scarce and desired by collectors," Albert said before returning his attention to his notebook.

The Asmat rowers slowed their pace as they rounded the next bend. Near the river's edge was a field of young palm saplings. Two bis poles lay between the rows. The boat rocked when Nick stood to get a better look. He caught a glimpse of them as they floated past the small opening in the brush before his view was obscured.

A chorus of barking dogs signaled they were approaching a village, presumably their first destination. Conch shells trumpeted, warning of their close proximity. Nick sat back down, hoping to see the displays of strength he witnessed during his last acquisition trip eight months earlier.

Roger perked up, as well. He called over to Nick, a smirk on his face, "Finally, land! That took long enough."

Nick tried to brush off his friend's irritation, unsuccessfully. The excitement of being on an adventure wore off for Roger their second night in Kopi when he was awakened by a family of cockroaches nestling in his damp armpit. The next morning, it had taken Nick hours to persuade Roger to stay on long enough to help with one collection trip, as he'd promised. If the first trip went well, Nick figured he could always find another willing assistant in Agats to help with a second one. He only hoped Roger could stand being in the rainforest for a few more weeks so he wouldn't have to cut this trip short.

As the river straightened, Nick saw warriors lining the bank, effectively blocking their entrance to the village of Ow. The men had feathered bands tied above their elbows and knees. A piece of bamboo covered some of their genitals. Most wore headdresses and necklaces made of shells, feathers, and twine. White, yellow, and red stripes and dots adorned their dark skin. They all had bows drawn and pointed at Nick's canoes. He knew it was nothing more than a show, but the sight of all these painted warriors sent chills up his spine.

At the front of Nick's catamaran was the oldest villager in Kopi, an elder who assured Albert Schenk he could guarantee them safe passage through the villages upstream. The man called out to his neighbors, singing his greeting. After a few melodious exchanges, the warriors lowered their weapons and began shaking their hips, indicating they wouldn't attack. When the men broke line, Nick could see a large opening and several huts built on stilts rising up behind them. Cowering underneath the structures closest to the shore were the women and children, huddled together in a ball.

The men continued to call and sing to each other as Nick's regatta pulled up to the shore. Before all of the canoes reached land, a cluster of children broke free from their mothers and ran into the water, shrieking in delight as Nick's men secured their boats.

The warriors and rowers began to chant in unison as Nick's catamaran pulled in close to land. He could hear drums beating in the distance yet saw no musicians. An old man steadied the dugout with one hand and offered Nick the other. Adorning his head was an outrageously large headdress made of bird of paradise feathers. A decorated skull with its jawbone attached swung from a palm frond rope around his neck. Nick took the older man's hand and sprang into the knee-deep water, his feet sinking into the squishy riverbed.

As he pulled his legs out of the muddy bottom and walked toward land, he got his first good look at the village of Ow. Huts built high off the glistening brown earth were clustered together around a circular clearing. The rainforest, a wall of solid green, rose up dramatically behind. The contrast in color always astounded Nick. Smoke twisted around the tops of most homes, rising from fires constantly burning inside the small huts. Human skulls were mounted on fence poles, hanging from rafters, and displayed on porches, some decorated and yellowed with age while others were gleaming white. A muddy path wound along a small group of structures built along the river's edge. Closest to the shore was the largest building in the village, which Nick knew was the Men's House. Guarding the entrance were two impressive bis poles, both easily fourteen feet tall with wings protruding out of their tops. Recently painted, the white chalk, red ocher, and charcoal lines decorating their surfaces were still bright despite the heavy rainstorms.

After Nick and his Western companions made it to shore, they were led to the clearing. The village's chief, a muscular man with a boar's tusk protruding from his nose, sat on a makeshift throne in the middle. According to Albert, he was in his sixties, though only the gray streaks in his hair gave his age away. *He looks majestic,* Nick thought. The intricate patterns adorning his body accentuated his muscular physique, and the crown of shells and feathers covering his head confirmed his village standing.

Behind the chief stood a group of young women wearing reed skirts and shell necklaces. Hibiscus flowers and feathers decorated their springy hair. Nick paused a moment to admire their perky bare breasts and full hips. As the three Westerners approached the village's leader, Nick smiled and made eye contact with the older man. The chief stared back, yet no smile crossed his lips. Instead, he patted a wooden bench placed on his right.

Once the Westerners were seated, the drums beating softly in the background grew louder as a group of musicians approached the shore. They held their long, exquisitely carved instruments in one hand and drummed with the other, all the while dancing and singing. A group of warriors began crawling over the muddy clearing before them, pantomiming a fight to the death, their terrifying motions perfectly synchronized to the incessant rhythm of the drums. Their intense performance crescendoed into a chaotic flurry of song and dance, then, stopped as abruptly as it had started.

After the shows of strength were over, the entire village sat before the Westerners, watching respectfully as their chief presented Nick, Albert, and Roger with headdresses made of shells and rainbow-colored feathers. Albert translated that these gifts were given so they wouldn't forget their visit to Ow. Nick nodded, smiling as the chief placed the crown on his head.

Once this transaction was complete, several villagers rose and ran to their huts. They soon returned with artifacts, artwork, and tools they wanted to trade for Nick's goods, still safely stored on his catamaran. One by one, the long line of locals presented their pieces and waited patiently for Nick to make them an offer. The chief picked up each shield, headdress, skull, armband, statue, paddle, and spear, holding each one up high as he proudly described its decoration and significance, clearly selling its worth to the inexperienced American.

Nick dutifully recorded in his notebook everything the chief said as Albert translated it. The Dutchman took no notes but did snap photos of everything presented to them. Nick handed Roger his Nikon and requested that he do the same.

At first, Nick asked his childhood friend's opinion of the objects, but Roger was clearly not interested in the Asmat's artwork, culture, food, or lifestyle. *His photographs will probably be a disappointment anyway*, Nick thought as Roger held up his camera and snapped a photo without adjusting the focus first. Instead of getting into an argument, Nick ignored Roger, leaving him to drink whiskey out of his flask, hoping the alcoholic beverage would improve his friend's mood.

Whenever a particularly beautiful skull, shield, or headdress passed before them, Nick signaled to Albert to start the negotiations, offering several sacks of tobacco, knives, fishing lures, and axes for the best pieces.

"I'm not going to translate that," Albert stated on several occasions. "You're offering far too much for it. I'm well aware your family can buy anything, but this is ludicrous. Do you realize your extravagant offer of ten hatchets per skull has already caused several tribes to take up headhunting again? Considering all that the Church and local government are doing to put a stop to these barbaric practices—"

"You are jealous you can't match my offer, that's all. And you're worried I'll drive the prices up. I don't believe for a second my acquisitions have anything to do with the recent spate of village skirmishes or headhunting raids. Several physical anthropologists active in this area have been accused of stealing ritual objects and looting gravesites for human remains. Arrest warrants have been issued for three of them. If anyone is to blame, it's them. It's no surprise, seeing how many of those vermin are photographing and measuring every native they come across. How such a racist pseudoscience is still respected and funded is beyond me. They should all be arrested, as far as I'm concerned."

Nick shook his head in the face of Albert's budding protest.

"Don't try to deny it. The governor of Dutch New Guinea told me about those barbarians and their sickening ideology during my last visit to Hollandia. Treating the locals as if they were objects to be studied—instead of as business partners—doesn't endear physical anthropologists to the villagers. Those thefts are likely the cause of these latest battles. A few hatchets and pots aren't worth killing for."

"You know nothing about the Asmat's religious beliefs or social structures. A few pots are more than enough reason to attack another village—that is precisely how tribal wars get started here."

Nick scoffed, waving his hand as if he was swatting a fly. "Are you going to translate my offer, or do I have to mime what I am willing to pay for that skull?"

Once the procession had passed, Nick inspected his selection of thirty masks, skulls, spears, and statues. "Is this everything they have for sale? Tell him I am interested in bis poles, like those we saw in the field outside their village. Though if they are already rotten, they won't do."

"Those are ritual objects." Albert enunciated the words as if Nick was an infant. "If you take those poles, the process cannot be completed, and their ancestor's soul will never be free. The poles rot into the ground and fertilize the new plants with their ancestors' energy and vitality. They won't sell them to you," Albert said in English.

"Ask anyway."

Reluctantly, Albert translated Nick's request. The indignation on the tribesman's face was confirmation—they were not for sale. Not to be deterred, Nick quickly asked, "Would they carve a new one for me, using these designs and motifs?"

Nick pulled five photos of bis poles out of his backpack and shoved them into the chief's hands. He'd taken them in Gallery Visser, his friend's ethnic art gallery back in Amsterdam. Gerrit Visser was one of the foremost dealers in Asmat art in the Netherlands. His son and Nick's good friend, Pepijn, was his assistant. When Pepijn mentioned several of their clientele had bis poles on their wish lists, Nick offered his services immediately. Collecting for both his friend's gallery and Harvard's ethnography museum was a way to motivate his own father to fund this acquisition trip sooner rather than later. Pepijn considered coming with Nick, but Gerrit's bad health made him reconsider. Ultimately, he decided it was better to stay in Amsterdam and learn the business before his father retired. He could always go on the next trip, both men figured.

"Are you actually ordering a bis pole carved to your specifications?" Albert stared at him, his mouth agape. "They will have no connection to Asmat culture and will lose their authenticity. At least the few made for trade are carved during a bis ritual and have some symbolic meaning."

"They will be made by Asmat carvers, right? That's all that matters to Pepijn and me. He gave me photographs of the designs most requested by his clients. The same goes for the poles I'm collecting for Harvard. First and foremost is their visual appeal. Their cultural or ritual significance is secondary," Nick stated matter-of-factly.

Albert cringed. "That dealer has corrupted you."

"No, Pepijn understands what Harvard's audience wants to see. They will be viewed and appreciated for their inherent beauty, as examples of what Asmat carvers are capable of. The paddles and headdresses are interesting, but bis poles are what make Asmat art unique. I can't leave here without acquiring several. If the locals won't sell me their old ones, then I'll order new ones."

Again, Albert reluctantly translated Nick's request, frustrated to see the chief's face light up in delight. He enthusiastically answered in the local Asmat dialect, then paused so Albert could translate. The Dutchman's face paled as the chief spoke. Only after Nick glared at him did he translate the chief's terms into English.

"They are willing to carve one for you using similar designs, but it will cost you fifty axes, three bags of tobacco, and ten steel pans. That is four times the amount I've paid for a pole," he added in disgust.

"Are you kidding? That's nothing compared to the cost of a Van Gogh or Matisse."

"No good will come of this," Albert said quietly.

"It's only money," Nick replied hotly, puffing up his chest. "And at these prices, I can afford several more."

Albert's face drained of color. He shook his head as he spoke. "You have no idea what you are doing. This will start a tribal war."

"I've flown halfway across the world to collect these objects and will not tolerate your insolence. Do I have to file an official report with your embassy, or are you going to do what you were paid to do?" Nick warned, not for the first time.

Albert stared at him, swallowing an evil thought before saying, "I will translate what you ask, only because I swore to do so."

"Tell the chief I want two poles carved, and I'm prepared to pay the same price for each," Nick said smugly, patting Albert on the back. "Now translate."

Zelda seeks guidance

May 17, 2017

"Marijke, do you have a minute?" Zelda asked. She hated interrupting her mentor's busy day of meetings but didn't know what her priorities should be. Police tape was still strung across the door to the photography studio. Even if it was open, Zelda had no reason to be there. In light of last week's events, she was unsure if data entry for the Human Remains project or collection research for the exhibition took precedence.

Marijke Torenbouwer's coffee spilled a little as her arm twitched. At first, her mentor seemed irritated Zelda had snuck up behind her at the coffee machine, but she recovered quickly. "Of course. Would you like a drink?"

"A cappuccino, please." Zelda took a porcelain cup out of the cabinet and handed it to her mentor.

As the machine rumbled to life, Marijke said, "I imagine you need some direction."

Zelda nodded, grateful she didn't have to start the conversation.

"I'm not sure if the Human Remains team has been allowed back into the depot or not"—Marijke sighed—"though you won't be able to do any data entry today. The servers are still down, and only a select few have access to a desktop right now. Until they know more about the group that hacked our network, both the police and our IT staff are reluctant to put the servers back online. Victor Nalong is going to love hearing about this interruption," she added sarcastically.

Zelda knew the police were busy interviewing all members of staff as part of their investigation into the network hack, the building's security breach, the robbery, and Janna's death. Thinking about the spunky photographer brought a tear to her eye. Her funeral on Sunday had been well attended by the Tropenmuseum staff, as well as museum professionals from cultural institutions spread around the country. Nothing like this had ever happened in a Dutch museum before, and it left everyone reeling, especially since the police still didn't have a viable suspect. Her family was still in shock, wondering aloud why they didn't know about her boyfriend's violent past and asking themselves what other secrets Janna had kept from them.

"Until the network is restored, we won't be able to get at our copy of the journal, meaning you can't continue with the transcription, either."

Zelda nodded meekly, keeping her eyes averted. She didn't dare tell Marijke about her paper copy. Of course, she couldn't work on the transcription at the museum without risking someone noticing what she was doing.

"And until Theodore Mayfield receives either the actual journal or a copy of the digital files, none of us are going to get any rest. The police are still combing through the IT department's files. It might be as late as Friday before we regain access," Marijke said, her voice infused with her frustration at having to wait two more days to get a resolution to any of the crises on her plate.

"Why don't you begin preparing for your archive visits? Have you scheduled any appointments yet?"

"I have an appointment at the Mission Museum in Steyl on Monday and another at Beeld en Geluid on Thursday."

"Excellent. Don't forget to check out Steyl's Asmat collection while you are there. It is stellar. Until then, be sure to familiarize yourself with their collections and the institution's history. Knowing how pieces were acquired is usually as important to understanding the collection as the objects themselves."

Zelda was elated she didn't have to work with dead bodies this week, and instead, she would finally get to do what she'd been training to do these last eighteen months—conduct archival research for an actual exhibition.

"Give me a call if you get into trouble," her mentor joked. "Don't forget to write up a report about each archive you visit and include the inventory numbers of any relevant photos or films we could use in the exhibition or multimedia displays. Did Janna have a chance to brief you on the types of media we would need... before she died?" Her mentor added the last few words under her breath as if she were afraid to say them aloud.

Zelda nodded solemnly. "She did." Two days before her death, Janna had emailed her the specifications required by the exhibition team regarding the size and quality of the films and photos. Zelda knew a few photographs would be blown up and included in the displays, though most would be shown on touchscreens dotted throughout the hall and in the multimedia tour.

"Good. After the project team has reviewed your findings and made their final selection of multimedia to be used in the exhibition, you can help fill in the official object loan contracts."

Zelda smiled broadly, thrilled to be an active part of this exhibition. "Excellent."

"Check back with me on Tuesday, would you? I will be curious to hear your impression of Steyl's collection."

Mission Museum Steyl

May 22, 2017

"Jesus Christ, Friedrich! Slow down!" Zelda gripped the dashboard and sank further down in her seat as her friend whipped around a Ferrari racing up the freeway.

"Calm down. I've got this under control," Friedrich said, his buzz cut gleaming, a smile splitting his narrow face.

Despite his Maserati-style driving, Zelda was grateful her friend made time to take her all the way down south to Steyl. By car, it was a two-hour stint. The same journey by train and bus would have taken twice as long. And because of her internship and his studies, they rarely got a chance to talk. Still, he didn't have to race to get there.

"We aren't going to be late or anything. I don't really have an appointment," Zelda said in a calmer voice, trying hard to relax. She instinctively sucked in her breath as he crossed lanes, barely missing a blue Audi in his path.

Without looking away from the road, Friedrich asked nonchalantly, "So, tell me about this journal. What secrets have you uncovered about Nicholas Mayfield?"

"Ha!" She snorted. "I wish I'd found something interesting to share." What could she say? She'd transcribed about half of the eighty-page document. Nicholas Mayfield's journal was a combination of scientific recordings and child-like rants. In the beginning, his entries focused on recording the names of villages he visited, local carvers he bought objects from and any information about the techniques

75

he'd seen them use. The entries, in the beginning, were written by a trained anthropologist interested in documenting unique aspects of the cultures he was encountering.

The collection he acquired sounded fascinating. He'd described all of the pieces so well that she could practically visualize them. So far, he'd bartered for a few hundred artifacts and carvings. In most of these entries, he'd also noted who the pieces were purchased for. Most were acquired for either Harvard Museum or Gallery Visser, though several of the more intricate pieces he'd intended to keep for himself.

However, these neutral, somewhat dry, artifact-related entries were very different from the increasingly derogatory observations he made about the Westerners he met along the way—missionaries, government officials, and anthropologists there to save souls, establish order, or collect information. According to Nicholas, they were all going about it the wrong way and ended up treating the locals as subservient primitives. Not even his American travel companion Roger was spared his abuse. Nicholas repeatedly wrote about his friend's inability to adapt to the climate or embrace the Asmat culture. Zelda figured these remarks were a product of his competitive spirit. His need to be the best at all he did shone through his journal entries.

"There are a few passages the curators may be able to use about one of the bis poles in the exhibition. He describes meeting the team of carvers pretty extensively," Zelda said, thinking back to one of Mayfield's earliest entries.

He described the Asmat carvers he'd commissioned bis poles from as talented artisans, as competent as any contemporary painter he'd met in New York. Nicholas seemed to value their creative efforts more than Western artists because they were actively producing these awe-inspiring objects to appease their ancestors, not for financial gain. In several entries, Nicholas referred to Asmat carvers as being better people than the Westerners he'd met on the island who were only there to collect data and start feuds.

The irony wasn't lost on Zelda. This was hypocrisy in its purest form, yet she doubted Nicholas ever realized that. Somehow, he considered himself and his actions as better than that of the others. For the hundredth time since she'd started transcribing his words, she wondered if the journal would bring his family grief or confirm what they had expected.

"Apparently, he wanted to buy two poles he'd seen rotting in a field outside the Ow village. The villagers refused, telling him those particular poles were sacred and had to be left to decompose in the forest."

"Do you think he took them anyway?"

"I don't think so, although I have found several archival documents that indicated theft was rampant. Several important anthropologists and government officials took poles and other ritual objects without asking permission or paying for them. I guess it was easy enough to export them out of the country without a bill of sale. The Asmat did barter for everything, and I've found no mention of invoices created which would document the transaction. Apparently, when ritual objects disappeared, the locals didn't suspect the Westerners. They blamed neighboring tribes for stealing the objects, which created tensions between the villages, and in some cases, led to headhunting parties."

"That's pretty messed up," Friedrich said.

"Yes, it is. Yet I don't think Nicholas stole those two poles. According to his journal, when the chief refused, he simply asked to have two new ones carved. The chief said yes but asked for a ridiculous number of axes and supplies in return for swift delivery. Nicholas didn't have any problem with the price tag, but the anthropologist guiding him did. And that, of course, is the current director of Rotterdam's Wereldmuseum, Albert Schenk."

"Oh, yeah, you said Schenk was Nicholas's translator and guide," Friedrich said, never taking his eyes off the road. Zelda was grateful. Traffic was heavy.

"Yes, assigned by the Dutch government to assist the American in any way possible. It sounds like Nicholas didn't let him forget it." Zelda knew the director and Nicholas were acquainted, so she wasn't surprised to see him named in the journal, but it was a shock to read Mayfield's unflattering descriptions of this now powerful man.

"And Nicholas's father set it all up, right?"

"Yep. I guess, when your family founded one of the most successful corporations in America, you can arrange just about anything."

"So what was Albert's problem, according to Nicholas?"

"It sounds like they were butting heads most of the time, and Mayfield was the kind of guy who was used to getting his way. He obviously didn't appreciate Albert's advice and wrote some pretty derogatory things about him."

"Like what?"

"That Albert was a phony and profiteer, a peon more worried about keeping prices down so he could make a profit when selling objects to a museum than really showing interest in learning about other cultures."

"Ouch."

"Yeah. I can imagine that's why he has been against including excerpts from Mayfield's journal in the exhibition. He must have figured Mayfield wrote some pretty nasty stuff about him."

"It would be fascinating to see what he thinks of those journal entries." Friedrich pondered, his interest surely originating from his psychology courses, which he was close to completing. A few more months of classes and he would have his bachelor's degree. Not that he would be finished with his studies. Thanks to his high marks, he was sure to secure a coveted position in the master's psychology program.

Zelda laughed. "I sincerely doubt he would enjoy reading it." Before Friedrich could continue his analysis, she rushed on. "And other than Albert, he's obsessed with a military-issued manual, *How to Survive on Land and Sea*. His friend Roger returned to New York only two months after they'd arrived. It sounds like Nicholas couldn't communicate effectively with the locals, despite his best efforts. And Albert avoided him when they were in Kopi. To kill time, he made hunting traps, fishing spears, and even built his catamaran according to specifications in that survival guide. I guess it makes sense. He was the only one in his family not to serve in the army, and it was a manual written specifically for survivalists and military. His brothers probably had copies of it lying around."

"Do you know why he didn't enlist?"

"He was deaf in one ear, so he couldn't."

As Friedrich nodded sagely, Zelda rolled her eyes, knowing what was coming next.

"That must have been difficult for him. Perhaps he felt inferior to his brothers, uncles, and father because of it," Friedrich speculated. "That may explain his interest in mastering those survival techniques. It was his way of visualizing his strength and ability, despite his handicap."

"I would assume so," Zelda said, remaining neutral, unwilling to get into a psychological discussion about Nicholas's possible inferiority complex. She'd once thought learning languages and flying remote control planes were what made Friedrich happiest. He enrolled in the psychology master program to please his parents, or so she thought. To her surprise, he embraced it with the same enthusiasm as he had his other passions and was consistently at the top of his class. She was sure he would graduate *cum laude*.

They had known each other for three years, almost as long as Zelda had lived in Amsterdam. Though Friedrich once saved her life, they had never been anything more than good friends. Thanks to their harrowing, shared experiences, he was like a brother to her now. Friedrich would do anything for her, and he knew Zelda would do the same.

The navigation system beeped and began instructing Friedrich in Hindi, his current language of choice. Zelda glanced at the screen and saw it was alerting them to take the upcoming exit. She noted with surprise that they were only a few miles from the German border. *The Netherlands is so small,* she thought, shaking her head in amazement.

Their exit brought them into a town called Tegelen. Signs for the Monastery Village Steyl appeared immediately, making their navigation system superfluous. The two-lane road wound through residential neighborhoods toward the outskirts of the village and into a wide green expanse of land dotted with horse pastures and farmhouses. The landscape suddenly rose, a sign they were entering the limestone formations of the Dutch Mountains found in the southernmost tip of the Netherlands.

Soon, an imposing building of red brick with white trim, surrounded by a tall iron fence, appeared on their right. Friedrich drove slowly enough that Zelda could read the brass plate informing visitors it was the Men's House. A few hundred feet later, they passed an almost identical building, though this one was for the Mission's sisters. The only difference Zelda could see was the fountain in front. Before she could tell which statue graced its center, a sharp bend in the road took them left and into the heart of Steyl.

"The entire village of Steyl is a protected monument," Zelda said. "Most of the buildings are still in the hands of the Society of the Divine Word. They're a religious order founded by a German named Arnold Janssen in 1875, according to their website."

"The village has a website?"

"Yeah, and a detailed one at that. Janssen's followers were entirely self-sufficient. They even built a steam generator to provide electricity to the village."

As Friedrich rounded another bend, their navigation system chirped again, indicating they'd reached their preprogrammed address. Zelda was not surprised to see their destination was similar in design to the other mission buildings they'd passed, except this one was longer and taller than the others were.

Directly across from the narrow road was an expansive garden. A few greenhouses and sheds were visible over the low wall enclosing it, as were signs pointing visitors toward the sacred caves dotted throughout. Twenty parking spaces sat in front of the garden's wall, and most were empty.

"I guess we should park here," Zelda said.

As soon as the engine was off, Friedrich sprang out of the car and stretched his lanky body. Zelda joined suit. After the long ride, it felt great to get the blood flowing through her muscles again.

Friedrich locked up, and they crossed the street to the Mission House. Before they entered, Zelda noticed a handwritten sign taped to the door indicating the museum was further up the road. *How many times did visitors ask before someone finally put that note up?* she speculated.

They crossed the street and walked along the sidewalk, which was curved to shape the natural bend in the cobblestoned road. A few feet later, they encountered another mission building. Painted onto three ground floor windows was "MU—SE—UM" in large white letters, followed by an arrow spanning another five.

Not that there was any chance of missing the entrance, Zelda thought. A sign as tall as her jutted out of the sidewalk with Mission Museum printed across the top. Their logo, a smiling Buddha and a butterfly, was underneath. The three large windows on this side of the building were covered in silhouettes of a butterfly, a shell, a drum, and a mask on the door. Zelda opened the mask, and a light scent of mothballs immediately filled her nostrils. A small reception and information desk was on their right with flyers, magazines, and calendars for sale prominently displayed. Behind the desk was a closed door marked 'Auditorium' and a large reading room, now empty.

A friendly, elderly woman greeted them in Dutch, her voice revealing a heavy German accent. *It made sense,* Zelda thought. The border with Germany was literally a few hundred feet away by land and water, thanks to the village's position on a bend in the Maas River.

"Welcome to Mission Museum Steyl. Two adults?" The woman

looked up at them expectantly.

Zelda and Friedrich simultaneously placed their *museum-jaarkaart*—an annual pass granting free admission to most of the museums in the Netherlands—onto the counter. With a nod, she handed them their tickets and an information folder.

"The museum's entrance is there." She pointed behind them. "In the auditorium, you can watch a short film about the mission's history."

"Thank you. We will definitely view it before leaving. I also wanted to ask, is Hendrick Groosman available? He knows I will be in Steyl this afternoon, and I hoped to meet with him."

"I will call to see if he's available." She dialed a number and quietly inquired. "He's wrapping up a meeting now but will be free in a half hour. Is that all right?"

"Certainly." Zelda smiled. "Thank you." She turned to Friedrich. "Should we start with the museum?"

"Sure." He nodded, following her lead.

To reach the permanent collection, they first had to pass through a large space currently housing a temporary exhibition about biomimicry and technology. Zelda hardly noticed the displays as she searched for the museum's entrance, but Friedrich apparently did.

"Whoa! I just read an article about this in *Science* magazine. It's incredible what researchers are able to learn by copying nature."

Zelda sidled up next to him and read the introductory text. She'd never heard of biomimicry or biomimetics. The text explained how engineers, chemists, and designers were using naturally occurring shapes, systems, and elements to solve complex human problems. It could be as subtle as modeling the nose of a high-speed train after the beak of a Kingfisher bird to reduce changes in air pressure. Or as complex as using the skeleton of a boxfish as the basis for the frame of a fuel-efficient car.

While she was reading, a screen at the back of the space caught her friend's eye. "Is that Leonardo DiCaprio's documentary?" Friedrich was already making a beeline for the screen. "I really want to see this." He took a seat and focused his attention on the film.

Zelda smiled as she shook her head. "Don't you want to see the museum first?" She knew art and artifacts weren't really his thing, but they did just drive two hours to see the permanent exhibitions.

"Oh, yeah. I guess so. A quick peek anyway."

They approached a doorway at the back of the room. A stuffed bear holding a golden staff stood next to it as if it were guarding the entry. Its presence disturbed Zelda greatly. The large brown bear's eyes bulged, and its limbs were bizarrely positioned because of the motors installed inside its carcass. A silver slit in his chest was for the coins. According to the text board next to it, the bear of Steyl was purchased in 1932. The animatronic mechanism inside made him growl and move ferociously. Thanks to his popularity, the bear went on tour, attracting attention and money for the order's missions abroad. Zelda stared at the grotesque creature, thinking about how quickly times changed. Though she was certain the bear was a topnotch *wonder of the world* when it first made its appearance, nowadays, it was downright creepy.

They passed by quickly and entered a rectangular hallway with three open doorways. Zelda was drawn to a room filled with cases of butterflies, beetles, praying mantises, and other insects collected by the order's missionaries. The iridescent colors and a pleasing variety of shapes lifted her spirits. Small slips of paper with the names Indonesia, S. America, and Africa were pinned inside the glass cases covering the walls. Zelda searched for New Guinea and found the name quickly in a case full of butterflies that were as big as her hand, their wings painted in blue, green, and yellow. *What a joy that must have been to see such a gorgeous insect in flight*, she marveled, attempting to imagine such a large and delicate creature in motion.

"It really stinks in here. Can we check out the ethnography collection now?" Friedrich wrinkled his nose, interrupting her awe-inspired daydreams. The room did reek of mothballs and was definitely the source of the overpowering scent filling the museum's halls. Zelda didn't care. She was enchanted with the displays. Friedrich, on the other hand, was already walking through the next door.

Zelda followed begrudgingly, gasping as she entered the dark space. Her eyes were riveted on a podium on the right side of the room. Through a large skylight, a halo of light shone down onto a plethora of jungle creatures. Zelda felt drawn to the light. Ignoring the rest, she walked toward the large beasts. A giraffe, tiger, rhinoceros, antelope, and several other large African mammals were displayed on a raised platform. None were posed as she was used to seeing them—pouncing or with teeth bared. The animals looked to be out on a leisurely stroll. Zelda figured this was a conscious decision so as not to alarm the parishioners.

From a cursory glance at their website, she knew the museum had been created to provide visitors a glimpse into the world the order's missionaries inhabited. *They have definitely done the animal kingdom justice,* she observed. Behind the larger animals were cases built into the walls housing smaller mammals and birds. She gazed into an aviary—birds of paradise, parrots, and cockatoos stared down at her from branches mounted on the wall. Their beaks were slightly open, colorful wings spread out and their heads cocked, forever in wonder.

"The animals are well preserved," Friedrich noted.

"You're right," Zelda said, surprised.

She opened the museum's information folder. "The museum's collection is comprised of objects acquired by missionaries in China, Argentina, Papua New Guinea, Indonesia, Togo, Ghana, Japan, Nigeria and more, as early as 1883," Zelda read aloud. "Ritual objects, ethnographic artifacts, and the carcasses of exotic animals were all sent back."

"Whoa! They are really old. I wonder how they keep them looking so good?" Friedrich wondered aloud.

Zelda skimmed the rest of the folder in search of the answer.

"I'm not sure, but check this out—the classification system used in the museum hasn't been updated since 1931, though pieces are continually added to the displays. Now the display cases are a time capsule, a sort of *wunderkammer* used to explain how museum exhibitions were once created and how Western missionaries saw their flock in the early 1900s."

Zelda looked to the left side of the room, at the four long cases containing the ethnographic collection, each easily ten feet tall and twenty feet long. The objects were split into displays dedicated to Japan, Indonesia, Papua New Guinea, and Africa. In contrast to the well-organized and somewhat sparse Japanese case, the other three were a crowded mishmash of objects placed according to what looked good.

Zelda's mouth fell open as she took in the gorgeous ancestor statues, lattice-carved paddles, colorful headdresses, turtle shell jewelry, woven armbands, carved flutes, and a multitude of spears filling the case labeled Papua New Guinea. Zelda couldn't believe how beautifully carved and decorated they were. She had seen many of the objects from Leiden and Rotterdam that were to be displayed in the upcoming Bis Poles exhibition, but these were superior in quality and preservation.

Friedrich called out, breaking her thoughts, "Zelda, you should see this." He'd already walked around to the other side of the long display case.

She sidled up next to him and followed the direction of his finger toward a sleeping bag made of woven reed. *To protect against mosquitoes*, according to the small slip of paper lying on top of it. She started to say something snotty when she noticed five hatchets displayed just above it on a glass shelf. Their large stone blades were attached to a carved wooden handle by a wide band of twine. She sucked in her breath as her eyes grew wide in astonishment. From her research, she knew these were rare commodities, most having been destroyed in the 1950s. She took in the flat stone blades, still dull despite obvious attempts at sharpening them. *How many times had these axes been used to kill or maim an enemy,* she wondered.

Her eyebrows shot up, and her mouth fell open when she read the sign placed between them: Stone axes (from the Stone Age).

"Oh man, Nicholas wasn't exaggerating."

How often had she read in Nicholas's journal about the Church's attempts to drag the Asmat out of the Stone Age? His frequent entries didn't reveal an obsession, as she suspected. This really was how the Church thought back then. It was somewhat relieving to see proof of their standpoint for herself, yet that sign still made her feel uncomfortable. It was strange to find this reminder of how Western missionaries viewed another people less than a hundred years earlier in a museum display.

"What do you mean?" Friedrich asked.

"Good afternoon."

Zelda yelped and sprang around.

Before her stood a short, bald man smiling up at her. "Hendrik Groosman. Sorry I startled you. You must be Zelda Richardson."

"Yes, of course. Hello." Zelda shook his outstretched hand enthusiastically. "It's lovely to meet you, Mister Groosman. This is my friend, Friedrich Rutz."

"It is kind of you to come all the way down from Amsterdam to see our modest Asmat collection."

"It's our pleasure," Zelda gushed. "I've heard so much about it that I wanted to see it for myself."

His smile faltered. "Yes, I imagine you have."

Zelda blushed. *Was this a new record for offending a person?* Why did she say that, knowing the legal claim on their collection had dominated the newspapers for months? "From my boss, Marijke Torenbouwer, I mean. She said you have the best collection of Asmat art in the Netherlands."

"In the world, really." Hendrik swelled with pride. "That was kind of her to say. Do you have any questions about the collection?"

"Excuse me," Friedrich broke in, "I'm going to let the two of you talk. Zelda, I'll be in the biomimicry exhibition."

Zelda chuckled. "No problem. We won't be long."

"Take your time," Friedrich said, already moving toward the room's exit.

She nodded as he walked away, secretly glad she had the curator to herself. This was her first real assignment. Meeting with Groosman like this made her feel like a real employee. Friedrich's presence reminded her she was not.

The curator gestured toward the glass case. "All of the objects in our museum were collected by missionaries during their travels and either sent or brought back. It has always been our way of preserving a small selection of relics for future generations while giving our parishioners insight into these diverse cultures and folks. Of course, nowadays, television and the internet enable them to learn far more than our meager displays could ever teach them."

Zelda chuckled dutifully.

"Though the classification systems have not been updated since 1931, we do continue to add unique artifacts to the displays." He pointed toward a carving hanging high up on the freestanding wall inside the glass case. It was a half-circle of wood, flat on one side. Rough depictions of three Christian crosses with martyrs nailed to them carved in relief, making it seem as if the shapes rose out of the wood. Standing next to each cross was an Asmat warrior holding a spear. The background had been painted orange, the crosses and figures brown. White lines created enough detail to recognize the shapes for what they were.

"The Asmat were encouraged to create carvings such as these as an alternative to carving ancestor sculptures or bis poles. It was an early attempt to keep their tradition alive and incorporate Christian iconography into their visual language."

Zelda had trouble keeping her face neutral. This crudely carved blob was a far cry from the intricate creations made to honor their dead. She wanted to spit in disgust yet nodded instead, avoiding eye contact at all costs.

"I'm sure you've heard about our legal battles with the Papuan government," Groosman continued. "We all prayed the outcome would be just. The courts have indeed agreed our priests did not steal these artifacts but received them as gifts from the Asmat they were helping," he said resolutely.

Zelda knew the Papuan government claimed the opposite; that the locals were tricked or forced into trading their most precious ritual objects for metal tools. Others must have been stolen, the government's claim argued because their ceremonial worth was too great. Their claim was supported by official colonial reports filed from the 1930s through to the 1960s, documenting suspected thefts and the resulting headhunting parties. The Papuan government argued these objects were part of the country's rich history—in part decimated by the missionaries and Dutch colonial officers who forbade the creation of new ceremonial objects—and should be returned.

The most controversial objects were the museum's seven decorated skulls, all covered in thick clay molded onto the bone as if it were skin. Cowrie shells served as eyes and painted lines recreated the mouth and cheeks. Several had hair made of reed attached. Zelda knew that the Asmat often kept the skulls and jawbones of their ancestors. It was common to display them in their homes, use them as a pillow when sleeping, or hang them around their necks as amulets. Ancestor worship was an integral part of both daily life and their rituals of the dead. The living often consulted with deceased loved ones, asking for their guidance and assistance in the physical world. Still, knowing this didn't make her less comfortable being in their presence.

At the very least, the skulls should be returned, the government rebutted when their case was denied. The Church did not relent. Gazing at these human skulls decorated so lovingly, Zelda tended to agree. You wouldn't trade your father's head for a pot or hatchet.

The Dutch court's ruling meant all of these Asmat artifacts would remain here in this museum instead of being returned to Papua. *They were created to be worn, worshiped, and used,* Zelda thought, her anger growing the longer she looked upon these human remains. *They shouldn't be gathering dust here and displayed as a trophy.*

Groosman walked around the case, gesturing toward a small bis pole, several masks, and the stone axes. "We are lucky to have any of these artifacts. Most stone implements and ritual objects collected from the villagers were destroyed. Thankfully, some of our priests saved many of the artifacts presented to them as gifts." Groosman gazed lovingly at the stone axes Friedrich had pointed out earlier.

They were scarce thanks to the Church's policies, Zelda thought, allowing the remark to burn on her tongue. Instead, she tempered her comment, asking, "Why did the Church sanction the destruction of cultural objects?"

The curator pursed his lips, his tone growing cold. "Our missionaries brought modern technology and industry to their converts, not only the word of God. Most Asmat were living in the Stone Age when we arrived. The Western world was rapidly encroaching on the island, and many villagers were taken advantage of. It was our mission to help ease them into the twentieth century so they could participate in the world economy." Groosman walked slowly around the case, staring into the display instead of at Zelda.

Their goals were quite lofty, but he still didn't answer my question, she realized, letting the topic drop. She didn't want to upset him before she'd had a chance to visit the mission's archives.

As they approached one end of the long cabinet, a pair of shields caught her eye, or rather, the hundreds of dog's teeth and boar's tusks lining their edges. The rest of the shields were carved flanks of wood painted with abstract images of ancestors on the front. These two were a latticework of woven palm fronds as tall as her five-foot-ten-inch frame. Both were covered in thick brown mud and decorated in a matching pattern of white dots and red stripes. The many tusks curved into needle-like points, most easily seven inches long. Zelda wondered if the Asmat sharpened them or if the tusks grew that way naturally. In the center of both shields were large bulges covered in a thick layer of clay. Zelda pushed her face closer to study them when she realized the shield was staring at her.

She sprang back instinctively, startled by her discovery.

"Impressive, aren't they?" Groosman said with a nod toward the shields.

Zelda gulped audibly as she read the notecard placed between them: Ancestor shield. Human skull.

Intellectually, she knew they were created with reverence to honor their dead. However, her Western morals and biblical upbringing were making it difficult to accept them for what they were.

"These were brought back by Father Terpstra," the curator continued. "The gifts he received are perhaps the finest in our Asmat display. In any case, he's contributed the most. But then, he was also stationed in the Asmat region the longest and was one of the first to make a genuine connection with the local populace," Groosman said in observation.

"That's incredible. I didn't realize he was one of your priests." Zelda recalled Terpstra's name from articles about Dutch missionaries she'd been reading for research. He was highly regarded by both the Asmat and Westerners, as far as she could tell.

"Yes, he is. In fact, a few months before the Dutch ceded its control to the newly formed nation of Indonesia, Father Terpstra opened the first museum of Asmat art on the island. It was in Kopi, the village he had been stationed in."

"Kopi?" Zelda asked, surprised he worked in the same village Nicholas Mayfield stayed in. Groosman didn't seem to hear her.

"It had been his dream to house their finest pieces in one space so the locals wouldn't forget their carving tradition," he said, again missing the irony of his statement. "It served as the foundation for the current Asmat museum in the capital of Agats. He also established twenty-five schools and ten hospitals, as well as trained numerous priests and nurses to carry on his work."

"Fascinating," Zelda mumbled, still wondering if he knew Mayfield.

"He is still alive," Groosman said suddenly as if he'd just remembered. "He lives in the Men's House down the road, but I saw him this morning praying in the chapel across the street. Would you like to meet him? He's quite old and fragile, yet his mind is still spry," Groosman asked much to Zelda's surprise and delight.

"I would love to," she said, curious to meet a man who spent years living among the Asmat and had done so much good in the region. And it would be the perfect opportunity to ask about Nicholas Mayfield.

Asmat baptisms

June 25, 1962

"With this toast, you receive the body of Christ," Kees Terpstra spoke his simplified blessing in Asmat dialect. His newest convert's eyes opened wide as he stuck out his tongue to accept his new religion and savior by way of cracker.

Kees finished the ceremony by sprinkling water over the young Asmat man's shoulders. His latest initiate glowed with pride, bringing a smile of satisfaction to his lips. This was the fifteenth baptism he'd performed today. *Another Asmat village embracing Christianity,* the priest thought happily. It had taken many attempts at contact before these shy villagers allowed him ashore, let alone listened to his speeches about his God and the Western world. He knew they initially saw him as a white devil and were perplexed by his mastery of their languages. Only after he'd shown a great interest in their daily life, ancestor worship, and complex rituals had they accepted him as a member of their village. He'd come to love and respect these people who were able to create a life full of meaning in a place most would deem uninhabitable.

His patience had born fruit. Since arriving on the island nine years ago, he'd converted forty-nine villages. Being a pastor to so many made his trips away from Kopi increasingly longer, but it was worth it and proof he was still worthy of carrying out God's work. A few years ago, he'd begun training assistant Asmat priests to help baptize converts as well as preside over funerals and marriages in villages where Catholicism had taken hold.

Kees examined the palm frond roof of the church still under construction. Despite the morning's heavy rains, he spotted no leaks. Next week, the walls would be complete, and the men could start on the school. He knew most villages initially converted to get ahold of the metal tools and medical supplies still scarce on the island. That was why the mission's schools and churches were so important. They were the best way to ensure the Church's lasting influence. By providing a well-rounded, Christian-based education, he was helping prepare future generations for the rapidly encroaching Western world as well as instilling Catholic values.

With the discovery of gold and silver deposits all over the island, it was only a matter of time before Dutch New Guinea was overrun with Western workers surveying for new roads to reach the mining sites deep in the interior. The Asmat were widely renowned as hard workers, and their reputation made them sought after. Yet, because of their naivety about Western products and their reliance on a barter system, they worked for weeks on end, only to be compensated with a sack of tobacco leaves or a few hatchets. It made him livid that these kind souls could be taken advantage of so easily.

Kees returned to his pulpit made of bamboo and reeds, spreading his hands wide to include all of his newly converted brethren in his message.

"You've brought joy into my life, dear friends. To welcome you into the fold, we will celebrate your new place among God's chosen ones tonight."

A murmur of approval arose from his audience of thirty. The villagers were well aware of the material benefits the Church brought with it. Most knew he had already ordered five swine to be killed and roasted.

Kees gestured toward ten crates stacked to his left. They were filled with steel pans, fishhooks, tobacco, and hatchets he'd brought from Kopi. He opened a lid and pulled out a large pot. "And these, dear friends, are also for you. Now that you are all brothers united by God, there is no reason to hunt or kill your neighbors. I urge you to trade your weapons for these tools and utensils. You will no longer need instruments of death on your journey with Christ." Kees smiled automatically. He had given this speech so often that he could recite it in his sleep.

The villagers knew as well as he did that this was not a voluntary trade yet was required as part of their conversion. The Church and colonial government were doing all they could to discourage their headhunting ways. As a servant of God, he agreed wholeheartedly. Yet, as an admirer of the objects created during the bis festival, he was dismayed by the Church's desire to wipe out their exquisite carving tradition. Logically, he realized the artifacts were created during rituals that culminated in murder. He understood the Church's position and obeyed their policies without question.

In the hope of finding a way to keep their artistry alive, he'd begun introducing Christian icons and symbols to the communities he served. But the resulting objects were ugly, soulless things that didn't have the same symbolic meaning for the Asmat—at least, not yet.

He gazed out at his flock, now fidgeting as they looked up at him expectantly. Of course, he thought, they were eager to complete their daily chores before the festivities began in earnest.

"May God be with you. Amen." He crossed himself before stepping down to shake hands with his growing brethren. Most inspected the open crate of goods before exiting. As they reverently gazed over the shiny steel supplies, Kees felt a twinge of sadness as he wondered how many artifacts he would collect tonight.

Paving the way

May 22, 2017

As they walked back to toward the entrance, Hendrick Groosman snapped his fingers. "I almost forgot. I have your research results ready for you. It's quite a thick bundle of information and photographs to go through. I've left it at the information desk. We can pick it up on the way out."

"Okay, great," Zelda responded as enthusiastically as she could, though her shoulders slumped visibly. She was so looking forward to conducting archival research, and this was her first stop. Truth be told, she knew the chance was practically nil before she'd stepped into Friedrich's car. Because the files she'd requested concerned official church business, most of the records were not public. Via email, Groosman made it clear he couldn't allow Zelda free access to the archives. Instead, he'd requested a list of keywords, which he'd used to check the mission's extensive records and make photocopies of all of the relevant information for her.

She'd hoped by coming all the way out here, Groosman would make an exception and allow her a peek inside. Otherwise, he could have mailed her the photocopies. On the other hand, she was dying to see their controversial Asmat collection, so the trip wasn't entirely wasted. The objects were more beautiful than she could have imagined and amplified her respect for the Asmat's artistry.

She pushed her disappointment aside, walking silently alongside him as they reentered the temporary exhibition space. They found

Friedrich examining a butterfly wing under a microscope, admiring the design mimicked by car manufacturers to improve their products' aerodynamics.

Zelda had to tap him on the shoulder to get his attention. "Hey. We are going to talk with one of the priests who collected part of the Asmat collection. Do you want to join us?"

He shook his head. "I'm good here, thanks."

Zelda smiled. "Okay, I'll find you when we are done."

"Great," her friend said before returning his attention to the microscope.

Groosman exchanged pleasantries with the older lady behind the information desk before asking for the envelope tucked underneath the cash register. He gave it to Zelda, allowing her to place it in her backpack before holding the door open for her. They crossed the street to the small square dominated by an enormous stone cross, and as they passed, Groosman gazed reverently at the photograph of the village's founder embedded in it.

"As I already explained, our archives are restricted access. Not all of the keywords you provided brought up any results, at least not ones I am able to share with you. Though I did find several photographs that you may want to use in the exhibition, including a few of Father Terpstra, Albert Schenk, and Nicholas Mayfield."

"Wait a second. They both knew Mayfield?"

"Of course. Albert Schenk worked in the same region as Father Terpstra for several years. Because of your research requests, I now know Schenk was living in Kopi when Father Terpstra decided to leave Agats and relocate there. Agats had grown into the colonial administration's regional hub, in part thanks to Father Terpstra's work. There were few villages left to convert in the immediate vicinity. I imagine they knew each other quite well, though I've never asked about their personal relationship. I also learned Schenk asked Father Terpstra to help arrange for Mayfield to stay in the same village. Mayfield and Father Terpstra apparently met on several occasions, though Kees was away from Kopi for weeks on end."

"Kees?" Zelda asked. The wheels of her mind were turning as she processed this new information.

"Father Kees Terpstra, the man we are about to meet," the curator replied, exasperated.

"How silly of me!" Zelda stopped on the sidewalk and rifled through the envelope, flipping through the pages until she found a photograph of the three men. "We found a similar picture in Nicholas Mayfield's journal," she exclaimed, suddenly quite excited to meet Terpstra. The name didn't click right away. However, she was certain this was the priest who Mayfield had expected to help him acquire bis poles. In his journal, Nicholas referred to him as Kees, not Father Terpstra. Only after that realization hit, did Zelda recognize her mistake in mentioning where she'd found the other photograph. She fumbled for words to cover her slip up. "I didn't realize there was a connection between them."

"Yes, well, I don't know how much of a connection they had. Perhaps you can ask Father Terpstra about it. Let's see if we can find him first," Groosman said, leading them past a café terrace toward a wrought-iron fence on the other side of the square. Zelda was relieved he didn't ask about Mayfield's journal.

"Father Terpstra was the first priest to successfully establish a mission post in Asmat territory. He was able to connect with the locals and win their trust by working with them instead of focusing on overtly converting them to Catholicism," Groosman explained, glowing with pride. "Thanks to his technique, other missionaries from the Netherlands, Australia, England, and America were able to set up posts in areas familiar with Terpstra and his message. He literally paved the way for the world's churches to help civilize the island."

They crossed through the open gate and onto the Mission House's expansive grounds. Hidden from the street was a large garden that ran along the Maas River's embankments. They followed a sign pointing toward the chapel. When the church's bells began ringing, Groosman changed direction. He doubled back and climbed a short staircase next to the gate. Using a key card, he opened a door marked Service Entrance as the bells chimed three times. "They serve coffee and biscuits in the Tea Room at three o'clock. I'll bet Father Terpstra is there."

The sturdy brick building was incredibly cozy on the inside. The walls were painted soft beige. Paintings of Dutch landscapes in gilded frames hung in the hallways. Only the faint odor of disinfectant reminded Zelda of being in a nursing home. Though in many ways it was, she reckoned. The Mission House was a sort of clubhouse for retired missionaries.

Groosman led her toward the back of the building to a large lounge. Wingback chairs and round wooden tables topped with porcelain plates and crystal glasses filled the room. The retirees were clearly well cared for.

Though the Tea Room was full of older men and women sipping their afternoon tea or coffee, Groosman spotted Terpstra immediately and made a beeline for the older man.

The priest sat alone at a table meant for six. As they approached, Zelda noticed his eyes were closed, his back hunched, and his neck poked out of his priest's collar. *He looks like a shriveled tortoise,* she thought.

The curator cleared his throat. "Father Terpstra." He waited for the priest's eyes to flutter open before adding, "This is Zelda Richardson from the Tropenmuseum. We were just admiring your Asmat artifacts, and she wanted to meet you."

He motioned at two chairs, offering one to Zelda. "Please, sit."

"The objects you brought back are some of the most exquisite I have ever seen," Zelda gushed.

The old man's eyes opened wide, glowing with intense hate. *Was it the interruption of his nap or the topic making him so angry,* she wondered.

"The court case has been settled," he said gruffly. His voice was deep and booming, a strange contrast to his withered body. "All of the objects were gifts, and nothing was acquired illegally."

In the pictures she'd seen, Terpstra was a towering giant. Because of his ability to connect with the Asmat, she suspected he was once charismatic. However, the shell of a man before her was none of those things. *What had happened to make this man so rancorous? Was it the court case or the accusations that he stole from those he supposedly loved?*

"Is that why the Tropenmuseum sent you? To strong-arm me into loaning my relics to your exhibition? Nothing's been decided yet," he snapped, referring to the loan request to display several of the Mission Museum's Asmat artifacts in the upcoming Bis Poles exhibition. Her mentor said Groosman had already assured the Tropenmuseum that Terpstra would sign the loan agreement as soon as the court case was settled in their favor. That was almost a month ago. Their request still hadn't been approved. In chagrin, Zelda now also wondered if her visit was supposed to function as a subtle reminder.

"No, really, I only came to pick up some documents, and as an afterthought, I took a look at the collection. I now understand why the Tropenmuseum is eager to exhibit them. They really are beautiful.," Zelda said, frustrated she'd angered the old man. "Hey, what was it like to be one of the first? Were you scared when you arrived?" she asked, hoping to change the subject and lighten the mood.

"Of course not. I was doing God's work. He sent me there to do the best I could to help the locals improve their lot."

"I understand that—"

"Do you? What do you know about our mission's history? You are an American, correct? Your accent is a giveaway. We aren't like you. We didn't force them to praise our God in exchange for our help. We moved into their villages and assisted where we could. We took the time to understand their culture and tried to help them adapt to ours, not impose it upon them."

The force of his words took Zelda back. He was right, she realized.

She'd never worked for or with missionaries—American or otherwise. Other than the basic research she'd done for the Bis Poles exhibition, she knew next to nothing about their work, methods, or beliefs.

"I am not sure what that has to do with—"

"Why did the Tropenmuseum send you of all people to conduct research into our archive?"

"It's part of my job. The documents are for the Bis Poles exhibition."

His eyes bulged as he leaned back in his chair. "Are you working on it?"

"Sort of," Zelda said, blushing slightly. She still had trouble admitting she was simply an intern yet knew she would be lying if she said she was an employee.

"Are they so desperate for help they let a foreigner conduct research in Dutch?"

"I am an intern. I've been assigned to the exhibition as part of my study. And I am not conducting research really, more gathering information, photos, and videos for the exhibition team to sort through."

"Unbelievable, leaving such an important task in the hands of an American." He spat out Zelda's nationality.

Hendrik Groosman cleared his throat and rose from his wingback chair.

Zelda did the same, adding tactfully, "I am sorry we disturbed your rest, Father." She stuck out her hand, but the priest ignored it, choosing instead to close his eyes and lay back in his chair.

Groosman shrugged his shoulders, then led them away from Terpstra's table.

"I am truly sorry," the curator said as soon as they were outside the building again.

It was Zelda's turn to shrug. "It's not your fault. I hope I didn't cause you any trouble."

"Of course not. I should have known Terpstra wouldn't want to talk about the past. He used to be so open about his time on the island, but this court case has been quite vexing for all of us. He has such deep respect for the Asmat people and their culture. I'm afraid the accusations that he stole from them have made him bitter." He escorted her back outside. "Good luck with your assignment, Zelda," he said, shaking her hand before returning to his office.

Zelda walked slowly back toward the museum and Friedrich, shaken by the priest's dressing down. He'd tapped into her darkest fears. There were so many native Dutch speakers searching for work, most of them more qualified than she was. Was she fooling herself into thinking she'd ever find a job here? Was all of her efforts learning the language, history, and culture of this country for naught?

As she passed the stone cross statue, she spotted her friend sitting on the café terrace, two wines already on the table. "Hi, Zelda," he called out, shielding his eyes as to see her better. "It's such a beautiful day that I thought we could sit in the sun for a bit before heading back to Amsterdam." His smile faded as she approached. "What's wrong?"

"The meeting with the priest didn't go as I'd expected. I have a feeling my mentor is not going to be happy with me," Zelda said with a sigh. All she was supposed to do was pick up the photocopies, not offend the priest whose collection the Tropenmuseum hoped to feature in their upcoming exhibition.

He looked at her quizzically.

Zelda shook her head. "I'll tell you about it on the way back. Can we leave?"

"Have some wine, and tell me about it now. I'm sure it wasn't as bad as you think."

"Okay, one drink," she grumbled as she took a seat. "Then I'd like to get out of here before I offend anyone else."

Breaking with the past

July 10, 1962

Nick knew a boat party was approaching when the dogs began barking their chorus of howls and whines. As a regatta of canoes approached Kopi, Nick couldn't help but gaze in wonder at the tall white man standing at the bow of the long dugout leading the way. Ten Asmat—dark men with turtle shell fragments jutting out of their septum, feathers and paint decorating their bodies—paddled him toward shore, singing in harmony, their oars dipping in and out of the water as one.

The man didn't stoop to steady himself as the thin bow glided toward land and slowly came to a halt in the muddy riverbed. Though he wore the typical dress of Western men—billowy white t-shirts and a pair of khaki shorts—it suited him more than the others. It was as if this tall stranger was born to live in the tropics despite his Caucasian skin.

He locked eyes with Nick, gazing at him with interest as he made his way to land. The stranger's stride was long and graceful. He stuck his hand out, smiling warmly. "Kees Terpstra, and you must be Nicholas Mayfield." His handshake was firm and welcoming. Despite the ninety-degree temperature and relentless humidity, his hand was dry.

"Welcome back to Kopi, Father," Nick said. "How was your trip?"

"It is always a joy to visit my flock." Kees smiled easily, the truth of his statement radiating from his face.

"You've been gone for weeks. I was wondering when you would return." Try as he might, Nick couldn't keep the insolence out of his voice.

Kees chuckled. "One of the prices of success, I suppose. That's why I am training priests to serve their own villages, nurses to assist in the mission's hospitals, and teachers to carry on our work educating the next generations. Until then, it is important to maintain a strong presence. If I stay away too long, some of my flock may be tempted to falter. Ridding the region of headhunting is a more difficult process than you would imagine. The bis ritual and their notions of spiritual balance are so ingrained into their daily life."

Nick nodded in understanding. Death and rebirth were such an integral part of their belief system that it was difficult to convince the Asmat to give up headhunting completely without rendering their spiritual lives meaningless. The Church was trying hard to give them something to replace it with but knew it could take generations before Catholicism supplemented their own beliefs. Though there had been sporadic mission and colonial outposts established in the region since the 1930s, it was only after Father Terpstra arrived in 1953 that the Catholic ideology took hold.

Kees glanced back at his boat before turning toward his hut. Nick followed his gaze and saw villagers unloading canvas bags of all shapes and sizes. By the looks of them, they weren't heavy, only bulky. Several decorated spear tips stuck out of a canvas sack and cassowary feathers spilled out of another.

"Why do you have so many artifacts?" Nick asked.

"These pieces are what I traded the villagers for supplies."

Nick knew the Asmat traded stone implements and ritual artifacts for steel knives, pots, and pans as part of the conversion process. Nick still had trouble believing the villagers parted so willingly with their sacred objects. Because the offers the Church made were quite lucrative, he supposed many villagers figured they could carve them again, not knowing both the Church and colonial government were actively discouraging the creation of new cultural objects and pushing hard for the acceptance of Western religion as well as its modern technologies in converted villages.

Though Nick offered more, the Church was in a better negotiating position, he realized, suspecting the priest probably had access to the same objects he'd been denied. "Can I take a look?"

Kees's smile faltered before he nodded and walked over to one of the bags sitting next to the river's edge. He opened the canvas sack and gently removed one of the most beautiful masks Nick had ever seen. The patterns and colors were a delight to the senses. He knew his patrons at Harvard would want this piece for their collection. Its ritual significance only enhanced its beauty.

"How much do you want for it?" Nick asked.

"It's not for sale," Kees said, putting the mask back into the bag and closing the drawstring tight.

"Why not?"

"Because it is my duty to destroy it," he said softly.

"Destroy it? I thought that was only a rumor," Nick said, shocked.

"It is my Christian duty to help civilize these people. These objects represent their past. They need to evolve beyond stone tools, primitive weapons, and ritual fears. Their destruction is an unfortunate part of the conversion process. Besides, if I don't destroy these relics, other tribes may attack ours to get at them and steal the villagers' vitality. Or those I bartered with may change their minds. Tomorrow night, I will organize a large bonfire and burn them all. Word will spread, and the villagers will know there's no going back," Kees explained, quite bluntly.

"You are destroying objects our museum will gladly pay you American dollars for, not axes and pans!" Nick exclaimed.

"I took an oath to the Church. This is my sworn duty. Only the pieces I receive as gifts are allowed to be shipped back to the Netherlands."

"This is ridiculous! I am going to file a complaint with my embassy.

There is no reason why these artifacts should be destroyed."

"Go ahead. This is official Church policy, and I just explained to you why it must be done immediately. I am working with the local colonial authorities and my church to establish a permanent museum in Agats. It will take time to sway everyone's opinion that the need to preserve the Asmat carving tradition for future generations outweighs their symbolic association with headhunting. When the time is right, God will allow it to happen."

Nick's deep frown signaled he didn't buy it.

Kees sighed and put an arm around the younger man's shoulders. "Please, this is not how I wished to welcome you to Kopi," he said cordially. "How are your own acquisition trips going?"

"No locals will sell me their ritual carvings or bis poles. I have to have them all made." Nick said, pouting.

"Perhaps I can help you purchase a few older pieces to supplement Harvard's collection. From time to time, I help Albert and other anthropologists negotiate for older objects."

"I would appreciate it," Nick said gratefully, hiding a smile as he spoke. This is why he wanted to stay in Kopi. This priest could help introduce him to the Asmat willing to sell him ritual objects not normally available to Westerners. The only downside was the priest was more often upriver instead of in Kopi. Nick had been here for six weeks, and this was the first time they'd actually met. He would have to convince Kees to help him before he left on another trip.

"Please, tell me about your adventures so far. Are you enjoying your stay in Kopi?" The priest propelled the younger man away from the shore and toward his modest hut.

Have faith

May 22, 2017

As soon as Zelda left the Tea Room, Father Terpstra walked back to his room and latched the door shut. The last thing he needed was an overzealous nurse bearing applesauce or coffee barging in. He picked up his phone's receiver and dialed a number from memory.

"Yes?" The phone's cell display informed him it was the Father calling.

"An intern from the Tropenmuseum was here picking up documents from our archives. She was asking all sorts of questions about my Asmat collection. Groosman said he gave her pictures of me with Nick Mayfield."

"The museum is creating an exhibition and research is part of the process. Groosman didn't grant her access to the archives, did he?"

"No, he'd already copied the documents before she arrived. Besides, she doesn't have proper clearance to access our archives. No one from the Tropenmuseum does. But why did she come to see me personally and ask questions about my work on the island? Is this the Tropenmuseum's way of pressuring me into loaning them my objects, or are they investigating my past? You have to find out. I already made it clear to Groosman I want no part of this exhibition. My work for the Church has nothing to do with bis poles," the priest ordered.

The phone remained silent.

"I will not allow this exhibition to ruin all we've worked for, all the Church has accomplished. No one must find out what really happened. My work will be discredited, as will yours. This generation sees everything as black and white. They don't understand the importance of gray. We have always done our utmost to protect each other. You need to take care of this situation," Kees pressed.

"There will be nothing to take care of if you remain calm and let me handle this. Give me a chance to find out what the Tropenmuseum is up to, and I will get back to you straightaway."

Now it was the Father's turn to remain mute.

"Have faith, Father." The man chuckled then hung up.

The priest glowered at the disconnected phone line.

Reprimanding Zelda

May 23, 2017

"Why did you attempt to interview Father Terpstra?" Zelda's mentor asked, her voice tinged with irritation.

"I wasn't interviewing him. The curator told me about the histories of the Asmat objects and that the priest who had collected the finest examples lived there. Groosman was the one who suggested I meet with him. I didn't ask."

"Whatever you said to Father Terpstra got him so riled up that I've had both him and the Bishop on the line all morning. The Mission Museum is now refusing to loan any of the objects we requested"—Marijke looked down at her notes to ensure she cited his words correctly—"'to an exhibition team run by foreigners who know nothing about Dutch history.' Thanks for that," Marijke Torenbouwer added with a smirk.

"But I didn't do anything!" Zelda wailed. "What was I supposed to say to the curator? 'No thanks, I don't want to meet the priest.'"

"Why did you tell Father Terpstra you worked for the Tropenmuseum?"

"I did not. When Groosman introduced me, he said I worked for the museum. I corrected him and made it clear I was only an intern. We woke the priest up from a nap. Maybe he didn't understand me completely." *And I was speaking in Dutch*, she thought ruefully, wondering if her own limited language skills had inadvertently created this mess.

"With the court case behind them, it was only a matter of days before the paperwork was signed. Now I'll have to go to Steyl to try to sort this mess out."

"I am truly sorry," Zelda said regretfully, sure her mentor would take her off the assignment now, abruptly ending her first real shot at conducting archival research for an exhibition.

"With everything else going on, I'd appreciate it if you do what I ask and nothing more. The police are still conducting interviews and reviewing the security tapes in the neighborhood. They still don't know how Janna's boyfriend got inside and if it was even him."

Since the photographer's death, security personnel continuously roamed the maze of hallways connecting the staff offices, as well as the museum's vast exhibition halls. It was unnerving being inside this enormous building without knowing what exactly happened to Janna Kolen. Footsteps echoed off the marble staircases and tiled corridors, closed doors led to hidden spaces and unexpected exits or entrances, and the museum was simultaneously an echo chamber and labyrinth. Zelda figured it would make the ideal location for a horror film.

And then there was the Anti-Colonial Brigade. Though they'd publicly claimed responsibility for the hack, the Tropenmuseum's own IT staff refused to believe it was them, and the police's investigative team seemed to agree. The group was too amateurish and unorganized to have inflicted this much damage on the museum's servers, which were still not functioning properly.

"Let me be perfectly honest with you, Zelda. If I had another choice, I would not let you leave this building until your internship was over, but I need these files and photos selected quickly and don't have enough time to do all the legwork. But for God's sake, don't interview or even chat up anyone, no matter what the situation," Marijke stressed.

Zelda nodded silently, her pride barely intact, and then raced out of the room.

Asmat rituals and ethnic art dealers

May 24, 2017

Zelda pushed back from the desk and stretched out her back. After two hours, she'd worked her way through half of the audiovisual material she'd requested to view. They were a fascinating mishmash of films, old newsreels, home movies, documentaries, and anthropological films of recorded rituals as well as interviews with colonial officers, missionaries, and anthropologists who were stationed there before 1963.

Her favorite recordings were the impressive dances and lengthy rituals performed by the Asmat. Most film fragments began with mesmerizing shows of strength featuring warriors roaring ferociously, their spears and shields at the ready. Their soulful cries and the melodious drumming created an energetic atmosphere tangible through the recording.

In other fragments, women sauntered into a clearing, presenting food to their menfolk. Their breasts were uncovered, though they all wore a grass skirt or underwear woven from sago leaves and held up by a wide waistband decorated with beads. Most had feathered bands tied to their wrists and elbows, necklaces made of bamboo, shells or bone around their necks, and flowers or beaded bands in their hair. After they had feasted, the women painted chalky white lines, stripes, and patterns onto the men's bodies before the clip ended.

It seemed that each gender had a special role to play in every ceremony. Zelda only wished the filmmakers had the foresight to note down the type of ceremony they'd recorded or the name of the village where it took place. Most films began around the same time the ritual did and ended when the reel was full. Only after the quality of recording equipment improved dramatically were filmmakers able to capture an entire ceremony or dance performance.

She'd found one film documenting an entire bis ceremony—or at least a visual summary of the six-week-long ritual. The forty-minute reel began with a group of Asmat men searching for the perfect tree. Once they'd found it, they began hacking at it with stone wedges and metal hatchets. The shaky, soundless footage then switched back to a shot of the men returning with the tree. Women hit them with sticks as they entered the village.

The scene changed again. Now they were inside a large hut, and eight men were carving and shaping the soft wood. Dances were interspersed with close-ups of the village's carvers cutting and scraping at the long trunk and root until three carved ancestors stood on each other's shoulders and a *tsjemen* protruded out of the highest man's abdomen. Once it was painted, the men carried the pole out of the Men's House, lifting it high up off their shoulders. A fantastic dance ensued. It seemed the entire village was celebrating its completion. Zelda wished they had recorded sound. She was certain the music was spectacular.

Finally, the pole was laid against a scaffold erected in front of the Men's House. After they had secured it to the bamboo structure with long vines, the film switched again. Now the camera zoomed in on the door to the Men's House. Warriors exited, one by one, before performing another dance. As their performance ended so did the film. Zelda sat back in awe. *How impressive it must have been to bear witness to such an event,* she thought, *to be in the middle of that chaotic conglomeration of thrashing bodies and vibrant songs.*

As much as she was enamored with the Asmat culture, after watching similar rituals performed by villages across the region, her interest in the ceremonies was waning. It was time for a break. The tiny cubicle, jam-packed with equipment capable of playing any kind of video, film, or audio tape she could imagine, was soundproof and suffocating. The only light emanated from a small spotlight shining on her notebook and the residual glow of the four monitors attached to one wall. As tempting as it was to stop for the day, requesting these tapes and recordings had been a fairly complex procedure requiring several emails and filled-in forms before access was granted to the Netherlands National Audiovisual Archives. She didn't know if the *Beeld en Geluid*'s archivists would allow her to return anytime soon.

She settled for a quick calisthenics routine, stretching and bending her body until she felt beads of sweat on her forehead. After wiping her face off with a tissue, Zelda glanced at the list of titles she'd requested, grateful to see interviews with a colonial officer, a prominent anthropologist, a few missionaries, and an ethnic art dealer were next on her list.

The term 'ethnic art dealer' intrigued her. She still wasn't exactly sure what that distinction meant. She was more accustomed to the terms 'ethnographic' or 'anthropological objects' and wondered what made a piece 'art' instead of an 'artifact.' And listening to talking heads would give her a break from the hypnotic drumming and dancing. She still wasn't sure which recordings of the ceremonies to select for the museum. The only real difference between them was their quality—the rituals were executed with the same precision and passion each time.

The singular exception was the frequent appearance of Father Terpstra in the films recorded by missionaries for their parishes back home. Thanks to his lanky, tall frame and engaging smile, he was unmistakable, even when wearing feathered headdresses and covered in chalk. The joy he took in being part of their rituals shone through the tiny monitor. Zelda could hardly believe this was the same grumpy old man who got her into so much trouble.

She glanced again at her list. Her mentor warned her to be selective, saying the average museum visitor wouldn't watch a lengthy video fragment. Three-minute excerpts were considered the maximum. She would put a star next to all the films Father Terpstra was in, figuring his enthusiasm may inspire museum visitors to watch a bit longer.

Knowing she had no choice but to continue, Zelda used her finger to find the reel number she was to view next before searching through the newsreels, nine-millimeter films, VHS cassettes, and DVDs for it.

Once found, she switched the monitor's input to the VHS player as the archivist had shown her a few hours before. She pushed play and sat back in her chair, curious to hear what this colonial officer—Tygo van Lissen—would say about life in the Asmat region of Dutch New Guinea.

The officer had been stationed in Agats from 1950 until 1960. Most of his ten years of service were spent traveling throughout the Asmat region settling disputes and tribal conflicts. He explained in a neutral tone how many of the problems were triggered by one tribe attacking another because they had received gifts from missionaries or Western mine workers surveying the region. Especially in the early 1950s when most villages had not accepted Christ into their lives and steel items were rare commodities, Van Lissen emphasized. Until Catholicism took hold in the late 1950s, most locals preferred to steal them than deal with the missionaries.

It sounded like the pioneer days with bandits attacking wagon trains as they headed west, Zelda thought. She took extensive notes of the points the colonial officer made, unsure if the project team would want to include this kind of background information in the exhibition.

The next tape on her list was a lengthy interview with prominent ethnographic art dealer Gerrit Visser, recorded in 1975 for a Dutch art program. The name Visser rang a bell, but Zelda couldn't place it. As his title suggested, he only dealt in ethnographic objects created by artists in developing countries. What made a piece art instead of an artifact seemed to be entirely up to his discretion.

Gerrit spoke of his gallery and its guiding principle—that the aesthetic beauty of the object set its value, not its cultural or religious significance. The gorgeous feather-covered armbands and headbands, richly decorated spears, and frightening figures carved into bis poles were the objects private collectors requested most. According to Visser, most of his clients weren't interested in the history of the object or its ritual use and didn't inquire about it.

It wasn't until the early 1960s—when more of these colonized nations gained status, respect, and finally, their own governments—that the worth of these objects changed, and they became more difficult to obtain. Aware that foreign collectors were removing the cultural history of their people from the country, the newly formed governments were often unwilling to allow older pieces to be exported. Any historical or cultural significant artifacts still in the country were taken off the market and showcased in newly established regional museums. His sources dried up almost overnight, leaving him scrambling to find a new direction. It was a difficult time for ethnic art dealers, Gerrit had remarked dryly.

In many countries, it took years for the indigenous governments to realize their unique artwork could contribute to the national economy. In Papua, it wasn't until the 1970s that the Asmat began carving bis poles, spears, and paddles with traditional motifs specifically for the growing tourist market and Western collectors. These contemporary pieces, created in the traditional ways and styles, were now the focus of Visser's gallery. Though he never said it in so many words, it was clear from Gerrit's body language and word choice that his gallery was flourishing in this new market.

After Zelda had viewed all of the interviews on her list, she was slightly disappointed to see none had mentioned Nicholas Mayfield. Granted, these anthropologists, colonial officers, and art dealers were being interviewed about their work and connections to Dutch New Guinea, not the American's disappearance, but still, she'd hoped to learn more about him today.

Every evening, she transcribed a few pages of his journal, though she hadn't got very far. *It worked better than a sleeping pill*, she thought. Nicholas wrote about his interaction with others but rarely about himself. It wasn't a diary of his inner thoughts, as she'd assumed it would be, but more of a notebook. By reading it, she didn't feel as if she'd gotten to know Nicholas better.

I must find out more about Mayfield and his disappearance, she thought. Not that it mattered whether he was a jerk or not. Once she finished transcribing his entire journal, she would present it to her mentor and let Marijke decide if any of the excerpts were useful. By then, the Mayfields should have his actual journal back and her having an 'illegal' copy would be overlooked—she hoped. Marijke had so much on her mind right now with Victor Nalong breathing down her neck, the police's investigation into Janna Kolen's death, the robbery, and the network hack.

Zelda checked her watch and was surprised to see it was only two in the afternoon. If she left now, she would have plenty of time to type up her findings before heading home. Tomorrow, she could search the national archives and internet for information about the missing anthropologist. With renewed energy, she popped out the last VHS tape and stacked it on top of the rest, glad to be finished with this task. All she had to do now was return the tapes and reels, then catch her train back to Amsterdam.

A missing collection

May 25, 2017

Zelda gazed out the open windows of her shared office in the Tropenmuseum. It was a gorgeous spring day. Fuchsias, amaryllis, and geraniums were out in force. The lilac bushes lining the fence in the parking lot below were starting to flower, their purple buds spreading a sweet scent that wafted inside. She breathed in deeply and reveled in their aroma, vowing to walk through Oosterpark today.

She'd spent the morning reviewing her summary of findings in the national audiovisual archives and the list of inventory numbers the Bis Poles exhibition team may want to use. A few minutes earlier, she'd sent it off to Bert Reiger and Marijke Torenbouwer, satisfied it contained all of the information they'd requested.

With that task behind her, it was time to find out more about Nicholas Mayfield. Janna Kolen had told her the basics, but Zelda didn't know much about the man or his family. In America, the Mayfields were a household name. The presidents of their many corporations were often on the news discussing their innovative breakthroughs or latest charitable donations. Yet the family valued their privacy, and details of their personal lives were not public knowledge. Besides, Nick disappeared before she was born.

Zelda thought back on Janna and the snippets of gossip she'd heard about Janna's junkie boyfriend, who was still being held in jail. She couldn't believe he could have got in and out of the Tropenmuseum so quickly and without being seen, even if he'd been sober. From the rumors circulating around the lunchroom, the few times he had visited Janna at work he was barely coherent. Was it really possible that he managed to outsmart the security personnel, cameras, and other employees in such a state? Even if he did, where did the journal and her camera equipment go? The police had found nothing in his filthy apartment except enough hard drugs to warrant holding him in custody longer. And what about the hack job? He couldn't possibly have known the museum and KIT were undergoing a cyber-attack at the same moment, could he?

Zelda told herself to focus on Nicholas Mayfield. The police were better equipped to solve Janna's murder than she was. She clicked open a web browser and typed in Harvard Peabody Museum. If she'd correctly remembered what Janna had told her about Mayfield's past, the poles and artifacts he'd collected during his last trip were shipped back to New York and the Netherlands after he went missing. The pieces he'd acquired for Harvard were now housed in a special wing of their anthropological museum, which bore his name. When it became clear he wasn't going to be found anytime soon, his family donated the extensive collection of photographs and films he'd taken during both of his trips to the island to their archive.

That's probably where his journal will end up, Zelda reflected as she searched through their online collection database—*if it's ever found.* Her search request brought up hundreds of photos, most taken during his last trip. She narrowed her search to 'Asmat' and '1962.' The first of fifty results linked to a page dedicated to his life and work as an anthropologist. The description on Harvard's website made Nick—as he preferred to be called—sound like a caring, interesting soul, whose passion for understanding other cultures motivated him to conduct research in New Guinea. *So different from his journal,* Zelda mused.

The description ended with a brief summary of the twenty-one-year-old's last days and the mystery surrounding his disappearance. The rumors concerning headhunters, crocodiles, and even kidnapping were all listed. Zelda read with fascination, amazed at how many theories there were and how far some reporters went to find out the truth, even traveling to Papua to relive his last days and interview local villagers who may have known Nick.

The last paragraph piqued her interest most of all. "According to local Asmat interviewed by the colonial authorities during their initial search for Nicholas, he should have had approximately five hundred artifacts in his possession when he disappeared. However, only three hundred objects have been accounted for. If the Asmat are to be believed, a significant portion of his collection disappeared around the same time as Mayfield."

A missing collection? How could only part of it disappear? In his journal, he did describe the hundreds of objects he'd acquired and from whom. In most cases, he also noted who they were for—himself, Harvard, or Gallery Visser. However, she hadn't taken the time to count them all. Perhaps she should.

It would also be interesting to see who the intended recipient of the missing pieces was. According to this website, everything he acquired was first sent to the Netherlands where Gerrit Visser removed the pieces Mayfield had collected for his gallery before sending the rest on to New York. Did Visser make an inventory list of all of the objects he'd received and those shipped on to Harvard? If he had, Zelda could compare it with Nicholas's journal entries.

It was only on the train ride back from Hilversum yesterday that she'd realized where she'd heard the name Visser before. Gerrit Visser was the father of Nicholas's friend Pepijn. The pieces Nick had acquired for Gallery Visser were, in fact, meant for Gerrit.

Zelda clicked on more search results, viewing the photos he had taken of his acquisitions while in the Asmat region, wondering how many objects she would recognize from Nicholas's descriptions. After viewing them all, she identified only a handful. What was oddest of all was the amount. There were only forty-six photos of Asmat artifacts and most were out of focus or poorly composed. Based on the many descriptions of acquisitions in his journal, she'd expected to see more.

She pulled out a fresh notebook and wrote Missing Collection. One more thing for her to-do list. As an afterthought, she added Pepijn Visser. He might be a good source of information if the museum ended up using excerpts from Nicholas's journal. Pepijn was the same age as Nick, meaning he would be in his seventies. Chances were high he was now the owner of Gallery Visser if it still existed and he hadn't yet retired. Zelda looked down at her notebook and sighed. How she wished she could discuss her findings with her mentor, but she couldn't, not without revealing she had a copy of Mayfield's journal.

Instead, she searched the online database for pictures of Nick in Dutch New Guinea. Twenty-seven appeared, arranged in chronological order. In most, he was smiling while standing casually alongside a bis pole, ceremonial house, or local villager. His expression always seemed to be a mixture of joy, pride, and surprise—as if he couldn't quite believe he was actually there. Almost all of the photographs were taken by Albert Schenk. *Not surprising*, Zelda thought, *since he was Nick's guide and translator.*

Two photos taken toward the end of his trip were particularly interesting. In both, his arm was draped over an Asmat man dressed in a lavishly decorated headdress and armbands made of Cowrie shells and cormorant feathers. A necklace of boars' tusks and dogs' teeth adorned the man's neck. Albert had taken a full body shot, capturing the painted stripes, circles and dots adorning both men's bare arms, legs, and face. Resting on Nicholas's head was a feathered headdress. Zelda wondered if it was one of the objects now displayed at Harvard.

Zelda studied the extensive patterns and decorations, wondering how long it took to apply. She started to click away when something niggled at the back of her brain, telling her to look again.

His clothes caught her attention. He wore the same baggy cargo pants and loose fitting shirt he always seemed to have on. Though in this shot, because his arm was around the villager's shoulder, his shirt hitched up, revealing his belt buckle. It was an unusually large and funky chunk of metal she hadn't noticed in other pictures. It seemed too big for such a skinny man hiking through the untamed wilderness, yet it looked familiar. So where had she seen it before?

She stared at the photograph, ruminating on its origin when she realized with a start where she had seen it—it was the same buckle they'd found in a bis pole crate in Rotterdam two weeks ago. The same crate they discovered Nick's journal in. Trembling with excitement, Zelda printed off two copies of the image, grabbed her notebook, and sprinted up to Marijke's office.

Restitution of our ancestors

May 25, 2017

"Good work, Zelda. It does appear to be the same." Marijke Torenbouwer smiled as she spoke. She and Zelda gazed at the belt buckle lying on Johan Dijkhuizen's desk. He was bent down, intently examining the clump of gold with a magnifying glass. "These swirls might be an N and M, though it is awfully hard to tell if they are meant to be letters or merely decorations."

Both Zelda and Marijke nodded in agreement, twisting their heads around to better decipher the image.

The curator picked up the photo of Nick that Zelda had printed off. "I will get in touch with my contact at Harvard and have them send us a high-resolution image. When they see our buckle, I'm sure they will agree there's a surprising similarity. They may be able to tell us more about its origin and if it is a common piece or unique to Mayfield."

"Sounds good, Johan," Marijke Torenbouwer said. "Let's send a photo to the Mayfield's lawyers as well. We should have shown it to Theodore when he was here last week. I guess in the wake of all that had happened, it was overlooked."

The curator's phone rang before he could respond. "Hello, Johan speaking. Yes, I'm with her now. We are almost finished." He looked to Marijke for confirmation.

Zelda's supervisor nodded.

He listened again, his expression growing grim before asking, "Do you want to tell her yourself?" He paused a moment then handed his phone to Marijke.

She eyed him curiously as she took the receiver, but he only looked away. "Yes? What! Not again." Marijke sighed heavily. "Okay, tell him I'll be right down." She hung up. "Perfect timing as always. That man is really starting to get on my nerves."

Johan nodded in understanding. "Victor is downstairs again, I take it?"

Marijke nodded wearily. "Third time this week. And my secretary is at a seminar in Leiden today." She turned to Zelda. "I know we agreed note-taking was not your primary task, but could you hold off on lunch and take notes of our meeting? The director will want to review them later."

Lunch and coffee breaks were sacred in the Tropenmuseum, so Zelda knew her mentor was asking a serious question. "Of course, I don't mind." Truth be told, she was thrilled. She'd wanted to meet the Papuan government's representative for weeks. He was a bit of a myth—often talked about and present somewhere in the building yet rarely seen. The museum's director and her mentor always whisked him into their offices before he could begin venting in public and cause a scene. From what Zelda gathered, most of the scientific staff was terrified of him.

She followed Marijke down two flights of marble stairs to the museum's vast Light Hall. The center of the three-story building was open, creating a cavernous room perfect for displaying large objects. Lining the edges of the space were bis poles, one displayed in front of each of the ten columns supporting the upper floors. As they walked past, Zelda glanced up at the ancestor poles she'd gotten to know so well. White and red painted men stared down at her with menacing grimaces. Happy children and abstract animals twisted into the latticed wings protruded from the uppermost figure's abdomen.

The hall, usually filled with a temporary exhibition, was cleared last week in preparation for the upcoming bis poles show. They crossed the space in silence, her mentor's heels clicking loudly on the stone floor. Most weekday mornings, the museum was quiet. A few older visitors mumbled to each other in hushed tones, gesturing toward the poles as they spoke. Once the schools began visiting in the early afternoon, the high-pitched squeals and chatter of teenagers echoing off the stone and marble walls would become almost unbearable. Zelda learned early on to do any research into the displayed collections before lunch—at least if she wanted to be able to concentrate.

When they reached the lobby, Victor Nalong had his back to them yet exuded a strength Zelda rarely experienced. It was as if his energy was tangible.

He turned to face her mentor. A pearly white grin split his dark-skinned face wide open. Zelda was caught off guard, expecting to see anger or disappointment etched on it. She started to smile back but extinguished her grin when her mentor said quite gruffly, "Victor, please follow me." Zelda's presence remained unacknowledged.

They wound their way back to her office in record time. Marijke refused to engage in polite conversation despite Victor's attempts. He wasn't particularly tall but had broad shoulders with thick, muscular arms and legs, Zelda noted. As soon as Marijke's office door clicked shut, his grin disappeared. "Have you finished your inventory yet? Or do you have another excuse lined up?"

Zelda was flabbergasted by his abrupt change in attitude. She hurriedly took a seat and pulled out a notepad and pencil, scribbling as furiously as she could. The director would definitely want to hear this.

"There are thousands of bones spread across sixty-five crates. You know they weren't carefully boxed up after that mishap at the hospital. Our forensics team is doing their best, but reconstructing all of those skeletons will take time."

Since gaining autonomy in 2003 from Irian Jaya—the Indonesian half of the island—the government of Papua had claimed artifacts,

123

ritual objects, and human remains held in galleries, museums, and universities across the globe. Though some of their requests for restitution were honored immediately, most were fought to some degree by the institution whose collection they were part of. Many claims ended up in court, at a high cost to the newly formed government. Considering their half of the island was in Dutch control for over three hundred years, the Asmat collections in the Netherlands were the most sought after.

Victor Nalong was a member of the Asmat Regency and, as such, was an official representative of the Papuan government. His country's vision of creating the first large-scale Asmat museum in Agats was severally hindered by Dutch court rulings that, so far, had not ordered a single object to be returned.

"You mean your team needs more time to measure and categorize my ancestors' bones for your museum's forensics database," he said. Marijke's face grew ashen. "We know about your project. You're no better than your predecessors, the vultures who misled my forefathers and desecrated their graves in the name of 'Western science.' These are my ancestors, not random skeletons," he raged. "We have a team of thirty competent anthropologists and medical specialists in Papua that can finish this job, probably more efficiently than your meager group. And with more respect, I might add."

"I have no doubt. Yet a number of the remains are not from Papua but other islands in Indonesia. Until we know which crates are from Dutch New Guinea expeditions and which are from collection trips to the Dutch Indies, we are unwilling to release them."

"Oh, yes, those scientific expeditions in which your physical anthropologists collected my ancestor's bones as if they were curiosities to be displayed and measured, without any respect for our beliefs or culture," he retorted.

Marijke frowned and folded her hands on her desk. "Poor word choice. Please, accept my apology. I am growing tired of having the same conversation every time we meet. I don't know what else I can say to make you understand we are doing the best we can with our limited resources. But you know all of this, so why are you really here?"

"The Papuan government wants resolution." Nalong jutted out his chin. "We demand the immediate restitution of our ancestors. Their remains will be going back with me when I leave in three weeks."

"You know that is impossible!"

"Our forensic scientists are more than capable of completing the procedures you've begun. We can return the other bones to their ancestral homes as easily as you can. And besides, we understand their need for restitution more than you."

"Is this an official request?"

"This is not a request. My government is done waiting for yours to return our ancestors to us. We demand restitution now. My flight is booked for June fifteenth—twenty-one days from today. I have already reserved cargo space for all sixty-five crates. I expect all of the remains to be packed and ready for shipment at that time." Victor's eyes grew hard as he spoke. There was no room for compromise in his voice. He rose as soon as he finished speaking, clearly having said all he wanted to say.

"I'll show myself out."

Marijke sat in her chair, motionless. Zelda didn't know what to do. She stayed put, quietly contemplating her next move.

"Unbelievable," her mentor finally muttered. "I need to talk to the director." She walked out without a glance in her intern's direction.

Zelda slowly gathered up her possessions and exited, closing Marijke's door behind her.

Setting priorities

August 2, 1962

The ebb and flow determined the traffic on the Lorentz River. Nick had been stranded in Kopi for three days, waiting for the currents to change and allow his heavily laden boats access to the villages upstream. Several bis poles, shields, spears, headdresses, and decorated skulls should be ready by now, yet he couldn't get to them. Nick glared at the fleet of canoes moored in the makeshift harbor, willing the waters to do his bidding. When no obvious change occurred, he kicked at a palm frond before slipping and sliding his way up the muddy shoreline and back to his hut.

Unused to being tied to the natural elements like this, Nick was frustrated by his lack of control. Though he did wonder if Albert wasn't stalling. If only he could speak any of the Asmat dialects, then he could ask the villagers himself if it was safe to travel upstream. At least he could try. They were so shy he had trouble getting any of these fierce warriors to make eye contact with him. The children loved to follow him around, observing his strange ways from afar but ran shrieking whenever he tried to talk with them.

His mood was not improved by Albert's steadfast refusal to share the names of his more lucrative contacts. He knew Albert occasionally sold artifacts to Harvard Museum, but he couldn't believe the man would be so petty. And Father Terpstra's promise to help him secure a bis pole was useless if they were both stuck here in Kopi. He knew the priest was busy planning his next trip. Nick only hoped

Terpstra would have time to negotiate on his behalf before departing on another month-long journey.

As he climbed up the tree trunk ladder and entered his hut, Nick glanced at the crates piled up in the corner, filled with trading goods. Perhaps he was offering too many axes per skull, but what did it really matter? Whatever he gave the Asmat, it was still a fraction of the objects' worth. Their artifacts and icons were exotic and hard to come by, making them the perfect item for rich Western collectors to want to obtain and museum-goers to gawk at. Heck, the boat and plane tickets needed to travel here from New York cost more than all of the items he'd had shipped over to barter with.

Nick gazed out of his hut's door as the sun rose further above the forest's deep green canopy looming behind the village. A gecko scurried up one wall and across the ceiling, pausing to look down at him and chirp before disappearing into the eaves. Outside, sunlight shimmered off the morning air, creating a thin mist that hovered above the red-brown earth and clung to the trees. The plethora of leaves, heavy with raindrops, sparkled in the shafts of light. Now that there was a break from the punishing rains, the birds were out in force. If he strained his good ear, he could hear the whistles and calls of black-tailed cockatoos, parrots, and several others he didn't recognize. He watched as they danced in the clearing sky, dipping and swooping to catch insects and small fish close to the river's surface.

He pulled out a cigarette and lit up, puffing softly. Since Roger left for New York last week, he'd been overcome by uncommon bouts of loneliness. Though he'd tried harder to talk with the villagers of Kopi, the few Asmat words he'd picked up from Albert weren't enough to get a conversation started. Most seemed frightened of him no matter what language he was speaking.

Not being able to communicate with the locals directly left him with no one in the village to talk to—especially since Albert was more an enemy than a friend. When Father Terpstra was in Kopi, he was constantly busy performing religious ceremonies, inspiring newly converted Catholics, baptizing newborns, and presiding over funerals. *If only Roger had been able to adapt better to the humidity and insects,* Nick brooded. His friend may not be cut out for the jungle, but he was a good listener.

To fill his time, Nick tried out the survival skills described in his guide—carving fishhooks from tree branches, setting traps for wild boar, and lighting fires with sticks and a stone. It was a test of his spirit and a way to remind himself of his worth. Being rejected for military service because of childhood asthma and one deaf ear was a blow to his ego he wasn't able to fully recover from. He'd assumed his father could pull some strings and get him enlisted anyway, but it proved impossible. Here in the jungles of Dutch New Guinea, he could prove to himself that he was as strong as his brothers and uncles who did serve.

A commotion of noise drew Nick back outside. Men were lined up on the riverbank in a makeshift chain, handing heavy crates down the line and into the catamaran, the same one Nick planned to use to go upstream when the currents changed. It was the only boat strong enough to transport all of his barter goods, and he had ordered its creation. In a way, he felt as if it was his.

What is going on? Nick wondered as he sprinted back down the muddy path toward the source of the crates. They were coming from Albert's hut.

"What do you think you are doing?" Nick roared. "You know I've been waiting days to use that boat."

"Priorities, Nick," Albert responded coolly. "These artifacts need to get to Agats. The next boat heading to Hollandia docks in three days. If I wait for the following ship, my artifacts won't make their connection onto a freighter leaving for Rotterdam in two weeks."

"I don't understand. I haven't seen you acquire a single object since I've been here. Where did you get all these things?" Nick gaped at the long line of crates being passed down by hand.

"My contacts are my own."

"You were ordered by both the American and Dutch embassies to share them with me."

"No, I was asked to translate your negotiations. No one ordered me to compromise years of work spent building up the locals' trust so you can buy anything your grubby hands touch. You are a bull in china shop, sweeping in and throwing your money around without considering the long-term consequences. You'll soon be gone, but I intend to stay. I refuse to destroy my livelihood so you can buy pretty things for your rich papa." He turned and strode toward the shore without allowing Nick a chance to rebut.

Nick started to chase after him until he noticed something peculiar. For the first time since they'd met, there was no shoulder bag crossing Albert's chest. The Dutchman was always recording village life by documenting spontaneous dances, carving sessions, and hunting trips on paper and film. His small leather satchel was filled with notebooks, a camera, and an endless supply of pens. This was the first time he'd ever seen Albert without it.

Now is my chance to search through it, Nick thought. He had to find out who Albert's lucrative contacts were. Nick was certain he kept some sort of records of the villages he bought his objects from. The museums he sold them to would require knowing their provenance. He'd already searched Albert's desk and chest of drawers yet found little of interest. There was nothing hidden inside his hut. Whatever Nick was searching for must be in that satchel.

He veered off toward his own hut and grabbed his camera before sneaking toward Albert's hut. He hung back, close to the rainforest's edge, watching the villagers shift crates to his catamaran. Once they were finished, Nick poked his head around the side of the hut and back toward shore. Albert was busy arranging the crates onto several boats, barking orders in an Asmat dialect.

Nick ran up the ladder and into the Dutchman's hut. Draped over a chair was his satchel. He opened up the small shoulder bag, not really knowing what he was searching for yet certain he would know it when he found it. There were a few sheets of paper, a measuring tape, and a camera in the main compartment. In a smaller zipped pouch were three small notebooks and several pens. Nick first scanned the sheaf of paper, but it was an article about the men's brutal initiation ceremony.

He then turned his attention to the notebooks. Nick felt a jolt of confidence when he opened the second one and found a list of artifacts spanning several pages. Next to each was the name of a village. Every entry noted the type of object, basic design, and its composition. Several originated from villages he and Albert had visited together, the same ones whose chiefs refused to sell anything of importance to him. *How did Albert arrange to buy these bis poles, paddles, spears, and shields? Was he meeting with the locals in secret? No, it wasn't possible.* He'd been by Nick's side the entire trip. Yet based on the dates listed, Albert had acquired many pieces while Nick was here in Kopi. *If only I'd learned the Asmat dialect,* he chastised himself again, cursing his inability to understand everything going on around him. For all he knew, Albert was negotiating with the villagers for these objects while he stood next to him.

Noises outside dissipated his indignation. Realizing he had little time, Nick quickly weighted the book open with a letter opener and snapped photos of as many pages as he dared. Only when he heard Albert's voice rapidly approaching did he throw the book back inside the satchel and scurry out the door.

"Hey! What are you doing?" Albert yelled as Nick raced away from the Dutchman's hut.

Nick turned to face Albert, feigning surprise. "There you are. I just wanted to let you know I will be reporting your hindrance of my collection trip to the American Embassy."

Albert sneered. "Tell them whatever you want. I'm sure the Dutch will reassure them that wasting thousands of their museums' guldens was more important than delaying your trip a few days." He climbed the ladder to his hut without waiting for a response.

Nick puffed out his cheeks in relief. Only after he'd entered his hut did he realize he hadn't put Albert's notebook back in the zippered pouch he'd found it in.

Exceptions to the rule

May 26, 2017

Zelda averted her eyes from the skeleton as she grabbed the clipboard hanging on the end of the rollaway steel slab. The crates full of bones suddenly became human when they were laid out on a table like this. She took the paperwork back to her desk, glancing over the top sheet as she walked. Like most in this room, the majority of bones were already colored in and their measurements noted.

The internal network was still down, which meant Zelda had to enter all of the data into an old laptop. It was one of five not connected to the network when the hackers struck. Once the servers were clean and online again, she could import all of the data into the museum's collection database.

The curator and his two assistants had already unpacked all of the crates and matched up most of the orphaned body parts. Last week, they'd begun the arduous task of measuring them all. While the researchers worked, Zelda entered all of the details into the Tropenmuseum's custom-built database about the skeletons they were finished with. It was painstaking work, but once complete, researchers would be able to access and cross-reference all sorts of information about the length, height, bone structure, diet, and longevity of these peoples.

Strangely, Bert and his team were doing the same sort of research that physical anthropologists did, as Victor had pointed out earlier. Yet the information gathered was not being used to prove Westerners' superiority over these islanders—as was the goal of physical anthropology—but to allow contemporary scientists to work out their average height or the effect of their diet on the development of their bones.

There was so much to do in three short weeks. Data entry became Zelda's top priority as soon as Marijke Torenbouwer told the museum's director about the Papuan government's demands. *Working down here full time wasn't all bad,* she thought as she stole a glance at Jacob, her sort-of boyfriend and Bert's right-hand man. He measured a femur, his lips pursed and eyebrows scrunched together as he jotted down a rapid succession of numbers. His intensity was one of the many things that attracted her to him.

They'd only been together a month, yet Zelda knew she was falling for him and hard. They hit it off so well that it was almost scary. Since she and Pietro split up two years ago, well-meaning friends had set her up on too many blind dates, none of which had panned out. Her friends told her she wasn't opening herself up to a relationship, but she just didn't feel a connection with any of the men they'd lined up for her.

After so many failures, she began wondering if there wasn't something wrong with her. Otherwise, why did none of her dates ask for a second? If she was honest with herself, Seattle wasn't much different. Other than a handful of short-lived relationships, she was usually the only person at parties without a plus one.

A week before she started her internship, she'd gone through another humiliating night of stilted conversation and uncomfortable silence. After her date ended that night by unexpectedly kissing her while shoving a hand up her blouse, Zelda swore off blind dates and men for the time being. Fate brought Jacob into her life. She'd best not screw it up by overthinking things and, instead, allow their relationship to grow naturally for once.

She turned back to her computer, reveling in the feeling of being in love when Jacob's raised voice made her look again.

"I know how to use a measuring tape," he snapped as Bert took the tool out of his assistant's hand and began measuring the bone himself.

"I don't know how this could have gotten into these crates. He can't be Indonesian nor Papuan. This femur is much too long and well developed, especially in comparison to the rest."

"There are always exceptions," Jacob persisted.

Zelda remembered him telling her on their third date that the bones of Japanese prisoners of war had accidentally been collected by eager anthropologists in the 1940s and sent back to the Netherlands labeled as *Asmat*.

The curator chuckled. "Unless he was a giant, I am guessing he was Caucasian," Bert said, analyzing it with knowledgeable eyes. He began his career in 1967 at the Tropenmuseum and was the only staff member old enough to have been trained in physical anthropology. When it was no longer considered an acceptable branch of science, he retrained as a forensic anthropologist. Nowadays, he spent most of his time on archaeological digs or reconstructing prehistoric sites and skeletons for museums all over Europe.

Angela, the second assistant, called out, "None of these bones are typical lengths for Asmat or Indonesians. That's why I grouped them together on this slab. We found this skeleton spread across three crates. They weren't properly cleaned before being packed up, which made it easier to spot." On a rollaway table to her left was a mishmash of bones, more brown than white in color. Even to Zelda's untrained eye, they were clearly longer and thicker than those she'd entered into the database.

"Was there documentation included in any of the three crates?" Bert asked.

Angela shook her head. "No, though I'm fairly certain they are part of the Van den Hof's shipment. The crate numbers correspond to his inventory list," she added, referring to the infamous Nazi grave robber.

Bert expertly rearranged the bones, quickly placing them back into their human form. He then measured the longest arm and leg bones, hips and jaw before examining their condition.

After a long silence, he said, "This was a tall Caucasian male. I would stake my reputation on it. His diet was richer in protein than an Asmat's would have been. Look at the structure of the marrow development. The lengths match up to a typical Western diet, probably North American or Northern Europe."

"A competing grave robber, perhaps?" Angela joked. Zelda shivered.

"I have not read any accounts of Van den Hof killing off his competition or anyone else in Dutch New Guinea for that matter," Bert said, his tone serious. He stared off into the distance, contemplating their origin.

"Could it be a colonial officer or missionary?" Jacob speculated.

"They were always buried in their own private cemeteries. I cannot imagine he would dare to steal bones from those graveyards and pass them off as Asmat. If he'd been caught, he would have been arrested and deported. Yet a local tribe would not have buried a white man's body among their own. At least, not under normal circumstances," Bert explained. "Were there any markings on the crates?"

Angela consulted the clipboard. "The crates were dated 'November 1962.' All three were undamaged during the flood at the Academic Medical Center, meaning they were packed that way in New Guinea."

"That's an odd coincidence, finding those bones in a crate marked 'November 1962.' Nick Mayfield disappeared in October 1962," Zelda chimed in.

"Are you actually suggesting this could be Mayfield?" Jacob asked incredulously.

"No, sorry. I shouldn't have said anything," Zelda replied sheepishly. She didn't know why she had said what she did. After spending hours reading about Nicholas Mayfield, he was clearly at the forefront of her thoughts. The curator looked at her strangely, making her even more nervous about speaking out of turn.

"Let's keep these bones separate from the rest and run a few tests.

We should be able to determine the age quite easily," Bert said before rolling the table over to his desk.

Fishing in Kopi

August 9, 1962

Albert watched the women fishing in a creek close to Kopi, waiting for the right moment to snap another photo. The high midday sun shone strongly through the thick canopy, lighting up his subjects as they pulled their hoop nets along the muddy riverbed, hoping to trap crabs and prawns. Albert snapped a series of photographs as they walked slowly backward, concentrating on their nets. The women of Kopi—as he called them in his journal—laughed shyly as he took their pictures.

Suddenly all of the women pulled their large bamboo hoops out of the water simultaneously and folded the frame in half, effectively trapping any marine life they'd caught. Albert zoomed in on the nets. The women quickly removed small crabs and prawns as big as his hand, then threw them into bags hanging across their backs. His stomach rumbled in anticipation.

In unison, the women unfolded their nets and continued their slow walk down the shallow creek. Once their sacks were teeming with dinner, they climbed up the muddy banks and sauntered back to Kopi, nodding at Albert as they passed by.

Albert sat down on a fallen tree and traded his camera for a notebook. In it, he wrote about how the women worked together as a team and the songs they sang out of comradery. He described the musty smell of decaying leaves, the chirps and whirls of bird life, the constant buzz of insects, the rushing sound of water, and how the muddy banks glistened in the sun and the green leaves reflected off the brown water's surface, turning the creek into an emerald tunnel.

Once finished, he placed his notebook and pen back in his satchel and wandered along the creek until it met the Lorentz River. A few dugout canoes glided by, their shapes silhouetted in the strong light. Behind them was the ever-present wall of green. Palm trees towered over the thick undergrowth, reminding Albert of telephone poles. The thought immediately filled his mind with images of home. Rotterdam's modern architecture and urban energy were the complete opposite of any village on the island.

How would the Asmat react if they were dropped in the middle of that vibrant city? Not well, he was almost certain. Chuckling at the thought, he wondered what would confound them most—the trams, cars, or the mere presence of roads. It didn't matter, he realized, since none of the villagers in Kopi would be visiting Rotterdam anytime soon.

A wave of apprehension rolled over him. In a few short months, he would have to return to that urban jungle and be forced to schmooze with rich collectors whose sense of adventure had been tempered by wealth long ago. He used to love giving those presentations, reveling in the chance to share his knowledge of the region with an appreciative audience as well as his superiors. He'd always thought his speeches were as important to his future as his scientific research and published articles. Yet, so far, his not-so-subtle hints about his ambition to be named curator had fallen on deaf ears. Eight years later, he was still collecting for museums to pay his bills. Well, at least officially.

Perhaps it was for the best, Albert thought. He gazed contentedly across the slow-moving river, watching as a crocodile slid from the muddy banks and disappeared into the thick brown water. In Dutch New Guinea, he experienced a freedom he'd never felt back in Europe. Here, he was the boss and could decide how to spend his days and set his priorities.

He had plenty of time to write, and his subject matter was unique. Despite their fierce reputations, the Asmat were incredibly shy. Even though he could speak most Asmat dialects fluently, it had taken months of hanging around in the background before the villagers grew accustomed to his presence. Now, many embraced him into their families, treating him like a long-lost nephew.

He only dared taking pictures of village life only after he'd explained the benefits to the community and gotten the chief's explicit permission to do so. His gifts of photographs did much to endear him to the villagers, who now summoned him to record their most sacred ceremonies so that they could have a physical memento. Their willingness to let him document these intimate rituals provided him with even more exclusive materials. He'd repeatedly been told his presentations and lectures were consistently the best attended. Yet even the most brilliant praise couldn't force a curator to retire or an assistant to quit. And until one did, Albert couldn't even get on that career ladder, let alone climb up it.

Until space opened up for him at any of the museums he collected for, he was more than content to remain here in Kopi. Well, he was until Nicholas Mayfield arrived. A dark cloud passed overhead, signaling the end of the short-lived sunshine. *Mayfield is my dark cloud,* Albert ruminated. The sooner Nicholas left Kopi, the better. As long as the American was here, Albert had to be extremely careful. With one well-placed call, Mayfield could ruin years of work and disrupt his main source of income.

Albert knew he shouldn't have moved those crates last week, but he'd had no choice. His storage spaces were full, and the shipping container was booked—that wasn't a lie. Though he was itching to shift another load to Agats soon, he knew the last shipment had piqued Nicholas's curiosity. The boy had been dumb enough to think Albert wouldn't notice him sneaking around, trying to follow him through the jungle or village unnoticed. Albert figured it was an attempt to discover his supplier's identity. The thought brought a smile to his face. Nicholas would never find out the truth about his supplier or his partner in the Netherlands. Nicholas wasn't able to move quickly through the rainforest, and he couldn't speak any of the local dialects. Without his help, Nick wouldn't even be able to commission those knockoff pieces his gallery owner friend and Harvard Museum were satisfied with.

No, it wouldn't be difficult to keep Nicholas in the dark. The American had one more collection trip planned before traveling back to New York and out of his life. *He would only be here a few more weeks*, Albert consoled himself. Then he could resume his activities without worrying about the boy snooping around. He had no choice but to wait until Mayfield left the island before attempting another shipment. Once Nick was gone, it was back to business as usual, whether Father Terpstra agreed or not.

A fifty-year-old dispute

May 29, 2017

Monday morning, Zelda rose earlier than normal, certain she was going to miss her train regardless. Citing a busy agenda, Albert Schenk had scheduled their appointment for nine a.m. sharp. She skipped showering and raced to Central Station, pushing her way through the throngs of clueless tourists to the train heading toward Rotterdam.

After grabbing a window seat, she lay back and closed her eyes. At least Marijke allowed her to keep her appointment with the Wereldmuseum in spite of the data entry work. Though she doubted she would be seeing the insides of any archives today. It took Zelda by surprise when Albert Schenk personally responded to her official request to peruse the museum's extensive Asmat photography collection, demanding they meet first. Despite calls from Marijke, he'd steadfastly refused Zelda full access to the collection or archives. Instead, he'd selected a number of images she could pick from. Zelda figured he was scared his staff would let her see photos of him in New Guinea or regale her with stories he didn't want shared. Hopefully, by the time she arrived, peer pressure would prevail, and she would be allowed to complete her final archive visit without hindrance.

His insistence that she view the photographs in his office made her even more nervous. She was under strict orders not to upset him. "Simply select the most relevant images and leave" was how Marijke Torenbouwer had put it. She was already terrified of slipping up and mentioning the journal or her transcription to anyone on his staff, let alone Albert.

True to his word, the museum director met Zelda at the front desk, shaking her hand politely before leading her back to his office. As soon as they were seated, he asked rather brusquely, "I understand you are interested in Nick Mayfield."

Zelda blushed, unsure how to answer. That was the last question she expected from him. Despite their numerous connections, he was surprisingly closed about the American and their time together in Dutch New Guinea. *Well, not really surprising,* Zelda thought. *From Nick's journals, it was obvious they didn't get along.*

"You helped Janna Kolen photograph his journal, didn't you?" Albert pushed when Zelda remained silent.

She hadn't realized her role as assistant was well known outside of the Tropenmuseum.

"In case you hadn't noticed, the Dutch museum world is small and interconnected."

Zelda nodded slightly.

"Did you read much of it?"

"Not really," she lied. "We only had a few days to photograph the pages, so I had to work quickly. I didn't have a chance to read more than a random sentence here or there."

Albert watched her carefully before nodding thoughtfully. "I was against using Mayfield's bis poles in the exhibition because they are not authentic. Did you know that?"

Zelda was flabbergasted. "You mean he didn't collect them in New Guinea?"

"He did, but he paid to have new ones carved. He even chose the designs, selecting images that suited his idea of what a bis pole should look like," Albert said, a wicked smile on his face as he observed Zelda's reaction. "Bis poles are created as part of a six-week-long ritual, and the design reflects the life of the recently deceased. You can't just order an ancestor pole to go."

"I had no idea," she sputtered, shaking her head mournfully. She didn't have to feign disappointment. Of course she knew from Nick's journal that he'd commissioned them. It wasn't Nicholas's actions that saddened her but Albert's words. Fifty years later, and he refused to let their dispute go.

"He paid too much for them, as well. His actions created headhunting raids and tribal disputes when villages he didn't visit decided to steal from those he did," Albert added, enjoying tarnishing Mayfield's name.

"That's not what—" Zelda stopped herself from completing the sentence. If Albert found out Karin Bakker asked her to transcribe Nick's journal, there would be hell to pay when she got back to the Tropenmuseum.

"What?" Albert asked.

"I mean, I'd read that museums bought newly made objects, too. Because once the missionary's influence grew, they banned the bis ritual and poles became scarce commodities," she replied innocently.

Albert's eyes flashed in anger. "There were still important objects to be had. One just had to know whom to ask. Nick was only concerned with filling crates. I was interested in acquiring unique pieces with real cultural significance. Those sorts of objects were more difficult to obtain because there were fewer to go around. It took time to build up the level of trust and respect needed before the Asmat would consider parting with them. You couldn't swoop in for a few months and expect locals to sell their most important pieces to you, no matter what you offered in trade. Obtaining them required finesse and a sense of diplomacy that Nick was incapable of. To him, money was the be–all and end–all. He thought if he threw enough at them, the villagers would do whatever he wanted without questioning him."

Zelda was shocked by his tone and anger. They must have hated each other, she realized, and this exhibition was bringing Albert's pent-up resentment back to the surface.

"Why did the locals part with their most important objects, then?"

"Sometimes, the Asmat carved several poles during a bis ceremony. When the ritual was complete, they would sell one to me instead of allowing it to rot. Any damage caused by the ceremony only added to its cultural value, as far as a museum is concerned."

"And aesthetics? Was that important?" Zelda asked, genuinely curious to see if his opinion had changed over the years.

Albert's face contorted with rage. "You sound like Mayfield. Beauty is in the eye of the beholder. I was acquiring objects for Dutch museums seeking to expand their collections with artifacts representing a diverse array of styles and periods. Quality above quantity has always been my motto. My contacts would rather have a handful of authentic objects than hundreds of made-on-demand pieces, no matter how great they looked. Nick and his art dealer friend didn't care about the history or ceremonial use of a piece. If it weren't aesthetically pleasing, his museum sponsors and donors wouldn't be satisfied." Albert sniffed.

He turned back to his desk and grabbed a DVD. "These are the photographs we are willing to display in the exhibition. The file name is the inventory number. Have Johan review them and fill in the official request forms. I will ensure they are approved immediately."

Zelda fumed inwardly, keeping her facial expression neutral. Albert must know that it was her responsibility to make the initial selection of photographs and not Johan Dijkhuizen, the head of the Bis Poles exhibition team. And why did he make her come all the way to Rotterdam to pick up a DVD he could have easily mailed to the Tropenmuseum? It was obvious to her now that he was never going to grant her access to the archives. This man was a true control freak. She was beginning to see why Nick Mayfield despised him.

Biting her tongue, she replied pleasantly, "Okay, thanks. It will be the end of next week before I have time to make the final selection, but I'm sure Johan will be in touch soon."

"Why is this task not a priority?"

"The human remains have to be returned to Papua in two-and-

144

a-half weeks, so I've been reassigned to help with data entry. And considering their strange findings—"

"What do you mean?" Albert leaned forward, locking eyes with Zelda.

"Bert Reiger and his team are still trying to figure out how that Caucasian man's skeleton could have gotten mixed up with the other bones," she replied, perplexed by his sudden intensity. As Albert pointed out, news traveled so fast in the Dutch museum world, she assumed he knew about it already.

"Impossible," Albert muttered, leaning back as if he was lost in thought.

Zelda frowned. "Of course, they aren't a hundred percent sure the bones are from a Caucasian. That's why Bert wants to run tests at Academic Medical Center to try to determine his ethnicity."

"What?" Albert grabbed his phone and barked, "Get Karin Bakker on the line now." He put his hand over the receiver. "You can go now. Don't forget the DVD."

Albert swiveled his chair away from the door, staring up at the ceiling while he waited to be connected to the Tropenmuseum's director.

Zelda pocketed the disc of images and slunk out of the room, confused as to his reaction yet almost certain she had gotten herself into trouble again.

Did you spill the beans?

May 29, 2017

Zelda's fingers flew over the keyboard as she typed in every detail she could recall about her meeting with Albert Schenk. Thankfully, she had made copious notes on the train back to Amsterdam. After that disastrous meeting with Father Terpstra, she didn't want to leave anything out lest her words were misconstrued once again. Because of Albert's odd reaction, she'd prepared herself mentally for another dressing down. Though why the Caucasian remains and Bert Reiger's tests distressed him left her confused. He didn't have anything to do with the Human Remains project, as far as she knew.

A ping from her phone disrupted her thoughts. Zelda grabbed it guiltily, mumbling her excuses as she unlocked the screen. There were seven others working in one shared office. To avoid the constant chirps of telephones announcing messages and calls, they'd agreed to set them to vibrate. Zelda received so few messages she'd forgotten to turn her ringer off today. Luckily, none of her co-workers said anything as she dug her phone out of her bag and opened it. A new text message from Friedrich filled the screen. "Coffee later?"

"Not today." She quickly responded, "Typing report now, date with Jacob later."

"Did you spill the beans?" was the reply.

Zelda chuckled. Friedrich did love to use corny American expressions.

"Nope. Stopped myself in time." Zelda sent her message off, then

146

added another as an afterthought. "BTW: Only 10 more pages then finished with journal transcription!" She added a string of emoji's, knowing he hated the silly graphics. They hadn't seen each other in a week, and she knew he would be wondering about the transcription. Zelda hit send again, rejoicing in the fact that she was almost finished with that irritating man's journal. Reading it made her cranky. He was becoming more paranoid and seemed sure everyone around him was misleading him. Though why, she still didn't know. Finishing her assignment would also make her backpack lighter. Since the robbery and Janna's death, she hadn't dared let her copy out of her sight.

Most of all, Zelda hoped the police would find his actual journal soon. Not only for Nick's family but because she was atrocious at keeping any secret and was tired of having to be careful not to mention it. And as selfish as it was, she was looking forward to being able to talk about his entries with her mentor.

Not that the museum would want to use much, though. There were only a few passages about the carvers Nick met that could be of interest to the exhibition team. Pretty much all of Nick's references to Albert Schenk were too derogatory to use. He mentioned Kees a few times, but they weren't particularly enlightening passages. It sounded like the priest was rarely in the village, and instead, he spent most of his time serving the community-at-large. The only other people Nick wrote about in his journal were his traveling companion Roger and his Dutch friend Pepijn Visser.

Zelda made a mental note to ask Johan Dijkhuizen if Gerrit Visser was going to be mentioned in any of the Bis Poles exhibition's displays. He was one of the premier ethnic art dealers in the Benelux, and his son was friends with Nicholas Mayfield. Perhaps that connection would be interesting to explore.

She glanced at the clock and saw it was already twenty minutes past four. In ten minutes, she was supposed to be in her mentor's office. Zelda typed in the last few notes about her appointment with Schenk and sent the email, glad to have that task complete. She printed off a copy and grabbed her notebook before speed walking up the stairs to Marijke's office. This was her last meeting of the day. A few minutes of chitchat and she was free to go on her sixth official date with Jacob. Zelda couldn't wait.

Considering blackmail

August 9, 1962

Nick gently bathed the print in the fixer, waiting patiently for the image to appear. To his delight, the journal's page was clear and the writing sharp, even at this enlarged size. He hung the last photograph up to dry, adding it to the line of nineteen others he'd already printed off. He was pleased to see four of them were easily legible. He'd been in such a hurry he hadn't had time to check the composition or focus. Four was enough to give Pepijn an idea of the list's extensiveness.

Tilting his head, he read the list of objects again, certain Albert was doing something illegal. It was the amount as well as the descriptions that bothered him. *How did the Dutchman get ahold of thirty bis poles and all those other ancestor sculptures?* Even with his vast array of trading goods, he'd had difficulty obtaining seven poles on commission. Not a single villager would sell him a pole carved during a ceremony, as Albert claimed to prefer.

Nick wondered again if the Dutch anthropologist was behind the recent spate of thefts reported by villagers. Though how he managed to steal so many pieces unnoticed was beyond him.

And even if he did, where did all these objects go? Before flying to Agats, Nick had spent a month in the Netherlands visiting the larger Asmat collections housed in Dutch museums and private collections. The objects listed on the pages he'd photographed were more than all of their collections put together. If Albert was exporting these objects back to the Netherlands, they weren't all going to museums. And the

Dutchman seemed to despise ethnic art dealers such as Gerrit Visser.

His thoughts turned again to Gerrit's son, Pepijn. At Harvard, his friend loved to regale him with tales of his father's exploits sailing the Fijian Islands, trekking through New Guinea's interior or hiking along the rugged coastline of New Zealand. Those adventures were what attracted Gerrit to ethnic art in the first place. It was the second bout with malaria that made the older man reluctant to travel to Oceania anymore.

While Nick was in Amsterdam, Gerrit had given him an introduction to Asmat culture, rituals, and artifacts. During their conversation, Gerrit's love of the Asmat people and their carvings shone through, as did his jealousy of Nick's upcoming trip. Gerrit also explained what made one piece more valuable than another to his collectors. As with most things, it was the quality of the craftsmanship and intricacy of the designs that determined the price, Gerrit emphasized.

Commissioned objects were the only ones Pepijn's father would sell. Despite all the regulations banning the export of older Asmat artifacts, they regularly appeared on the black market, offered for an absurdly high amount to private collectors willing and able to pay. After being repeatedly accused of selling illicitly acquired objects, Gerrit refused to sell any older pieces in his gallery.

Nick sat back and wondered what would happen if Albert was selling artifacts on the black market. He was in the perfect position to get them out of the country and seemed to have the right connections, both here and in the Netherlands.

That would explain the large number of pieces on his inventory list. But where was he getting them from? If he could prove Albert was selling them, he might be able to blackmail the Dutchman into revealing his sources.

Or perhaps he should think bigger, Nick realized as another idea took hold. His father made it clear mining rights here could be worth a fortune, if only the Dutch government's monopoly could be broken open. Until then, only Dutch companies were allowed to survey potential sites. If Albert was smuggling artifacts out the country, he must have help, both here and in the Netherlands. If Nick could prove colonial officers were involved, his father might be able to embarrass the Dutch government into allowing his company a foothold in the region. If Nick helped his father secure a lucrative mining contract, his own position within the Mayfield family would be strengthened along with it. He would no longer be the sickly branch on the family tree but a hero worthy of the Mayfield name.

Nick could feel his heart begin to race as the thought took hold. It was imperative he find out whom Albert was working with—for his father's sake as well as his own. But where should he start? His flight back was in three weeks—a world of time in New York City yet a blink of an eye in Dutch New Guinea. He would write Pepijn in the morning and see what his friend could find out about Schenk's activities and connections. *Perhaps I should change my flight to stop in Amsterdam on the way home,* Nick contemplated. It would require some finagling, but dollars should smooth over any difficulties. In the meantime, he must find out who Albert's supplier was, who was helping him—and most importantly—how he could spin this to his advantage.

Can't this wait?

Floris's computer began pinging like crazy. Surprised by the sudden interruption, he paused Warcraft and switched back to his desktop. When his mind registered what his search queries had found, Floris forgot all about his game. He read the results carefully before picking up the phone and dialing.

His call was answered on the third ring. "Can't this wait? I have a meeting," answered a male voice gruffly.

"No, it can't," Floris answered in a shrill voice before relaying the reason for his call. His explanation was met with silence. He began repeating himself when the deeper voice interrupted.

"I heard you the first time. Damn it, I thought you'd destroyed every copy!" He was quiet for a moment before continuing in a calmer tone, "Are you sure she only sent an SMS referencing a journal and her transcription? Not an email, as well?"

"I've checked. Her emails are all work-related. She's only communicated with him via SMS, three text messages in total. I've forwarded them to your email, along with the recipient's name and phone number."

Floris waited while his boss clicked open his web browser. "It is rather vague. I will find out if she's got a copy of Mayfield's journal and if she was asked to transcribe it. Right now, I have a more pressing crisis to deal with. Run another search of the Tropenmuseum's network and her Sent Mail, will you? We have to be certain no other

152

copies exist."

"I already replaced their photos of the journal with corrupt files. There is no way anyone will be able to open them again," he whined. When his complaints were met with more silence, he responded, "I'll run another search."

The line went dead.

Date night

May 29, 2017

Zelda wrapped her long hair into a bun before pulling out a few wisps around her neck, as they did in her housemate's fashion magazine. Not normally one for dressing up, she'd borrowed Elisabeth's latest *Vogue* and flipped through it until she'd found a hairdo she could actually replicate in time for her date with Jacob.

They'd met at the Tropenmuseum a month ago during the welcome party for interns. Marijke had introduced her to all of her future co-workers, including the Human Remains team. Zelda's heart just about stopped when Jacob gazed down at her with his big blue eyes and gently shook her hand. When he asked her out for a drink, she hadn't hesitated, agreeing to meet him at a bar across the street from the museum after work the next day.

They'd hit it off immediately and snuggled closer and closer on the long black benches of Café Eden until two co-workers showed up and ruined the mood. If they hadn't, Zelda was sure she and Jacob would have spent the night together. In hindsight, she was glad they didn't. Things had moved too fast with her last boyfriend, as their spectacularly embarrassing breakup attested to. She didn't want to make the same mistake again. And Jacob's teaching schedule and PhD research left little time for their budding relationship to blossom. *It was better to take it slow*, Zelda cautioned herself, lest her heart got broken again for no good reason.

She was powdering her cheeks with one of Elisabeth's rouges—unsure if she was overdoing it or not—when the front door opened, startling her. The Clarion compact fell to the floor, chunks of burgundy powder spreading across the bathroom floor.

"Shit," Zelda mumbled, hurriedly gathering up the crumbling clumps as heels clicked in the hallway. She thought Elisabeth had yoga tonight. Or was that Thursdays?

"Zelda? Are you in the bathroom?" a lilting voice sang out.

"Yes, I'll just be a minute." She leaned over to close the door, two seconds too late. Her housemate, Elisabeth P. Jansen, was already standing in the doorway. Her raised eyebrows and thin sneer made clear she knew what Zelda was up to.

"That cost me twenty-two euros."

Zelda blanched. She'd never spent more than ten euros on any piece of makeup. "I'll get you a new one tomorrow."

"Is that my *Vogue*?" Elisabeth grabbed her magazine off the countertop. Water dripped off the cover. "It's wet! I haven't even read it yet."

"Sorry. When I washed the foundation off my hands, I must have splashed water onto the counter," Zelda babbled, grabbing the thick magazine and dabbing at it with her towel. Her housemate made her nervous enough on a good day. The girl was perfect in every way. Model thin with a short-cropped bob that reminded Zelda of a flapper, Elisabeth was always dressed in the latest fashion and accessorized to the hilt. In the ten months that they'd lived together, Zelda had never seen her wear the same clothes twice. The only chink in the woman's armor she'd found so far was her middle name. Zelda still didn't know what the *P* was short for but figured it must be something hideous. Otherwise, Elisabeth would flaunt it, instead of being so secretive about it.

Elisabeth's parents bought her this apartment when their only daughter started studying economics and modern languages at the Free University in Amsterdam. Zelda never dreamed she would ever live in such a beautiful neighborhood in the heart of the city's center. Her bedroom windows overlooked the Amstel Church—the only wooden church in the city—and a gloriously empty square surrounded by old trees, sporadically used as a basketball court. Usually, the only noises they could hear inside were birds roosting.

Their apartment building was quite modern, which was a welcome change from her old studio on the Stadhouderskade. She'd been searching for months for a cheaper place to live when a fellow museum studies student mentioned Elisabeth was looking for a housemate. For Zelda, it was love at first sight. Her bedroom was a large and cheery space with a tiny balcony overlooking the church and Reguliersgracht. And it cost less than her studio. The only drawback was Elisabeth. Thankfully, their schedules were so different that they rarely saw each other.

Zelda sighed in irritation. She was already anxious Elisabeth would not renew her yearlong lease next month, and this incident with the rouge and magazine wasn't helping. "I'm really sorry. I have a date tonight, and I needed some inspiration."

"How exciting!" Elisabeth practically squealed with excitement. "You haven't been on a date since you moved in."

Zelda started to add that it was their sixth date, but she knew Elisabeth wouldn't care. She was out with a new guy every month. In comparison to her housemate, Zelda was living a nun's life.

Elisabeth examined Zelda's short black dress, favorite necklace, and high heels intently before pursing her lips and scurrying off to her room. When she returned, she was holding a pair of chunky silver earrings that complimented Zelda's necklace perfectly.

"You always wear that thing. Try accentuating it with these."

"Thanks, that's nice of you." Zelda was baffled by her housemate's sudden interest. Was this all it took to reach the girl—dates and dressing up? She slipped the earrings in. They did draw out the circle of red and blue stones encrusting the silver medallion. She'd bought the chunky pendant in Nepal during her first trip outside the United States, a journey that changed her life and, ultimately, brought her to the Netherlands.

She knew Elisabeth wouldn't understand her emotional attachment to her necklace. But loaning her these earrings showed she actually noticed Zelda's existence.

"What time is your date?"

"In a half hour. He's taking me to Pasta e Basta. I mentioned I wanted to hear the singing waiters someday, so he booked a table." Zelda blushed.

"Great. George will be over in an hour, and I hoped we'd have the place to ourselves. Have a good night," Elisabeth said.

Zelda stood still, mouth agape, unsure of how to respond. Elisabeth didn't wait. She was already back in her bedroom and closing the door. *We are never going to be friends*, Zelda thought, wondering if renewing her yearlong lease would be such a good idea after all. Instead of fretting about her living situation, Zelda turned back to the mirror and carefully applied mascara to her long eyelashes.

Break-in at the Tropenmuseum

May 30, 2017

Zelda raced up the Mauritskade, pedaling past the Hotel Arena, Zoological Museum, and KIT building in record time. She only slowed a little when she biked around the Tropenmuseum to the staff parking lot at the back. She'd had such a great time with Jacob last night, she had trouble sleeping, her spinning thoughts keeping her awake until the morning sun broke over the treetops outside her window.

The waiters at Pasta e Basta had regaled them with arias and ballads all evening long. The only drawback was they weren't able to hold a real conversation, but it was worth every minute. From his relaxed grin and butterfly kisses, Zelda had the impression that Jacob had enjoyed the food and performances as much as she did, which made his request to spend the night even harder to fend off, she mused. Though she couldn't help worry she'd upset him by saying no, he did seem to understand her desire to wait a little longer before getting physical.

She would mail him later and see if he was available for lunch, she decided. That would be the best way to check his mood. Satisfied, she walked along the bike racks until she finally found a free space. Before she could chain her bike up, her phone began to ring. She ripped her bag open, "Yes, this is Zelda."

"Hi, are you in the building?" her mentor asked. *Geez, I'm only ten minutes late*, she thought. She knew Marijke was a stickler for being on time, but this was pushing it.

"I'm right outside, locking up my bike. Do you want me to come to your office?" Instinctively, she glanced up toward the top floor, knowing Marijke's window looked out onto the parking lot. A few moments later, her mentor's face appeared.

"Stay where you are. I'll be down in a moment." Her mentor locked eyes with her from above then ended the call.

Puzzled, Zelda stashed her phone and sat down on a park bench. Hidden behind the Tropenmuseum's monumental façade were a small pond, the Grand Café's terrace, the entrance to the storage facility, the Tropen Hotel, and a gate leading to Oosterpark. Zelda wondered why Marijke called when a uniformed police officer standing in front of the storage facility's entrance attracted her attention. Before Zelda could work out what he was doing there, her mentor exited the museum and rushed over to her.

"We need to get down to the Human Remains lab," Marijke said without further explanation or even a *hello*.

"What's going on?"

"There's been another break-in. This time, they hit the storage facility," Marijke said as she charged toward the depot's entrance. "The police want to interview everyone who has worked on the project."

Zelda did her best to keep up, though her feet were dragging as her mind raced with possibilities. What would any thief want to steal from that lab? It was filled with skeletal remains, a handful of oversized objects, and the museum's archives. Not exactly the kinds of things thieves would normally steal—nor would most value. Bewildered, she jogged a bit to catch up to her mentor.

After they approached the entrance and gave the officer their names, he radioed down their arrival. A few moments later, the giant, ten-foot wide elevator door opened. Another officer was already inside.

When the elevator opened again, Karin Bakker's voice resonated through the concrete hallway. "How is this even possible?"

"It's not like we left the door open. This was a professional theft!"

Bert Reiger yelled back.

Zelda gazed across the gathering of curators, assistants, and police investigators. Her boyfriend stood in the far corner, crying softly. She was still too stunned by the news to feel anything but confused.

"And there is no indication the lift was used yesterday after five p.m.?" Karin asked.

"None whatsoever. The cameras show no one approaching the entrance, and there is no registration of a key card being used to access it," Bert responded.

"Have we been hacked again?" the Tropenmuseum's director inquired. Zelda feared her question was rhetorical.

"Whoever did this, they must have access to a sophisticated hacker and a large crew," the lead investigator answered. "There is no digital trace of them entering the storage facility or of their movements in the parking lot. Your security systems must have been sabotaged and the video feeds circumvented. Those cameras are monitored by guards twenty-four hours a day."

"And the anti-colonial hackers?" Karin asked.

"We have two of their members in custody, but they refuse to claim credit for this robbery. They also now deny any involvement in the anti-colonial messages spread across KIT's social media channels or your network hack. They maintain another group is setting them up," the investigator said, disbelief evident in his voice.

"What about Victor Nalong?" Marijke Torenbouwer interrupted. "Do we know where he was?"

"We've already spoken with him. He was at his hotel all night. We checked their internal security cameras and confirmed he never left the building. And no, there are no human remains or suspicious crates in his hotel room. We already searched it. He's at the station now, making an official report of his movements," the lead investigator responded.

"We did find footage from a neighboring café that shows a moving van exiting the Tropenmuseum's parking lot at two in the morning.

The license plate was covered in mud and illegible. We tracked its movements through the city but lost sight of it after it exited the IJ Tunnel. We are searching street cameras in the region for any potential sightings," one of the police officers said.

"The director of Rotterdam's Wereldmuseum was also quite upset," another investigator offered, checking his notes as he spoke. "According to Bert Reiger and your director"—the officer nodded deferentially at both parties—"Albert Schenk threatened to remove the objects his museum agreed to loan for an exhibition if the bones weren't returned to Victor Nalong immediately."

Marijke Torenbouwer sighed. "Yes, we spoke yesterday. I still don't understand his reaction. There is little chance the Papuan claim on the remains would have hurt the publicity surrounding the Bis Poles exhibition, as he asserts. We intended to resolve this problem long before the exhibition opens. It doesn't matter. Albert's retirement party was last night, and most of the Dutch museum world was in Rotterdam celebrating with him. He couldn't possibly have been involved."

Zelda was flabbergasted her mentor seemed to think either Victor Nalong or Albert Schenk were possible suspects. The whole situation was surreal. The entire storage area—thousands of meters of space—had been picked clean. There wasn't a single vertebra or stray notecard in sight. All of the skeletons, empty crates, boxes of notes and archival materials as well as their laptops, desktops, backup hard drives, USB sticks, and research material had vanished. She couldn't believe it possible to clear out such a large space without anyone noticing, even in the dead of night. Although the elevator's shaft was situated behind the museum, she realized. From the street, no one could have seen what they were up to.

Zelda weaved her way to where her boyfriend listened in silence, tears still in his eyes. She grabbed his hand and squeezed, knowing there was nothing she could do to ease his pain. His entire PhD project had been stolen from him, eighteen months of irreplaceable research gone. It had taken months of planning, project meetings, and programming to make it this far. He was so close to completing a new database-driven collection inventory system for forensic researchers. But without the bones, he had no data to input, correlate, index, test, or verify. Therefore, no PhD project.

If only she had been able to type in more of their data, Jacob might have had enough to salvage the project. But there hadn't been enough time to enter into the database all of the information and measurements they'd collected. Jacob and Angela spent their time piecing the skeletons together and measuring the bones, not on data entry. She felt a wave of guilt, though quickly realized it was pointless. The Tropenmuseum's servers were still down, and none of their computers had been hooked up to KIT's network. Meaning she'd been backing up her work on a portable hard drive, which was now in the hands of the thieves. It didn't matter how much she'd typed in—Jacob had nothing to work with.

The only way he could complete his current PhD would be to start again at another museum, but collections of undocumented bones weren't something researchers came across on a regular basis. Most human remains had been removed from museum storage depots and exhibitions decades earlier when physical anthropology was no longer acceptable. Even if one of the few with such a collection would allow him to catalog it, considering how strapped he was for cash, she wasn't sure he could swing an extra year of full-time research. If he had to take a part-time job, it would delay the completion of his project that much longer. His required ten hours per week of teaching university lectures already sucked up so much of his research time. And besides, part-time PhDs were seriously frowned upon. He might lose his mentor's sponsorship over this.

"Should we get out of here?" Zelda whispered softly into his ear.

He nodded slightly. "Please."

Zelda approached the officer closest to them and made her request. He asked them a standard set of questions, and they explained how neither of them was anywhere near the museum last night. Once they'd written down their contact information, they were free to go. Another officer escorted them back to the elevator shaft and up to the parking lot.

Zelda grabbed Jacob's hand and led him to their bikes. He moved like a zombie, sluggishly stumbling his way toward their transportation. She unlocked her bike while he pulled himself together. Her heart broke as she saw how difficult it was for him to get his emotions under control. He wasn't dumb. He knew as well as she did that this might be the end of his PhD and, with it, years of hard, potentially meaningless work. She wrapped her hands around his neck and murmured, "I am so sorry."

He nuzzled his face into her neck. "Come back to my place." She could feel his tears catching in her hair.

It was Zelda's turn to nod, understanding his need to connect, happy to be there for him. She waited for him to unlock his bike then followed him out of the parking lot.

Nick Mayfield's journal

May 31, 2017

Zelda raced up the wide marble stairs, dreading being late for her meeting with Marijke Torenbouwer. Her tardiness yesterday went unpunished only because of the police investigation.

Her secretary wasn't behind her desk, and Marijke's door was cracked open. Seeing as it was five minutes after eleven, Zelda knocked and entered without waiting for a response. Her mentor was standing next to her desk, facing the window, talking on the phone. Zelda started to back out when Marijke whipped around and slammed the receiver down. "What are you doing here?" she demanded, clearly startled.

"It's eleven a.m., and time for our weekly meeting."

"Didn't my secretary call you? She was supposed to cancel all of my appointments today." Marijke frowned.

"Oh, that's odd." Like most interns, Zelda didn't have a permanent desk or telephone extension but used whatever computer station was free at the moment. She pulled her smartphone out of her purse. Her cheeks reddened. "Sorry, I forgot to turn my phone on." She switched it on and typed in her code. Five new messages appeared.

Zelda knew she should feel bad for being late, but she couldn't feel bad about anything right now. Her night with Jacob may have messed up her morning routine, but it was worth every second. Despite all of the problems of the day before—or perhaps because of them—their first night together was nothing short of spectacular. She only hoped that once he realized his world wasn't over, he would still want to be with her.

"I am going to be in meetings with the board of directors all day trying to sort out this journal situation before Nick Mayfield's relatives arrive and demand my resignation."

"What happened? I thought the IT department was working on getting the journal files restored?" Zelda asked, genuine concern in her voice.

"They have been, but it is hopeless. All of the photographs you took are corrupted beyond repair, meaning we have no record of the journal. The police have yet to find any clues leading to the book itself, and Mayfield's family is furious. So, if you don't mind, we'll have to reschedule our appointment."

Instead of leaving, Zelda removed her backpack. "Marijke, I have a confession to make." She opened her bag and took out her copy of the journal. "I made this copy because it was easier to transcribe the journal using the printouts, rather than the scans on the screen. I know we were warned not to take it out of the museum, or we would be fired. I understand if you want me to leave."

Marijke fell into her chair as her eyes opened wide in disbelief. "Why didn't you say anything earlier?"

"Because I figured the IT department would have restored the digital copies or the police would have found the journal by now." Zelda hung her head in shame.

Marijke rose, grabbed her by the shoulders, and kissed her three times. "You may have saved my job." She took the stack of paper out of Zelda's hands and slowly flipped through the loose sheets.

"Susan!" her mentor yelled. Her secretary, back from her coffee break, scurried into the office.

"I need five sets of this document photocopied—now. Then take it down to the IT department and have them scan in all the pages at high-resolution. It's the journal, Susan. Zelda had a copy of it this whole time! I have to call the director so she can tell Mayfield's lawyers the wonderful news."

Susan rushed off to the copy center in the basement.

"Thank you, Zelda." Her mentor flashed a winning smile before she rushed out of the room and down the corridor to Karin Bakker's office.

It was only after she'd left that Zelda realized the letter and photos they'd found inside Mayfield's journal were still in her backpack. Because she hadn't transcribed them yet, she'd kept them apart in a manila folder. She would have finished that task last night if she hadn't spent the night at Jacob's place, she realized, blushing.

She looked over her mentor's desk and wondered if she should leave the folder there. But after all the trouble the journal had caused, Zelda figured it was better to hang onto it until she could deliver the letter and photos in person. And Marijke would be busy with Karin for quite some time, she suspected.

Besides, the journal was what the Mayfield's wanted, not the mysterious list and cryptic letter. No one here at the museum understood their significance, anyway. And she doubted Nick's family would, either.

Give back what is not yours

May 31, 2017

Zelda checked her messages as she left Marijke's office, surprised to see an unknown number had left three voicemails. She dialed in and listened aghast as an unfamiliar voice told her to call the police station on Leidseplein right away. In the last message, a Detective Sergeant Smit left his direct telephone number.

She guessed they must have more questions about the bones, though why they would be so desperate to reach her was confusing. She had only been in the Human Remains lab a few times and knew next to nothing about the research project as a whole. Zelda walked to a quiet corner of the hallway and called the detective's number. When Sergeant Smit picked up, Zelda gave him her name and waited as he shuffled through paperwork.

"Thank you for getting back to me so quickly. For the record, are you Zelda Marie Richardson?"

"Yes. But I haven't remembered anything useful about the robbery."

"Excuse me?"

"The robbery at the Tropenmuseum last night. That's why you are calling, right?" Zelda asked.

"I am not assigned to that case. Please, I need you to confirm your identity for me. What is your address?"

"Kerkstraat 343, apartment F," Zelda answered automatically. *What was going on?*

"And you lived with Elisabeth Petunia Jansen at that address?"

"Yes." Zelda almost burst out laughing—*Petunia*! She always suspected Elisabeth's middle name was something horribly old-fashioned, but Petunia was worse than she'd imagined. No wonder her housemate kept it a secret. Zelda's chuckle caught in her throat, abruptly replaced with a sense of dread. *Why was the detective speaking in the past tense?*

"I need to speak with you about an investigation. Can you come to the Leidseplein station?"

"Yes, but I would prefer to go home and shower first." Zelda sniffed at her unwashed clothes. She'd been embarrassed enough to show up at the Tropenmuseum in crumpled clothes, frizzy hair, and streaked makeup, but when the police were involved, she preferred to make as good an impression as possible. "I'll be there within an hour."

"I am afraid that's not possible." The detective paused before adding gently, "your apartment is a crime scene."

Zelda blew her nose loudly, filling a fifth Kleenex. "But why?"

"We don't know yet. We hoped you could help us understand why. Do you know if anyone had a motive to harm her?"

"No. Elisabeth was one of those people everybody loved." Zelda sniffed. Well, everyone except for her. They had been housemates for almost a year yet never confided in each other, let alone hung out together. Zelda had tired of little Miss Perfect's constant stream of advice long ago. Elisabeth always knew the right club to go to, which bouncer to wink at to jump the line, the best biological markets to buy fruit from, the next hot fitness craze, and even the most effective way to clean chalk off their sink.

Zelda looked over at the detective, who patiently waited for her to collect her thoughts. A wave of shame rolled over her. Why hadn't she tried to be a better housemate to the girl?

"We believe Elisabeth interrupted a robbery-in-progress last night. She fought back but was no match for a knife," the detective said quietly.

Zelda's body convulsed at the thought of her housemate being stabbed to death. She raced to the corner of the interrogation room and threw up into the wastebasket. The detective exited the room, quickly returning with a cup of water and a roll of paper towels.

When Zelda wiped off her face, rage won over her shame. "What about her boyfriend George? Or was it Jim? Damn it, why can't I remember! Could he have done this to Elisabeth?"

"Security camera footage from your street confirms George Dunhill walked Elisabeth home at eleven p.m. He's stated they had drinks at Lowie's Café on the Utrechtsestraat." Zelda knew that was Elisabeth's favorite hangout because the bartenders always gave her free cocktails. "Elisabeth didn't want to call it a night, but he had to start work at six a.m. The security footage also confirms their verbal transgression. After Elisabeth entered your building, he biked back to his own apartment."

"So he didn't see or hear anything?" Zelda sniffled.

"No. He's stated he saw nothing to indicate there was anything amiss. Elisabeth used her key to enter your building, so the door was locked. He didn't see anyone suspicious hanging around outside the building or in the square where he'd parked his bike. His housemates confirmed he returned to his apartment twenty minutes after biking away from your home. And his employer can prove he arrived on time."

How close had George come to being killed, she thought with a gulp. Zelda's face grew pale as she realized her own luck. If she hadn't slept at Jacob's house, would they be bagging up her body, as well?

"Do you know what this text means?" the detective asked gently, laying a photo of her living room on the interrogation room table. The usually neat and tidy space was almost unrecognizable. All of Elisabeth's knickknacks, travel souvenirs, and framed photographs lay scattered and broken. Her stylish furniture had been destroyed. Mounds of dirt and leaves from her precious plants littered the floor. Elisabeth would have been livid to see her house torn asunder. The thought turned Zelda's sniffles into sobs.

"Can you read this text? Does it mean anything to you?" the detective asked again, pointing at a message scrawled onto the living room wall in what looked to be thick red crayon. Zelda wiped at her eyes and focused on the words. Written across the yellow wallpaper her housemate had spent weeks picking out were the words "Give back what is not yours."

"It's lipstick, taken from your bathroom."

It was too purple for her complexion, Zelda realized. The lipstick must have belonged to Elisabeth. She stared at the trashed room and scrawled message, completely numb. First Janna and now Elisabeth. Why were people dying all around her? She wondered how much more she could take before breaking down completely.

She drew in three deep breaths, telling herself to calm down and help the detective for Elisabeth's sake. "That's the same text the Anti-Colonial Brigade added to the Tropenmuseum's website when they hacked it. It must refer to the Human Remains project at the Tropenmuseum, but it doesn't make any sense to target me. I don't have any say in the restitution of the bones or Asmat objects or anything else for that matter. I'm just an intern. Why would someone think I did?" Zelda wondered aloud, tears streaming down her cheeks. If this break-in was related to the Tropenmuseum, then Elisabeth was never the target—she was. Zelda wouldn't be safe until they knew what the thieves were searching for.

"I've spoken with the team leading the Tropenmuseum robberies. They confirmed you were working on the Human Remains project and helped to photograph Nicholas Mayfield's journal before Janna Kolen was murdered. You must admit, it is a strange coincidence that you are connected to both crimes."

"Are you kidding me?" Zelda stared at him, simultaneously disgusted and astonished by the officer's comment. "I was assigned to both projects by Marijke Torenbouwer. It's not like I asked to work on either."

The detective nodded, but his eyes remained cold. Did the police really suspect she was somehow involved?

"You won't be able to go home until we've finished processing the crime scene." Smit paused before continuing in a softer tone. "You will want to get in touch with your landlord to have the blood stains removed before you return. Is there somewhere else you can stay?"

Zelda's wails echoed off the concrete walls. Visions of Janna's body and the blood-soaked floor of her photography studio rushed into her head, her face now replaced with Elisabeth's. Did she suffer or die quickly? Zelda hoped for her sake her death was painless, but she knew that was a stupid, worthless thought. The girl was dead.

And how was she going to tell Elisabeth's parents their only daughter had been murdered? They were her landlords. She'd met them once when they'd driven in from Hilversum to spend the day with their daughter. They were as perfect as Elisabeth, which irritated Zelda at the time. But they clearly adored their child and doted on her constantly. Their luxurious apartment attested to that. This news was going to devastate them. No, she couldn't make that call.

And even after the apartment was cleaned, Zelda knew she could never live there again. How could she ever go back, knowing Elisabeth took her last breath there?

A letter to Pepijn

June 1, 2017

Zelda leaned back on Jacob's couch and closed her eyes. The words *Give back what is not yours* and images of her destroyed living room filled the black.

Her eyes popped open. "Give back what? I already gave back the journal. What more could you want from me?" she asked aloud. Home alone, she was relieved no one answered.

Jacob was at the university meeting with his study adviser, trying to find a solution to his PhD problem. Unless he found a collection of undocumented human remains to use as source material, finishing his current research project would be impossible.

When she'd biked over to his place last night, she'd been so anxious about asking to stay the night that she'd almost switched direction and booked a hotel instead. Yet her fears subsided when he welcomed her with open arms, listening quietly as she told him about Elisabeth and comforting her as best he could. His generosity and sensitivity touched her deeply, wiping away any misgivings she'd felt after their first night together. As twisted as it was to admit, the Tropenmuseum robbery and Elisabeth's death brought them closer together.

Jacob even offered to let her move in. As much as she wanted to say yes, she knew it would be better not to. They needed to get to know each other first. She didn't want to make the same mistakes with Jacob as she had with Pietro.

Right now, she couldn't think about finding a new apartment.

Every odd creak, bell, or random noise set her off, turning her into a panicking mess until she could locate the source. She wished the police would call and let her know they'd arrested a suspect in Elisabeth's death, but she didn't see that happening in the immediate future.

Zelda forced herself to meditate on the confusing text again. What were the robbers searching for? The message scrawled on her living room wall made no sense, no matter which way she looked at it. She prayed Elisabeth's murder wasn't connected to the Human Remains project or Bis Poles exhibition—though there was no reason for her to be targeted by anyone angered by either project. She knew almost nothing about the remains, only what Bert and Jacob had told her. Even if someone discovered she'd had a copy of Nick's journal, she'd already given it to Marijke. And the Tropenmuseum's director had arranged to hand the journal over to the Mayfield's lawyer next week.

Frustration caused her to throw the police photo across Jacob's living room. Guilt made her pick it up and gently lay it down on his coffee table. It was a photo of Elisabeth's apartment, after all.

She gazed at the picture. Thankfully, Detective Smit contacted Elisabeth's family, sparing Zelda the agony of delivering that heart-breaking news. Elisabeth's mother called her soon after, weeping uncontrollably as Zelda relayed every kind word she and Elisabeth had exchanged. She'd even invented a few to try to make her mother feel a bit better. Though Zelda doubted the grief-stricken woman heard her—her pain was too raw.

Two deaths in two weeks' time had drained Zelda emotionally. Knowing how close she'd been to becoming a victim left her reeling and confused. In both cases, Janna and Elisabeth interrupted robberies in places she'd just left or where she should have been. What if Janna hadn't needed the IT department's help? Or Zelda hadn't slept at Jacob's? Would she also be dead, or could she have somehow prevented either death from occurring?

To stop herself from weeping, Zelda closed her eyes and breathed in deeply, sucking the air far down into her lungs. Taking a week off to deal with everything that had happened was a smart move, she thought, glad Marijke understood.

She promised Elisabeth's mother she would call a professional cleaner and knew she shouldn't delay, but she was having trouble saying the word 'murdered' aloud without breaking down. Somehow, booking the cleaners online seemed disrespectful to Elisabeth's memory. Zelda picked up the phone again and then dropped the receiver, not ready to deal with it. The police had released the apartment only a few hours ago. She couldn't imagine Elisabeth's parents were chomping at the bit for the cleaners to get started. Would they be able to set foot in the apartment again? Zelda realized she should offer to box up Elisabeth's possessions, though the idea brought tears to her eyes.

Instead of making the call, she sprang up and grabbed her backpack, emptying it of the notebooks, manila folders, research articles, and history books stashed inside. Only after everything was out on Jacob's kitchen table did she realize she had no toiletries. A new toothbrush would be nice to have before bedtime. A trip to the supermarket was in order.

Jacob's pajama pants and oversized t-shirt were so comfortable, and she wasn't ready to get dressed and face the outside world just yet. Instead, she pulled out the letter Nick Mayfield wrote to his friend. She and Janna Kolen had read it once when they'd discovered it, but Nick referenced people and events that she'd not yet heard of, making it seem quite cryptic. Now that she'd read the journal and knew most of the players, she hoped it would make more sense.

After snuggling back down on the couch, she unfolded Nick's unsent letter to Pepijn Visser. She skimmed the long brief, thankful his handwriting was easy to read. It was clearly the continuation of a conversation they had been having. After Nick summarized what survival tactics he'd tried out and mastered, he relayed his suspicions to his Dutch friend.

"I'm closing in on A.S. and believe I've found confirmation of his deeds. Quality above quantity—ha! He is such a hypocrite. Can your father find out who A.S. is selling his objects to? See enclosed inventory list. For comparison, put together a list of everything he collected officially, would you? I'm still searching for his suppliers and customs contacts. If he is involved in illegal practices, my father will want to know so he can use it as leverage."

Selling objects? Illegal practices? My God, he suspected Albert of smuggling artifacts! Zelda realized. Her initial excitement tempered rapidly when she reread the last line. Thanks to the internet, Zelda now knew that when Nick disappeared, his father was the president of Mayfield Enterprises, a conglomerate of mining, steel, and construction companies, founded generations ago. Based on the number of results she'd found, they were a powerful family of politicians, businessmen, and lawyers who were often in the American news. Zelda didn't understand what information an anthropologist could have discovered on a far-flung island in the Pacific that would interest his powerful father so greatly. And how could he use an artifact smuggling operation for leverage? And to what end?

"I have commissioned several pieces for your father's gallery, as agreed. Last week, I changed my ticket to fly back to Amsterdam so we can meet. My acquisitions will be shipped back six weeks later. Sixteen spears, ten paddles, twenty ancestor sculptures, four bis poles and five shields are for your father, carved with the designs and iconography his clients prefer. I also picked up a few dozen headdresses and armbands; I hope the feathers survive the trip intact. We can soon have a beer to celebrate. See you in November. Yours, Nick"

Zelda meditated on the letter's contents. "Quality above quantity," Zelda read aloud. That was what Albert Schenk kept hammering on about, she realized. It was also a repeated theme in Nick's journal, and one of the reasons he despised Albert. *And the initials 'A.S.' fit,* she thought. But did Nick really suspect that Albert was involved in smuggling Asmat artifacts out of the country? To what gain? He was about to be named curator at Rotterdam's ethnography museum, his bright future just beginning.

Zelda read the letter a third time, more confused than enlightened. She and Janna assumed the enclosed inventory list was a record of the objects Nick collected for Visser's gallery and Harvard. According to this letter, it was Albert's list. But everything he'd collected was for important museums. There were paper trails to follow, export documents and import certificates to check. How did this prove he was smuggling artifacts?

Pepijn Visser was the son of Gerrit Visser, a good friend of Nick Mayfield and an ethnic art dealer. He may be able to help her understand what Nick was trying to prove and why. She would have to Google his name and see if she could find out more about him and his gallery. She was staring off into the distance, contemplating what the letter could mean or why Nick's father would care, when the phone rang and just about scared her to death.

Quality above quantity

August 16, 1962

"In the morning, the tides should be flowing in our favor," Albert Schenk announced. They stood by the river watching a dugout canoe full of men returning to Kopi. Two crocodiles were laid out in the bow, their long heads lolling over the boat's side. The sun wouldn't begin setting for another hour or so, yet the plethora of smoke plumes wafting out of most huts attested to the fact that it was almost dinnertime.

"They were flowing in our favor last week, but you'd already sent the boats out to Agats." Nick sulked, still perturbed that Albert's shipment had taken priority over his own expedition.

The Dutchman shrugged. "You could have taken the smaller boats."

"You know my bis poles won't fit in those canoes. They are far too long and heavy."

"That's why locals tie them to the sides and pull them back," he snapped back. When Albert caught Nick's scowl, he quickly added, "The men should be back with the catamaran tonight. Another crew can row us upstream tomorrow."

He turned away from the shore and began walking toward his hut. Nick jumped in front of him, hands on his hips. "Why are you trying to delay me?"

Albert sighed in exasperation, staring at Nick as if he were crazy. "The jungle and that ridiculous survival book are making you paranoid. The container ship was leaving, and Rotterdam already paid for my collection's passage. I couldn't allow their money to go to waste," he explained rationally.

"I thought you determined when objects were shipped back, not them?"

Albert's face grew red. He started to speak, but he shook his head and walked around Nick instead.

Nick ran to catch up. When he sprang in front of Albert this time, his sneer softened into a smile as he held his palms up in a truce. "We need to discuss my expedition. Why don't we have dinner together?" He knew Albert preferred to eat alone and work on his many scientific articles about the Asmat.

"I have two articles to type up," Albert answered.

"You can let them sit for one night, right?"

Albert pulled a handkerchief out of his pocket and wiped the sweat off his forehead. "I'm not sure. We will be village hopping for at least two weeks. I really should send them off before we leave."

"A drink when you're finished, then?" Nick insisted. Albert dabbed at his brow again. Nick realized he'd never seen the man sweat before. "Are you feeling all right?" Contracting malaria and dengue fever were real possibilities here in the rainforest. For Nick, it was reason enough to cover himself in DEET and wear long-sleeved shirts and pants, despite the heat. Or was the Dutchman hiding something, and his guilt was making him perspire?

"One drink," Albert said gruffly as he turned on his heel and headed back to his hut.

Nick was boxing up the last of the axes when he heard boots clambering up his ladder. He glanced toward the hut's open door. The sun had gone under long ago, and the moonless night engulfed the village in blackness. The only light came from the many stars and a few bonfires dotted along the riverbanks. Most were slowly burning down to embers as the village prepared itself for bed.

"All ready for tomorrow?" Albert asked as he crouched to enter Nick's domain. Once inside, his gaze locked on the many crates stacked up inside. "I hope we don't get raided on the way up. You do realize what a strain these will put on the boats, don't you?"

Nick felt himself tensing up. With difficulty, he kept his voice neutral. "This is what I promised to pay for the objects I ordered. You keep warning me how dangerous the locals are when provoked. I doubt they would look kindly on us if I tried to short them."

"We should make two trips, so we have a chance at evading any raiders. Otherwise, we will be a floating target, vulnerable to any attack."

Nick turned away from Albert, grinding his teeth to avoid snapping back a response to the older man's latest reproach. He dug through his suitcase and pulled out a bottle of bourbon.

"Maker's Mark, Kentucky's finest and my favorite." He poured them both large glasses of alcohol, not bothering to ask if Albert even drank the stuff. "How many trips did it take you to transport all of your artifacts back?" Nick's innocent tone contrasted sharply with his defiant expression.

"My acquisitions are more sporadic because they aren't commissioned," Albert responded as sweetly before taking a swig. "The objects I collect are only acquired after long and careful negotiations. Quality above quantity, remember?"

"It sure looked more like quantity over quality," Nick grumbled. "Which villages do you collect from again?" He topped off both of their drinks.

"Overall. The locals get in touch with me when they are willing to part with a pole or statue. They know my museums prefer artifacts that have religious and cultural significance." He emphasized 'my,' another jab at Harvard's preference for aesthetically beautiful artifacts, regardless of age or purpose.

"Why didn't you introduce me to any of them, as was your directive?"

"You know why. You would have ruined years of work." Albert was sweating terribly. Nick wondered again if he was getting sick. The

179

Dutchman swallowed his drink in one gulp. "Besides, they are useless to your art collector friend. He wouldn't be able to acquire the export permits needed to ship them back or sell them in his shop."

"I think you are lying about your sources," Nick said, shaking his head as if he were disappointed with the Dutch anthropologist. "You won't tell me because you can't. You transported too many artifacts to Agats to be telling the truth about acquiring them legally."

"What you saw being transported to Agats was the result of months of bargaining," Albert raged. He stood and grabbed the half-full bottle, sloshing bourbon over the side of the glass as he poured himself a generous shot.

"Then where do you store it all? Why do I never see crates in your quarters?"

"Are you planning to rob me? How I conduct my business is none of your concern." Albert downed his third drink then turned toward the door.

"Albert, wait," Nick called out, grabbing his shoulder.

The Dutchman shook his hand off. "The colonial authorities assigned me to assist you on your collection trips, but that doesn't make me your slave or servant." Albert stormed out of the hut, stumbling down the steps as he went.

Once outside, Albert righted himself and stared up at a carpet of stars twinkling high above. Bats crossed overhead, their dark shadows and beating wings swooshed gracefully by. The smell of burning embers was still strong even though the shoreline was now dark. Albert knew most villagers stayed indoors, close to their fires, in order to avoid mosquitoes.

Using his flashlight to guide him, Albert walked away from Nick's hut and toward the shore. He plopped down on a log and stared out at the water, watching the pinpoints of light from above ripple across the gentle waves. The village's dugout canoes bobbed softly in the rocking water, their silhouettes almost invisible in the darkness. In preparation for tomorrow's expedition, Nick's catamaran was tied close to shore.

Albert sucked in the humid air, allowing it to fill his lungs over and over until his bout of dizziness disappeared. It felt good to be outside, despite the constant buzz of insects feeding on his blood and sweat. He wiped his face off, disturbed by how wet his handkerchief was. He'd been feeling poorly all day, and the alcohol wasn't helping. His time on the island had made him lax. He couldn't forget the malaria parasite infecting New Guinea's mosquitoes was the most fatal known to man. Yet the stream of perspiration pouring out of him, headaches, and increasing nausea made him fear the worst. As a precaution, he'd begun taking anti-malaria pills again, but if he'd already been infected, they would do little to help improve his condition.

If he were lucky, his sudden symptoms were a reaction to Nick's upcoming trip, not a mosquito bite. *The American was asking too many questions*, he thought. For years he'd been able to smuggle artifacts back to the Netherlands undetected, protected by the museum's export certificates and sealed containers. Two or three artifacts in a box marked on the shipping manifest as containing one were easy to arrange. But if Nick kept nosing around, he could ruin his trade. Albert refused to let this spoiled brat threaten his livelihood any further.

But what could he do about it?

The last thing he wanted to do was accompany Nick upstream. Not only would they be sitting ducks for raiders in both directions, he knew he couldn't take weeks of Nick's interrogations and accusations without snapping. Of course, he couldn't share his supplier's name with the American. If Nick ever discovered what he and his accomplices were up to, God only knew what he would do with the information. He'd certainly use it to ruin them all.

Perhaps if he could scare Nick off, get him out of New Guinea sooner than planned. Right now, six weeks seemed like a lifetime. Albert was certain he would leave the island soon after his friend Roger flew back to New York, if only out of sheer loneliness. He'd made a point of avoiding Nick at all costs, to ensure he didn't become Roger's substitute. Yet, despite the isolation, Nick already hinted he might stay longer to go on another collecting expedition further upriver. However, if his barter objects were gone, he would have nothing to trade. Dollars and his father's reputation meant nothing here.

Albert stared at the boats rocking in the waves and knew what he had to do. First, he collected twigs and leaves, scooping up a handful of mud last. He looked around again yet saw no inquisitive locals spying on him and heard no dogs growling in territorial protest. The only sounds were the lapping water and flapping wings of flying foxes as they fed in the sky above.

He crept over to the makeshift catamaran, knowing it was crucial to Nick's expedition. He crawled into the stern of the left side and took his Swiss army knife out of his satchel. An inch above water level, he used the corkscrew to bore holes in the left and right side of the stern. The soft wood gave easily.

Once the holes were the size of a small coin, he filled them in with twigs and leaves, pasting it all together with mud. When he was finished, he crawled into the second canoe and repeated his actions. Once dried, the mud would be similar in color to the canoe's shell, he reckoned. He only hoped the villagers and Nicholas would be too concerned with loading the boat to notice.

After Nick's crates were placed in the boat, the weight should ensure that the holes would dip below the surface and slowly fill the craft. If Nick stored the bags of beads in the stern, as he'd done last time, it would slow the discovery of the holes down even further. If he were lucky, the boat wouldn't take on enough water to sink until they reached Flamingo Bay.

All I have to do is feign a fever and let nature take its course, he thought smugly as he crept back to his hut.

Lashing out

June 1, 2017

"The journal just ends?" Friedrich asked.

"Yeah. He did disappear a few days later. I doubt he knew it was going to be his last entry," Zelda quipped. She spread out a napkin on the park bench between them, to serve as a table for their sandwiches, glad Friedrich had invited her for an early lunch before he had to start work.

"Good point." Friedrich grabbed the larger of the two—stuffed full of extra lettuce, ham, cheese, egg, and cucumber—and shoved it into his mouth. Zelda picked up the normal version of the *broodje gezond*, or *healthy sandwich*, and took a significantly smaller bite.

"Their wasabi mayonnaise has got quite a kick," her friend murmured appreciatively.

Zelda agreed with a nod, gazing out at the water fountain in front of them, watching the circle of spray dance on the pond's surface as she ate. Wide paths crisscrossed Oosterpark. Bikers, joggers, and pedestrians moved along at a steady pace, yet gave each other room to maneuver, which was a rarity in Amsterdam.

"Do his entries remain scientific throughout?" Friedrich asked between bites.

"After the boat incident, he barely mentions the Asmat or his purchases. Most of his entries are fixated on Albert. He really hated the man, but it's not clear why. Sure, he was giving him a hard time, but you would think Nicholas could rise above it. At the end of the

183

day, he got all of the objects he wanted."

"What boat incident?"

"His catamaran sank shortly after he'd embarked on his second collection trip. He lost all of his barter goods, so his trip was delayed until more could be brought from Agats. Somehow, he sees Albert as being responsible for his catamaran sinking, but frankly, his rants border on manic. I think he was alone for too long and was getting paranoid. I mean, why would Albert Schenk ever have reason to purposefully sink Nick's boat? It doesn't make any sense."

"It's too bad you can't ask Albert about it."

Zelda laughed. "No, I'm not going to risk my internship by being so bold."

Friedrich chuckled, taking another bite before asking, "Did he write anything more about that priest or other Westerners in his journal?"

"A few passages are dedicated to the priest, but not as many as Albert. Nick seemed enamored with Father Terpstra at the beginning of his trip and was full of praise for all the Church was doing to help the locals. But toward the end, he becomes increasingly irritated that Kees won't sell him artifacts in his possession, choosing to burn them instead. It was part of how the church and the colonial government tried to stop the headhunting, by destroying any objects associated with their rituals of the dead. Terpstra helped negotiate for a few ceremonial bis poles and shields, but not as many as Nick had expected. After that, he accuses the Catholic Church of tricking locals into incorporating Christian iconography into their artwork and essentially ruining their carving tradition. We saw a few of those kinds of objects in Steyl, remember? As far as Nick is concerned, the Church is destroying the Asmat culture, and he's going to tell his professors at Harvard about it."

Friedrich snorted. "This coming from a man who ordered bis poles made according to his specifications."

"I think he was lashing out because the priest wasn't doing more for him."

"It sounds like he was used to getting what he wanted and couldn't handle any form of disappointment or delay. I wonder what his upbringing was like, being part of such a successful and powerful family."

"I don't know what his family life was like," Zelda said before Friedrich could sidetrack the conversation with an analysis of the psychological reasons for Mayfield's behavior. "Nick does seem to view the world from his own unique perspective. After the boat accident, his journal is all about Albert. Nick was preoccupied with something he suspected the Dutchman of doing and was determined to discover the truth about it."

"What do you mean?" Friedrich asked before popping the last bite of his sandwich into his mouth.

"Well, I don't know exactly. He writes about Albert being a hyp-ocrite. And how, after searching through all of his possessions, he'd finally found proof of his deceit, whatever that means. Unfortunately, his journal passages were too vague for me to understand what he meant exactly."

Friedrich stared out into space, saying softly, "I wonder what he thought Albert was doing."

"Well, I think I may know now. I found an undelivered letter in his journal, addressed to a Dutch friend of his. Nick suspected Albert of doing something illegal with Asmat artifacts and wanted Pepijn's help proving it."

"Do you have the letter with you?" Friedrich asked.

Zelda handed him Nick's undelivered message to Pepijn Visser. "Read it yourself."

She took another bite of her sandwich and watched kids play tag on the grass field before them while Friedrich read.

"Okay, that is strange," Friedrich said. He pointed at the middle paragraph of Nick's letter. "Nick asks if his friend can find out how many objects A.S. sold to the museums he's supposedly working for. At least, I assume that's what 'collected for officially' means."

"I think so, too. And I love how he assumes Pepijn will have the information ready by the time he arrives in Amsterdam."

"Nick sounds like a man who was used to getting what he wants," Friedrich said.

"The whole journal is like that. I don't know if his family will be happy or sad to read this," Zelda observed.

"This letter doesn't clarify things, does it? We still don't know what exactly Nick suspected Albert of doing," Friedrich added.

"I have to assume smuggling. But how would Albert have done it? He was in Dutch New Guinea eleven months out of the year. If he were smuggling artifacts out of the country, he would have needed a contact in the Netherlands who helped him find buyers or at least store them for him. It's too bad Nick disappeared before he could send it. Though it does sound like this letter is a continuation of a previous conversation, not an accusation sent out of the blue. I wonder if his Dutch friend knew why Nick was asking for this information or why he thought Albert was doing something illegal," Zelda said.

"Do you think he will even remember Nick after fifty-odd years?" Friedrich scoffed.

"I am certain he will. How could he not? Nick Mayfield's disappearance was an international media event that dragged on for months. Considering he was collecting artifacts for Gallery Visser, I wouldn't be surprised if his friend Pepijn was questioned by the police, as well."

"You do have a point, Zelda. You don't forget that sort of thing easily."

"It is worth talking with him. He may know why Nick considered the inventory list to be so important." The description on Harvard's website flashed through her mind. "And he might even know more about Nick's missing collection," Zelda added, her next course of action clear.

Surveying the jungle

Nick hacked at banana leaves blocking his view, certain he'd spotted another hut in the distance. With every step, his feet sank into the muddy path, slowing his progress to a crawl. Thorny ferns and palm plants pulled at his clothes and skin. A labyrinth of creeping vines and young saplings crisscrossed the path, fighting for space in the sporadic bands of sunlight breaking through the thick canopy. The rain was blinding. Lightning streaked across the sky at regular intervals, a rumble of thunder following close behind. At least the heavy rainfall meant a reprieve from the constant buzzing of insects. Only a few mosquitoes swarmed determinedly around his head. The DEET kept most at bay, though the bugs seemed to understand that the rains were washing the repellant off.

There. Nick's pulse raced as the flits of light lit up the hut's outline again. He chopped at a creeper pulling at his throat, slicing it in two with one satisfying swing. "I'm closing in, Albert," Nick sang aloud. Not that he needed more motivation. His rage fueled his progress. The holes in his canoe's stern were perfect circles. There was no way its sinking was an accident. He was certain Albert had something to do with it, yet didn't know how he was involved. Did he order the Asmat to do it? Or creep down in the night and drill the holes himself? His fever was too conveniently timed to be a coincidence. Albert must have been faking the sweats when he was in my hut, Nick surmised, setting up the scene for his sudden fever and nausea.

After his catamaran sank, Nick became convinced he was on the right track, that Albert really was doing something illegal. Otherwise, why would the Dutchman have tried to get rid of him? Though he could hardly believe Albert would risk killing him in order to drive him out of Asmat country.

The bartering goods lost to the Arafura Sea were nothing significant, and another load of supplies was already on its way from Agats. As soon as it arrived, he could head upstream and collect the commissioned objects waiting for him. And this time, he would make sure Albert did nothing to hinder him.

Nick stopped a moment to catch his breath. Swimming back to shore sapped the life out of him. He hadn't yet regained his former strength or stamina. He'd been barely conscious by the time he finally reached land, twenty-seven hours after his catamaran left Kopi intact. He'd washed ashore far up the coast, his only luck being he'd landed in a missionary post with a well-supplied hospital. If villagers, who didn't know he was working in the area, had found him, they might have killed him for his head. As both Albert and Father Terpstra repeatedly warned him, the Asmat didn't look kindly on strangers. It had taken a week of intravenous drips before he was able to stand again, unassisted. After he'd returned to Kopi, he'd made it his mission to discover Albert's storage space and supplier.

The only place left to look was in the forest surrounding their village. Albert kept no artifacts in his own hut or any other building as far as Nick could tell. He'd already checked every hut, house, and storage shed in Kopi. He'd tailed Albert several times, but the Dutchman always managed to slip away.

Convinced Albert was keeping his stash in the jungle close to Kopi, Nick had marked off sections on his map and began to search each quadrant for his hidden storeroom. He'd started with the tufts of forest closest to a waterway, figuring it would be easier for Albert to transport them in and out of his hiding place undetected. There were a surprising number of huts and structures dotted throughout the forbidding forest, which were currently used by Western anthropologists and surveyors as well as local hunters.

His first day out, he'd found five huts, all filled with a macabre collection of chemical baths and rotting bones being prepared by physical anthropologists for their trip back to Western museums. Most of the crates were filled with glistening white skeletons. Some included notes about the villages they'd come from. The putrid stench was usually noticeable from several feet away. Strands of barbed wire strung up between the stilts kept most animals at bay.

Father Terpstra told Nick there were dozens of huts in the area currently used by physical anthropologists to prepare their specimens. Several took up temporary residence in them, using them as makeshift labs and storage spaces as they traveled the region searching for more bones to collect. So far today, he'd come across another three huts. None were occupied, though they all held crates of bones ready for transport.

The rain lessened slightly, spurring him on. Albert Schenk's secret storage place must be close, he was sure of it.

As the trail began to descend into a shallow valley, Nick stopped to survey his surroundings and catch his breath. He wiped the mud off his watch's face. It was only three in the afternoon. He'd been hiking for five hours now. Though the light was already starting to fade under the thick jungle canopy, he decided to walk another hour before turning around. He'd purposely stayed on what appeared to be the main trail. With a little luck, he should be able to find his way back to Kopi, even in the darkness. His flashlight's beam was strong, and the batteries were new. In a worst-case scenario, he could always spend the night in one of these huts, he reckoned, though he wasn't really comfortable with the idea of sleeping among all those skeletons.

After a short pause, he resumed his walk—chop—tour of the rainforest. Forty minutes later, he saw a small structure on the other side of a narrow stream. He smiled broadly, glad he'd finally found it.

Hoping to avoid leeches, he tucked his pants legs into his socks before stepping into the warm current. He steadied himself on the fallen tree trunks jutting out of the muddy brown water as he slowly crossed the waterway. The water ran faster than he'd anticipated.

As he climbed up the slick bank and approached the small hut, Nick tried to imagine how Albert would react to knowing he'd found his secret stash. Nick only hoped he would find some indication of who Albert was working with as well.

Would artifact smuggling alone be enough to help his father gain access to the island's vast mineral reserves? Nick didn't know. He supposed it would depend on the extent of Albert's deception, who his partners were, and his father's ability to bluff.

Perhaps he could use the smuggling as blackmail to force Albert to reveal the name of his supplier. Nick refused to believe the locals willingly parted with as many ritual objects as Albert's notebook suggested. But first, he needed to find Albert's storeroom. Until he did, he had little leverage over the Dutchman.

As he approached the fourth hut of the day, he noticed a weak light emitting from one window. Nick's pulse raced. Was it Albert or one of the physical anthropologists at work? He had to find out before he announced his presence. Nick hoisted himself up into a palm tree, balancing on the thick stems while he searched for a higher vantage point. When the leaves holding up his right foot cracked under his weight, Nick instinctively grabbed onto the trunk. A thorn sank deep into his palm. Nick cried out in pain, realizing too late that the hut's occupant could hear him.

"Albert?" called out a familiar voice.

Nick pushed himself against the tree's trunk, hoping the man wouldn't spot him.

A spotlight shone down and found him in no time. "Nicholas Mayfield? What are you doing here?"

Nick waved his bloodied hand awkwardly. "Father Terpstra, I could ask you the same."

The priest climbed down the ladder as Nick hopped onto the

ground. Kees Terpstra noticed blood dripping onto the ground. His calling overcame his surprise. Gently, he took Nick's hand and examined the wound. "Come with me. We need to bandage that."

Gallery Visser

June 1, 2017

Finding Pepijn was easier than Zelda thought it would be. She started by googling Gallery Visser, hoping it existed in some form, only to discover it was still open, and he was the current owner. According to the search results, Gallery Visser was one of the oldest and most renowned ethnic art galleries in the Netherlands. It was still housed on the Prinsengracht in the same space his grandfather established it back in 1932. She glanced at the opening hours, not surprised to see they were only open from eleven until three or by appointment. Most galleries kept odd hours, she'd learned, because they made their money during art fairs and from clients they'd met at them. Walk-ins were more often looky-loos than serious buyers. Zelda checked her watch. It was already one o'clock. Rather than make an appointment, she could pop by and chat with Pepijn today if she hurried.

After a quick shower, she grabbed her backpack, unlocked her bike, and headed off to the center of Amsterdam. Her journey took her across the lively Utrechtsstraat and toward the old canal houses of the Golden Bend. As she turned onto the Prinsengracht, Zelda slowed to watch the afternoon sunlight sparkling off the canal, giving her mind a chance to catch up with her actions. As usual, she'd acted before thinking things through. What exactly would she say to Pepijn? This was certainly going to be a bizarre and unexpected conversation for the poor man, no matter how she started it. Though she was sure he would remember his American friend, she wondered if Pepijn would be willing to discuss Nick's life with a perfect stranger or be able to shed some light on Nick's cryptic accusations and the inventory list.

Zelda locked her bike to a lamp pole along the canal and took in the monumental building Pepijn's gallery was in. Situated on the corner of the Passeerdersstraat and Prinsengracht, it was rather small for the neighborhood, only three stories tall and a few feet wide. Back in the 1800s, it wouldn't have been one of the grander homes on this strip of the canal. However, it was well maintained and quite adorable from a tourist's perspective. The light brown paint covering the façade was accented with forest green shutters. A garden of colors rivaling a Monet filled the two wrought-iron balconies. The bottom floor housed the gallery. The large window on the left displayed several painted masks. On the right, there were framed pieces of fabric richly embroidered with stylized birds. Zelda had purchased one in Panama years ago. Hanging above the door was a piece of wood, the name Gallery Visser carved into it. She buzzed the intercom, hoping the owner hadn't decided to leave early.

A few seconds later, an older, well-dressed man approached the door. He smiled broadly as he opened it. "Welcome to Gallery Visser. Please, come inside." He stepped back, allowing her a wide berth.

"Thank you," Zelda said, her voice cheery. The small shop was a jumbled mess of exotically beautiful objects assembled from all over the world. The walls and display cases were filled with carvings, statues, headdresses, shields, spears, masks, pottery, and a mini–bis pole. Many pieces she recognized as Native American, Peruvian, Mexican, Nigerian, Indonesian, and Asmat. It was busier than any museum display she'd seen, yet, somehow, Zelda found this presentation more appealing. She had to stop herself from stroking the brightly colored feathers and shiny beads in the headdress hanging closest to the door.

"Can I offer you a coffee or tea?" the gallery's owner politely offered.

"Tea, please," she responded automatically, not yet able to tear her eyes away from the objects. They appeared to be new, their intricate designs still crisp and the paint bright. In museum displays, objects often missed a few feathers or adornments, their paint chipped and designs worn down from ritual use.

Realizing her request for tea may have given him the wrong impression, Zelda followed the man toward the back of his gallery. "I'm sorry, sir. I should have asked first, are you Pepijn Visser?"

He stopped filling the kettle and turned toward her, a questioning look on his face. "Yes."

"I am not here to buy art but to ask you a few questions about Nick Mayfield. Is it all right if we have a cup of tea together?"

Pepijn's face transformed into a mask of rage. "Why can't you bloody journalists leave the man alone? Get out of my shop—now!" He let the kettle drop with a clang and strode toward the door, holding it open.

"No, please, you don't understand. I work for the Tropenmuseum. I'm a collection researcher, not a journalist."

Her response caught him off guard. "What?"

"The Tropenmuseum is hosting an exhibition about bis poles. During my research, I found an undelivered letter addressed to you in Mayfield's journal. It's quite cryptic, and we hoped you could help us decipher it. That's why I am here." Zelda hoped her words implied she had the Tropenmuseum's blessing so Pepijn didn't think she was acting on her own.

He let the handle loose, and the door slowly closed. "Do you have this letter with you?" he asked, his tone calmer yet still guarded.

"Here." She pulled Nick's letter out of her bag and handed him the page.

He accepted the sheet of paper then walked toward his desk to grab his glasses. After reading the first few sentences, he stopped and looked up at Zelda, a grin on his face. "This is most definitely from Nick. You found this in his journal? I knew about the Bis Poles exhibition yet but had heard nothing about this. Has his body been found?" he asked, sinking into his chair as he spoke.

"No, his journal was in a bis pole crate stored in the Wereldmuseum's depot." Zelda relayed how it was found a few weeks earlier in Rotterdam's storage department.

"Of course! I didn't realize the book the media mentioned was his personal journal." Pepijn's voice softened as he looked away shyly. "You'll have to excuse my initial reaction to your presence. It's been fifty years, but I still get journalists snooping around, looking for a connection between us or for a lurid story to share. When Nick is mentioned in the news, I tend to tune it out. There has been so much speculation, unsubstantiated rumors, and unfounded allegations about his disappearance printed as fact. I can't bear to read those kinds of stories anymore." He held up the letter. "Let me read this through."

He sat down and slowly read the front and back. When finished, he placed the document on his desk and stared off into the distance. Zelda swore she saw tears forming in his eyes.

She concentrated on his collection, allowing him time to get his emotions under control. She could only imagine how weird it must be for him to read his friend's words written fifty-odd years earlier. A few minutes later, her patience was rewarded.

"Nick was always so demanding. Even at university, he acted as if he was in charge of the class, not the professors." Pepijn chuckled. "We met at Harvard my freshman year during our introduction to humanities class and kept in touch when I returned to the Netherlands. I was one of the few who could cut him down a notch and get away with it, probably because I was a foreigner. I'm sure his bullheadedness was the result of being a Mayfield. His family was used to getting what they wanted. But he's a good man, or was. I refuse to believe he disappeared of his own free will. He wasn't the type to run from his name. No, he embraced it wholeheartedly."

"Did he write to you often?" Zelda asked.

"About once a month. My father commissioned him to collect several pieces for our gallery. I became his assistant a few months before Nick traveled to Dutch New Guinea the first time, in 1961. Nick's letters were usually short updates about his most recent purchases and the villagers he'd bought them from."

Zelda nodded toward the paper in his hand. "In this letter, Nick mentions he suspects a person he refers to as 'A.S.' of being involved in illegal activities. I now believe he is referring to Albert Schenk. Do you know what Nick was specifically investigating or concerned about? And how Albert Schenk may fit into the picture?"

Pepijn's eyebrows scrunched together as he contemplated Nick's letter. He opened his mouth to speak, then shook his head, and asked angrily, "Albert Schenk is one of the organizers of the exhibition. Why don't you ask him?"

"I doubt he would tell me the truth. Besides, he doesn't know about the letter."

"How can he not?"

"He knows we were photographing the journal but not that we found this letter in it. He's been against including any information about Nick in the exhibition, and my boss wants to keep this letter under wraps until we can figure out what it means," Zelda lied, hoping Pepijn wouldn't call Marijke Torenbouwer and check her story. Her mentor and the bis poles team knew about the letter, but no one deemed it important. Even in the gossipy museum world, she doubted this bit of information would have been worthy of the grapevine.

"I can imagine Albert wouldn't want Nick to be a part of his exhibition." Pepijn brooded, leaving Zelda to wonder if he would ever tell her what he was really thinking.

Just when she was beginning to believe this was the end of their conversation, the ethnic art dealer spoke again. "Nick was convinced Albert was smuggling Asmat artifacts off the island and selling them to rich Dutch collectors." Pepijn shook his head as he spoke, making clear he didn't believe a word of it. "I knew from his previous letters he and Albert didn't get along, but this is ridiculous."

"What do you mean exactly?" Zelda asked.

"He repeatedly wrote about Albert reprimanding him for paying the locals too much and refusing to introduce him to his more lucrative contacts. In reality, Albert was his competition, but he couldn't afford to pay as much as Nick could. It sounded to me like Albert was trying to get Mayfield to leave before he ruined the local economy."

Zelda nodded in agreement.

"However, Nick had no proof to back up his accusations. His letters were increasingly rants about everything Albert did or said. In the end, I didn't take Nick seriously. Instead, I chalked it up to a clash of egos. Albert isn't a wallflower. He wouldn't have liked Nick ordering him around. Yet in this letter, Nick says he'd found proof of Albert's wrongdoings. Do you know what he is referring to?"

"These photographs were folded inside the letter." Zelda dug the four prints out of her bag and handed them to Pepijn. "We think this may be Albert Schenk's inventory list or at least part of it."

The dealer studied them intensely before bursting out, "That son of a bitch! Nick wasn't being petty. There really was something strange going on." Pepijn was angry, his face red with emotion.

"Sorry, you've lost me," she said, concerned about his sudden change in attitude.

"There are sixty-seven bis poles listed here. Albert may have collected a total of forty for Dutch museums. Where did the others go? And how did he acquire so many?"

"Are you certain it was forty? Albert did collect objects for several museums in the Netherlands over the course of a nine-year period."

"Young lady, it is my job to know the ethnography museums' collections by heart. Otherwise, how do I know which holes in their displays need filling? Granted, most of my current clients are private collectors, but I do sell pieces to museums from time to time."

Zelda was at a loss for words.

"Tell you what, let's find out for certain." He turned his computer's monitor on and opened up Adlib, a collection database system used by museums in the Netherlands. He searched several museums' collections, rapidly creating a short list of bis poles in Dutch museums.

"Albert collected twenty-five poles for Rotterdam, eleven for Leiden and two for Amsterdam. So that leaves twenty-nine poles unaccounted for. And this list is incomplete. Based on the dates, it looks as though Nick only photographed a portion of Albert's inventory. Who knows how many containers of objects Albert shipped back."

"I don't understand why this list is so incriminating. He was there to collect objects and was apparently successful at it, so what is the big deal?"

"What is your name again?"

"Zelda Richardson."

"Well, Zelda, if he were collecting them legally, they should be in a museum's collection."

Her puzzled expression spurred him on.

"The Papua Ordinance Act of 1923 forbade the collecting of historically or culturally significant objects by private collectors and artifact dealers, such as my father. Anthropologists were only allowed to export them if they were acquired for a registered cultural or scientific institution. Anything Albert collected of historical value should have been placed in a museum." Pepijn paused for a moment before adding, "The ordinance was not always followed to the letter, and some older pieces did get through. Sometimes, museums didn't have room in their budgets to purchase all of the objects collected for them, so the extras were sold. Though, by the late 1950s, ancestor artifacts were nearly impossible to come by legally. And my father prided himself on only selling pieces with the proper paperwork and import certificates. He didn't want to feed the black market by purchasing objects that were most likely smuggled into the country."

"Are you saying there was a black market for Asmat artifacts here in the Netherlands?"

"My dear, there is a black market for everything if you know where to look," he scoffed. "That sort of practice is what gave our gallery a bad reputation in the 1950s. You have no idea how often my father was accused of dealing in illegally acquired Asmat artifacts. That is why, in 1962, he decided to stop selling older Asmat pieces, and instead, he specialized in the higher quality pieces carved for tourists and collectors, those valued for their beauty instead of their religious significance. That's what his clients preferred anyway. Though honestly, I doubt most private collectors could tell the difference between a new or old piece. Only a handful could or cared."

"1962 is quite specific. Wasn't that the year New Guinea became part of Indonesia?"

"No, the Dutch turned it over to the United Nations in 1962 but control of the region wasn't transferred to Indonesia until late 1963," Pepijn said.

"Oh, yeah." Zelda's mind was buzzing. *Strange coincidence that*, Zelda thought. *Gerrit Visser stopped selling older Asmat artifacts the same year Mayfield disappeared, the Dutch left New Guinea, and Albert returned to Rotterdam.* Zelda kept her thoughts to herself, wanting more time to process everything before she dared share her concerns with Gerrit's son. "Okay, so if Albert wasn't collecting these objects for a museum but selling them off to rich collectors, he would have risked being deported from Dutch New Guinea and possibly arrested."

"And any pieces he had acquired for museums would have also become suspect. No institution wants to be accused of having stolen objects in their collection," Pepijn added.

"But why did Nick care? Was it simply the competition between them? These seem like pretty serious charges your friend was making, and his trip was almost over," Zelda reasoned.

"It was more than Nick's need to best Albert. He probably saw this as a way to win over his father. Nick was the only man in his family not to serve in the military, and I know it ate at his soul. That's why New Guinea fascinated him. It was the last frontier, a place where he could prove himself."

"What does his trip or artifact smuggling have to do with his father?"

"The Dutch were fighting hard to keep their control because of the lucrative gold, oil, and silver reserves on the island. Colonial governments were being toppled all over the globe, and Indonesia was screaming to be established, yet they refused to relinquish their authority. The rest of the world wanted in. American, British, and Australian companies were actively searching for an entry into the region and a way to profit from those mining rights. If Albert was involved in smuggling and selling illegally acquired artifacts, Nick's father may have been able to use the information to leverage a contract. Especially if a colonial official was involved, as Nick suspected. That would explain how Albert exported all of these objects and never got caught by customs."

"That seems like a stretch." Zelda frowned. "I can't imagine the Dutch government would give up their monopoly so easily."

"I'm sure they would have if given a choice between awarding Nick's father a mining contract or to have it become known a Dutch anthropologist and colonial officials were actively participating in international artifact smuggling."

"Okay, let's say it's true. Even if Albert was smuggling pieces to the Netherlands, who would buy them, knowing they had to keep them out of the public eye?" Zelda asked, completely confounded. She couldn't even imagine the logistics involved in such a smuggling operation, especially one that had gone on for so many years.

"I can't imagine one collector could have purchased them all. Based on this list, he must have smuggled hundreds of objects back and finding enough buyers would have taken time. Albert was only in the Netherlands a few weeks a year, so he must have had help here in the Netherlands from someone he had regular contact with. Someone working for a museum with access to their list of sponsors would be a good place to start."

"What do you mean?"

"Dad took me along to listen to Albert speak a few times. His photographs and descriptions brought the region and its people to life. Dad also saved several of Albert's articles about Asmat village life, headhunting rituals, ancestor worship, and the like. In the 1940s and early 50s, my father had gone on acquisition trips in the Asmat region. They shared a common love for New Guinea," Pepijn reflected. "Now that I think of it, perhaps Albert did not need a middleman. Thanks to his presentations and articles, he would have come into regular contact with donors and sponsors, many of which were private collectors. That could explain how he found his clientele."

Zelda's eyes widened in disbelief as Pepijn's words sank in. What began as conjecture was slowly becoming a reality. Did Albert Schenk really sell illegally acquired objects? It was almost too surreal to be true. *If Nick had been certain he had proof, would he have confronted Albert? If he'd threatened to tell Albert's superiors about his suspicions, what would the Dutchman have done to protect his reputation,* she wondered. Albert certainly wouldn't be the director of any museum if this had come out back in the 1960s. Even a rumor that he'd been involved in smuggling would have ruined his budding career and his chances at a curator's position.

Oh, God, Zelda suddenly thought, was Albert a murderer? Is that the secret he'd been trying to keep all this time and the real reason why he didn't want anyone to read Nick's journal? Would he have killed her housemate to protect his sins of the past? Zelda choked up at the thought. She didn't want to be responsible for Elisabeth's death.

"This inventory list alone wouldn't have been enough to destroy Albert or secure his father's mining rights. And Nick never did discover who Albert's supplier was, how he got them out of the country, or who purchased them. Without definitive proof of all three, Nick's accusations would not have stuck. Nick was no fool. He would have known that. That must be why he asked in this letter if I might know who Albert could be selling artifacts to. If Nick could have convinced a prominent collector to admit he'd bought an illicit piece from Albert, it would have been enough to start an investigation and certainly have ended his chances at furthering his career."

Pepijn was right, Zelda realized. As excited as she was to know what the inventory list meant, without more proof, they were no closer to finding out the truth than Nick Mayfield had been. If only she could meet with one of Albert's clients. But how would she go about finding them? And even if she did miraculously manage to do that, how could she convince them to admit they purchased illegally acquired artifacts?

It was as if Pepijn read her mind. "I remember asking Dad if there was any truth to Nick's accusations. He said there would always be a black market if rich collectors were willing to buy illicit objects. He even mentioned a few clients he suspected of doing so, though he had no proof. I've digitalized our active client list, but no one in recent memory has tried to sell me traditional Asmat art. Before my father retired in 1981, it happened quite often." He rose and opened a large filing cabinet, searching through the many hanging folders as he spoke. "Dad kept a client list, in which he noted every piece they'd bought or sold and when. His regulars were quite loyal. Some had been clients for more than thirty years. One, in particular, springs to mind. Let me see if I can find him in Dad's ledgers."

Zelda nodded eagerly. "That would be great."

Pepijn soon found what he was searching for. He pulled a ledger marked 'H-M' out of the cabinet before shutting the drawer with his hip and returning to his desk. "Norbert Meerman," Pepijn stated as he opened the book and searched for the man's name. His grimace told Zelda there was more to the story.

"Why do you remember him so well?"

"He's the reason my father retired." Pepijn shook his head instead of saying more, choosing to find the entry first. She moved her chair closer to his desk and watched as unobtrusively as she could, not wanting to irritate him by looking over his shoulder. From what she could see from her seat, most pages contained one name at the top in capital letters, followed by a long list of objects and dates. Between the listings were several blank pages. Zelda presumed so more clients or objects could be added. He flipped through the pages too quickly for her to read any of them.

Toward the end of the book, he stopped. MEERMAN, NORBERT was written across the top of the left-hand page. A list of objects covered the first and part of the second page dedicated to his collection. "Here it is. How did that story go?" he asked rhetorically, tapping a finger on the desk as he scanned the long list of objects written under Meerman's name. Zelda stretched her neck a little to see what he was reading. At the bottom of the second page were long paragraphs of text. After reading through the notes, he exclaimed, "Oh, yes. That's how it went."

Pepijn turned the ledger around so Zelda could read it more easily. "See these notations at the bottom? It says here Norbert Meerman tried to sell my father five Asmat shields on December 15, 1980, but Dad wasn't interested. We'd already switched focus to contemporary Asmat art, and the ones Meerman was offering were much older. He insisted my father could find a buyer for them, even though he had no export certificates or other documentation to prove their provenance. When my father refused to sell those five, or anything else in his collection, Norbert stormed out and never returned." Pepijn glanced at his file. "He had been a loyal client for more than twenty-five years. That's what upset my father so."

"Upset him?"

"He hated to think one of his long-time clients—a friend really—would have bought illegally acquired objects in the first place. And he was offended that Meerman then tried to use his gallery to whitewash them."

"Are you certain they were illegally acquired?" Zelda gasped.

"Positive. Otherwise, he would have had the proper export documentation. That was the only logical explanation."

"Do you think he would talk to me?"

"I'm afraid not. Norbert Meerman died of a heart attack shortly after he came to my father's gallery. That's why I remember him so clearly. Meerman's wife blamed my father for his death, claiming the stress of their last conversation and its ramifications ultimately caused his fatal heart attack."

"I'm so sorry."

Pepijn shrugged. "His widow had five small children to raise and was lashing out. After Meerman died, Dad lost interest in everything related to the gallery—his clients, artwork, and even his collection trips. He retired a few months after Meerman died and bought a house in France."

"That's too bad." Zelda didn't really know how to respond but felt as if she was supposed to say something comforting.

Pepijn jutted his chin out. "I'm not sorry he retired when he did. The last few years in the gallery, he seemed bored by developments in ethnic art and less interested in promoting contemporary works. On my last trip to Nice, he was happier than I'd seen him in years. He rediscovered his passion for art, food, and travel. And I was able to run the gallery how I wanted, which has brought immense pleasure to my life. In many ways, Meerman's death was a blessing in disguise, for my father and me both."

Pepijn pointed to the last paragraph written into the ledger. "Dad also noted that the shields were bequeathed to the Wereldmuseum in 1981, which is frankly strange. If Meerman didn't have documents proving their provenance, no museum should have acquired them," he said, his puzzled expression turning to astonishment as a realization entered his mind. He turned back to his desktop and searched online. "Albert was named the director of the museum in 1977, which would explain how those objects got into the collection system."

Zelda could feel the anger welling up inside as the level of Albert's deceit hit home. How many objects had he sold off to rich collectors willing to look the other way when it came to the artifact's provenance? If what Pepijn said were true, then everything Albert had ever acquired for the museum or added to its collection would become suspect. The ramifications were too horrible to consider.

She willed herself to calm down and look at the situation rationally. She needed to tread lightly. Her own budding career depended on it. Before she told Marijke Torenbouwer or anyone else at the Tropenmuseum what she and Pepijn suspected, she needed to find out more about Meerman's collection. She didn't want to be accused of trying to sully Albert's distinguished career. She would certainly never be welcome in any Dutch museum again if she did.

"Norbert Meerman did have a large family. I'm certain some of his children still live in Amsterdam." Pepijn turned back to his computer and typed Meerman's name into the city archives.

Zelda felt he suddenly looked weary and drawn. What happened to the regal gentleman he'd appeared to be when she'd arrived thirty minutes earlier? As he clicked through Meerman's personal records, searching for his children's names, she asked, "Pepijn, why are you helping me?"

He kept his eyes on the screen as he answered. "Because if Albert Schenk was smuggling artifacts, he should pay for what he did. People like him give galleries like mine a bad name." His shoulders sagged as he added, "And I need to know if Albert did hurt Nick. I let my friend down by not following up on his suspicions all those years ago. I doubt Albert had anything to do with his disappearance, but I need to know what he was up to as much as Nick did. If only to honor my friend's memory and help his family find peace after all these years."

She hadn't thought about how Pepijn must feel, discovering his friend wasn't exaggerating or acting paranoid. He'd doubted Nick for more than fifty years, discounting his accusations as nonsense, only to discover he had been telling the truth all along. And Albert, a man he'd known for several decades, may have had something to do with Nick's disappearance. How confused and hurt he must be right now.

He printed off a single page before handing it to Zelda. "Meerman's oldest daughter Renee lives on the Singel, a few blocks from here."

"Wait, how did you get ahold of her address? I thought only the information about deceased persons was accessible to the public?"

"That's true. But she's the proud owner of Renee Translates." Upon seeing Zelda's blank stare, he added, "Her business information is online, including her business address, which is probably also her home."

"That's creepy."

"That's the Dutch Chamber of Commerce for you. Look, I know it is a lot to ask, but there is a chance Renee Meerman remembers her father's Asmat collection. There is no guarantee she will talk to you about Albert or their artifacts, but someone has to try." He paused, locking eyes with Zelda. "Would you be willing to talk with her?"

Zelda's eyes widened at the thought. She wasn't comfortable barging in on the woman and asking painful questions. However, her own life was still being threatened, and she needed answers. Until she knew who killed her housemate and why, she wouldn't be able to rest. Nick's letters and journal weren't enough to arrest anyone. If she accused Albert of anything, it had to be well-founded. The man was one of the most respected museum directors in the Netherlands.

"Why don't you come with me to see Renee? After all these years…" Zelda's voice trailed off, not really sure it was a good idea but hoping his company would strengthen her resolve to follow through and contact Meerman's daughter.

"I doubt my presence would be helpful. In fact, any child of Norbert Meerman would probably refuse to see you if I tagged along." He closed his eyes momentarily, shaking his head against the memories. "Please, do let me know what she says about Norbert's Asmat collection. For Nick's sake."

Zelda nodded solemnly. "Of course. I'll stop by in the morning and let you know what she said."

Only after she'd unlocked her bike chain did Zelda remember Nick's missing collection. She glanced back at the door. Pepijn had turned the sign to *Closed*. *He probably needs time to digest everything*, she realized. Now was not the time to add to his confusion and inquire about the missing artifacts. *Oh, well, I can ask him about it tomorrow,* she thought as she peddled away.

Ancestor worship

September 8, 1962

Nick followed Father Terpstra inside the small hut, glad to be out of the pelting rain. His clothes clung to his skin, a layer of red mud covering most of his body. When the priest handed him a towel to dry off, he accepted it gratefully.

As he scrubbed at his sopping clothes, Nick looked around the hut. A small bed, nightstand, and two chairs lined one wall. Crates similar to the ones he saw transported to Agats a few weeks earlier were stacked up against another. Headdresses and a few decorated skulls piled up in front of spears rested in one corner. More crates and packing materials were stacked up next to a large worktable in the middle of the room. On top of the table lay a pair of shields almost as tall as he was, one wrapped in dried reeds and leaves, but the other hadn't yet been packed up for transport.

Curiosity drew Nick closer. The shield's intricate decorations took his breath away. It was one of the most beautiful Asmat creations he had ever seen. The woven reed covered in thick clay, stripes and dots painted in charcoal and red ocher decorated its surface, and hundreds of dogs' teeth and boars' tusks poked through the reed, creating a fierce ring around the shield's oval edge. In the center was a clay-covered face. Cream-colored Cowrie shells filled the eye sockets, and the mouth was painted in a thin red grin. *It must be an actual skull,* Nick realized in astonishment. *This was the real deal,* he thought, *not a piece made for tourists or collectors, but to honor an ancestor.*

Father Terpstra ushered him to a chair and grabbed his first aid kit. Without further ado, he pulled the thorn out and allowed blood to rush out of the wound for a moment before pouring disinfectant over it. Nick screamed in pain. The priest dried off his patient's hand and wrapped it in a thick bandage. "It's quite deep. You'll need to get it stitched up, but I don't have the right supplies here. Once we get back to the village, I'll take you over to the medical hut and get you fixed up. Here, let me get you some bourbon for the pain." He poured them each a large glass of alcohol from one of the five bottles of liquor on the nightstand.

"That's my favorite, thank you."

Father Terpstra chuckled easily as he handed him a double shot. "A good guess on my part."

Nick gulped it back, feeling the pain recede immediately. He closed his eyes and relaxed into his chair, glad he'd run into the priest way out here in the jungle. The thought tickled at his brain until his eyes jolted open. As he took in his surroundings, his relief turned to dread as he realized what he was seeing. Hundreds of exquisite Asmat artifacts filled the hut. The table was a packing area. The crates matched those Albert was using to transport his collection to Agats.

"Father, why did you think I was Albert?" Nick asked slowly, unsure if he wanted to hear the priest's response. After all his talk of helping these people, Nick wanted to believe Kees was an upright and honest man.

"I don't know. It's the first name that popped into my head," he said, avoiding Nick's gaze as he fidgeted with his empty glass.

"Aren't you scared locals will find this hut and steal the objects for their vitality—isn't that what you called it?"

Kees grabbed Nick's empty glass and placed both back on his nightstand. Gazing up at the ceiling, he kept his back to the American as he spoke. "This is my meditation hut. The locals give it a wide berth."

"It looks more like a packing station to me. What are all of these objects doing here, Father?"

The priest whirled around, his face a mask of indignation. "I told you, trading steel utensils for ritual objects is part of the conversion process."

"I thought it was also the Church's policy to burn them all, as you did a few weeks ago?" Nick glared up at Kees.

"These are from my last trip upriver," he said, unconvincingly.

"Then why are you packing them up so well? If you are going to destroy them, why go to all this trouble to protect them?" Nick rose from his chair and examined the open crate next to the table. Several artifacts were already wrapped and placed inside. He removed the objects, one by one. After tearing off the protective packaging, he placed them on the table until there was no room left.

"These are stunning," Nick said, more to himself than to the priest. He picked up a small carving of an Asmat woman and ran his fingers along her elaborately carved body.

Father Terpstra remained silent, watching the American warily.

Suddenly Nick's whole body froze visibly as the truth slapped him in the face. He stared at the priest, his eyes wide. "My, God, you are Albert's supplier!"

"It's not what you think," Terpstra whispered, his whole body shaking.

"You're selling these objects to collectors for a profit, aren't you? The same objects you refused to sell me because you were sworn to destroy them. What did you put on the bonfire, exactly?"

The priest fell onto his bed, nestling his face in his trembling hands as tears flowed down his cheeks.

Nick ignored him, choosing to open more crates. He carefully freed several more objects from their packaging, openly admiring one before grabbing another. When he found a decorated skull, complete with hair and painted on facial features, he lifted it up high. "Harvard would love to have this."

Father Terpstra met Nick's gaze and shook his head. "I can't sell them to any museum. I can't explain how I acquired them," Terpstra pleaded.

"You're right." Nick smiled. "I'm sure your superiors would not be pleased to hear about your side project, nor would the international media. You must have a contact at the export office helping you, too. And Albert must have a contact in the Netherlands, someone working in one of his museums, I bet. It's not possible to sell all of these objects in a few weeks' time." He glared at Kees, daring him to contradict him. The priest's face was awash with emotion, yet he said nothing.

"But this doesn't need to be made public." Nick quickly added. "My father would love access to the island's mineral reserves even more. There is enough gold and silver for all of us. When I tell the Dutch colonial authorities about your scheme, I am certain they will be more than willing to offer his company a fair share. Otherwise, 'Dutch museums and Catholic Mission Active in Illegal Artifacts Smuggling' will make a lovely headline."

"You don't understand! I've done much soul-searching and decided my superiors are wrong. Because we have banned their rituals, artifacts such as these are no longer created. They have lost their significance in a post-headhunting world, but these carvings are too unique to destroy. They must be saved for future generations. I cannot give them to any institution that demands proof of provenance. Selling them to private collectors is my way of protecting them."

"You are abusing God's power! The villagers only part with these objects because they want your bartered goods and the promises of more to come if they get baptized. How will the international community look upon the Netherlands once it becomes known colonial officers and God's missionaries are taking advantage of the Asmat's inferior bargaining position?"

Father Terpstra pushed his palms together. "You'll do more than destroy me and Albert's reputation. You'll undo years of honest work and the progress we have made. Without us, the Asmat would still be stuck in the Stone Age, raiding each other's villages for heads. Most in this region have accepted Christ and renounced bloodshed. We are doing good work, God's work."

"How dare you hide behind the Church!" Nick raged. "You and Albert must be turning quite a profit. What do your superiors have to say about the extra monies flowing into your mission?"

"My superiors don't know where the money is coming from. They think it is an anonymous benefactor."

"How much do you get from each sale?"

"Albert and I split the profits equally," the priest said in a resigned tone. "But my share is used to build new schools, medical huts, train locals, and pay for extra tools, utensils, and food. All of it goes back into the community."

"They aren't children, and you aren't their father. You weren't honest with them, nor did you let them decide what to do with the money. You are profiting from them."

"No, it's not like that. How can I make you understand?" Kees pleaded.

"I have a copy of Albert's inventory list and contacts. I'll let the colonial authorities investigate and decide," Nick said resolutely.

"Please, you'll destroy everything my church has accomplished. It's not your place. You don't have the right!"

Nick turned to leave, his mind made up. "You have no right to sell them," he said, determination etched on his face.

Kees grabbed Nick's arm as he strode toward the door, pulling him off balance. As Nick spun around, he swung his fist toward the priest, grazing his chin. Terpstra retaliated, his fist connecting with Nick's jaw. The American's head flew back as he fell hard against the worktable with a sickening thud.

Terpstra watched as Nick's anger changed to surprise then froze, his head seemingly suspended in mid-air. His eyes widened as blood began streaming out the back of his neck and onto the floor. Nick gurgled softly before his body went limp, gravity pulling him and the Asmat shield he'd fallen onto, crashing to the floor. When it hit the ground, three boar's tusks, their curved horns still stuck deep under his skull, broke off.

The priest crossed himself before daring to touch Nick's neck, searching for a pulse. It was so faint that Terpstra knew the American had little time left on this earth. There was nothing he could do to save the young man. If he removed the tusks, Nick would only bleed out faster.

He knelt next to the American and held his hands tight until the light faded from his eyes. He felt again for a pulse yet found no sign of life.

Kees muttered a prayer for the American's soul and gently closed Nick's eyelids before sobs racked his body.

Shady provenance

June 1, 2017

Zelda stood before Singel number 146, working up the courage to ring the doorbell. Renee Meerman's office was in a large canal house in a well-to-do neighborhood. Based on the number of names listed next to the front door, it appeared to be divided into ten apartments. Several had company names next to them just as Renee's did. Zelda's finger hovered over her bell, unable to ring it. What could she say that would convince the woman to let her inside? Certainly not the truth. Norbert Meerman's daughter surely would not invite her in if she did.

Several scenarios ran through her mind, from pretending to be a potential client to faking a bicycle accident. Zelda crossed them off her mental list until only one was left. She took a deep breath and pressed the buzzer next to Renee Translates. After what seemed like a lifetime, a woman's voice crackled over the intercom. "Hello?"

"Good afternoon," Zelda said cheerily, "Is this Renee Meerman?"

"Yes?"

"Hi, I am a researcher at the Tropenmuseum. We are including information about several important Asmat art collectors in an upcoming exhibition. Your father is one of them. I had a few questions about his collection if you have a few minutes to answer them?"

"Oh, he would have been honored. Please, come inside. Second floor."

The door began buzzing. Zelda pushed it open, her relief at being let in slightly stronger than the guilt she felt for lying her way inside.

She quickly ascended the wide staircase to the second floor. Meerman stood in her doorway, a welcoming smile brightening her pretty face. She was in her forties with long blonde hair and a smart blue suit, which was topped off with a ruffled white blouse.

"Hello, I am Renee."

"Thank you for meeting with me. I'm Zelda Richardson." Meerman's grip was firm.

"Please, follow me." The older woman led her to the living room, gesturing at a pinstriped couch. "Would you like some tea or coffee?"

Zelda didn't have time for pleasantries. "Ms. Meerman, I haven't been completely honest with you. I do work at the Tropenmuseum, but we are not including your father in our exhibition. I'm sorry I lied, but I have questions about his Asmat collection only you can answer. It is extremely important you tell me how your father acquired his Asmat artifacts and why he couldn't prove their provenance."

"How dare you imply my father did anything wrong! I want you to leave right now," Renee said, her voice full of indignation and her hands on her hips.

"I can't, not until you tell me the truth. Someone killed my housemate, but I'm pretty sure they meant to hurt me. And I am afraid Albert Schenk is involved. I believe he was smuggling artifacts into the Netherlands and selling them to private collectors. If your father did buy any objects from him, I really need to know. It's the only way I can prove Albert was involved and have him arrested. Otherwise, it's just his word against mine, and I don't stand a chance. Please, I am so sorry I lied to you, but it truly is a matter of life and death."

"Why do you think Schenk was involved in smuggling?" the older lady asked, wide-eyed.

"I have documents and letters from the 1960s that show he was exporting more objects back to the Netherlands than he'd noted on the shipping manifests. And Pepijn Visser has a list of collectors who tried to sell his gallery Asmat artifacts without export certificates. Your father's on it." Zelda knew she was stretching the truth, but she needed Meerman on her side. "You are the first person I've found who can shed some light on Albert's practices. Would you at least tell me why your father left his Asmat collection to the Wereldmuseum instead of you and your siblings? And if he couldn't prove the provenance to Gallery Visser, why did Rotterdam agree to acquire them?"

"It's been more than thirty years," Renee Meerman exclaimed, the shrillness in her voice revealing her nervousness. "What does it matter anymore? Surely, you can't have him arrested for misrepresenting an artwork's provenance. It's been too long, and I don't have any evidence."

Zelda's face lit up at the word *evidence*. "Ms. Meerman, if what I think is true, then it won't matter if it happened three or thirty years ago. Albert Schenk's reputation would be tarnished beyond repair, and the collections he's assembled for several Dutch museums would come under serious scrutiny. I think that's why he tried to scare me off, but my housemate got home first. Now she's dead."

Zelda didn't have to fake her fear or the tears flowing down her cheeks. She needed this woman to break her silence and give her enough proof to put Albert behind bars.

The older woman pursed her lips and twisted the ruffle of her blouse in her fingers yet said nothing.

"Only you can tell me what really happened," Zelda pleaded.

"Are you certain he hurt your housemate?"

"Getting surer by the hour."

"That man is pure evil!" Renee looked away, clearly wrestling with her emotions and memories. After a long silence, she said, "I don't know about any murders, but Albert Schenk did arrange the paperwork for my father's Asmat collection. It was part of their deal."

"What deal?"

Renee began pacing back and forth across her living room. "Are you recording this?"

"No," Zelda responded, surprised.

"You should. If Albert had anything to do with your housemate's death, he must be held responsible. For once."

Zelda dutifully pulled out her smartphone and started the voice recorder app.

Renee sat down on the edge of her couch next to Zelda. "My father was always fascinated with ethnic artifacts, though Asmat art interested him the most. He traveled through Dutch New Guinea while working for a mining company surveying potential sites in the 1930s. He bartered for several pieces during his travels and continued to collect more when he returned to Amsterdam, mostly through Visser's gallery."

She paused to play with the stitching on her garment again. "When business was good, my father donated money to the Wereldmuseum. They had the best Asmat collection in the Netherlands. My mother told me that in the late sixties, Albert offered to sell Dad a collection of five shields he said Rotterdam could not afford to acquire. My father knew Schenk from openings and fundraisers. They enjoyed swapping stories about their adventures and got to know each other pretty well.

"Mom said that Dad got quite excited when the five shields were delivered, and he saw how richly decorated they were yet also worn from use. Private collectors rarely got a chance to acquire objects created as part of a death ritual or ancestor worship. He'd tried to export similar pieces twenty years earlier and had been denied an export permit based on their ritual use.

"Unfortunately, Schenk couldn't provide any documentation for them, despite his claims they were intended for Rotterdam's museum. If they had been declared at customs—as they should have been—he would have had an import certificate. Schenk somehow convinced my father it was all aboveboard, claiming it was a simple mistake by a customs official that they weren't recorded on the shipping manifest.

217

Selling them was a way to recover his costs and help my father acquire a collection not usually available to private collectors. Dad should have had alarm bells ringing in his head, but it was too late. He wanted those shields, and Albert offered them for a steal."

Renee Meerman glanced over at her bookcase filled with family photos before continuing. "Over the years, Dad bought several 'extras' from Albert—thirty-five in total. None had paperwork. My father didn't care. Those pieces, in combination with the ones he'd collected and purchased from Gallery Visser, meant he possessed one of the most complete private collections of Asmat art in the Netherlands. Even though he couldn't show it off to the general public, he and his collector friends knew, and that was enough."

My God, Zelda thought, if Albert sold these thirty-five objects to Meerman so easily, how many others did he sell to private collectors under the same pretext during his nine years on the island? I bet several of Meerman's friends were also clients. If only I could get my hands on Albert's complete client list; who knew how many important Dutch collectors were involved? Before Zelda could work out how many objects Albert may have smuggled back and the ramifications of knowing who purchased them, Renee resumed her story.

"Dad bought older pieces from Gallery Visser as well, usually after a collector passed on and his family wanted to sell off his collection for a quick profit. Gerrit Visser didn't want them in his gallery because he focused on contemporary artwork. Dad got first dibs. As far as I know, he bought everything Visser offered."

Zelda nodded, still distracted by Renee's earlier remarks.

"In the late 1970s, Dad's business ran into financial trouble, and even at the low prices Schenk was offering, he couldn't afford to purchase any more artifacts.

"When his business went bankrupt in 1980, Dad had to sell most of his assets to pay his debtors. He'd built up a large collection of artifacts from around the world, but those five Asmat shields were the showpieces. It broke his heart to do so, but he approached Visser and tried to sell them. Without an import certificate, Gerrit Visser refused to buy them or help my father find a seller. Of course, he could tell they shouldn't have been in my father's possession in the first place. Visser was always aboveboard."

"Dad had no savings. He spent all of his money on art. His Asmat collection alone was worth hundreds of thousands of guldens. If he could have sold them, he would have had enough money to pay off his debtors and start again. He tried a few other dealers, but Visser must have warned them. They all refused to sell any of his artifacts in their galleries," Renee said, bitterness seeping into her voice.

Zelda now understood why Pepijn was reluctant to come. Renee probably wouldn't have said a word about her father's art if he had. She clearly held him at least partially responsible for what happened to her father.

"Somehow, Albert found out my father had approached several dealers. He came to our house one night right after Mom put us to bed. I heard shouting and my father scream. I was terrified. I was just a little girl, but I'll never forget running into his study and seeing Dad on the floor, his nose bleeding and Albert Schenk towering over him."

"My God! What did you do?"

"Nothing." A tear came to her eye. "I was only eleven. I remember Albert warned my father to keep quiet and say nothing about how he'd acquired his Asmat objects, how that was part of their bargain."

"A few days later, Dad suffered a fatal heart attack. I think Albert's threats, his inability to sell his collection, and losing his business was too much to take."

Zelda felt herself tearing up, thinking about that little girl losing her father far too young. Yet, as much as she wanted to console Meerman, she needed to find out the truth about Albert Schenk's actions. Her own life depended on it.

"Ms. Meerman, I know you are hurting, but I still don't understand why Rotterdam accepted his Asmat art into their collection. Any museum should have rejected them for the same reasons Visser did," she asked gently.

"Albert came to my mother's house two days after Dad had died. Albert told her Dad's Asmat collection had been bequeathed to the Wereldmuseum and showed her the paperwork proving it. He had export certificates dated 1922 when private citizens were still allowed to collect them. As the director of the museum, he had to sign off on the acquisition. The forged paperwork made it possible to enter them into their collection database. Once they were in, there was no reason to question their provenance."

Zelda nodded solemnly, recalling how Pepijn Visser had said the same thing.

"Albert offered her some money to tide us over if she turned the collection over without incident. She agreed straightway. Albert crated up Dad's Asmat collection and took it away that same afternoon. I remember he had to arrange for a van to come by because there were so many objects to move. I don't think he gave Mom much money, but I know she was glad to have Schenk out of her life. She knew he'd threatened my father and was frightened when he came to the house. I remember she called my uncle to come over and stay with us as soon as he left."

Zelda nodded, absorbing all that Renee was sharing. Suddenly, her head jerked up. "Wait, Albert took all of your father's Asmat pieces? Not just the thirty-five?"

Renee hesitated as her eyes shot to the left, remembering. "No, I'm certain he took them all. Well, except for the ten pieces Dad collected in Dutch New Guinea. Mom made sure Albert didn't touch those. My younger sister Nella has them now. I was never a fan of Asmat art."

"Why would he take the objects your dad purchased from Gallery Visser, as well? And why did he have copies of their documentation?"

"I don't know. He said it was part of their deal."

Zelda's face drained of color. Albert did have an accomplice here in the Netherlands, she realized. And it wasn't a museum director but an ethnic art dealer. Gerrit Visser must have been selling Albert's artifacts to trusted clients.

But if Gerrit was helping Albert move these objects, why was Pepijn helping her? Would he have known if his father were selling pieces on the black market? Zelda shook her head at the thought, figuring she was getting paranoid. Renee was only eleven at the time. She was probably mistaken about Albert taking the pieces he bought from Gallery Visser. Pepijn Visser was clearly despondent to learn Nick's suspicions were probably correct after all. Once she shared this tape with him, he would help her figure out the truth, she was sure of it.

The physical anthropologist's hut

September 9, 1962

The putrid stench of rotting flesh filled the small hut. Kees Terpstra had been inside too long to notice it anymore. Over the course of the afternoon, preparing Nick's body, his sadness and anger had numbed his senses. He looked over at Albert, wondering if the man felt any remorse. All Kees could read on the anthropologist's face was irritation as he searched through the American's backpack.

Kees crossed himself before gently lifting the bones that once made up Nick's legs, now scraped clean of skin, fat, and muscles. He placed them in a tub of bubbling water and bleach, careful not to splash the acidic liquid onto his clothes. After six hours of simmering, they should be cleaned of enough tissue materials to cook in water. Once the bleach had been boiled out, he would bathe them in alcohol before allowing them to dry. All in all, it would take the rest of the day and night to prepare Nick's skeletal remains for transport.

Kees was thankful the physical anthropologists who used this hut had pinned instructions for cleaning bones to the wall as a reference. He'd vaguely recalled how the process worked from a tour given with pride by one of the many bone collectors working in the region. But in his time of need, the detailed instructions were quite handy. He only hoped none of the anthropologists and explorers currently working in the region would stop by before their work was done.

As Kees stepped back from the tub and removed his gloves, an exasperated sigh escaped Albert's lips. "What did Nicholas say exactly?" Spread out on the floor around him was the American's possessions: his journal, a well-worn copy of *How to Survive on Land and Sea*, a Nikon camera, several pens, rope, and a measuring tape.

Kees leaned against the hut's reed wall and pinched the bridge of his nose as he recalled Nick's final conversation. "He had a copy of your inventory list, which proved you were shipping back more objects than you were declaring."

"How did he get ahold of my notebook? I always have it with me," Albert said, glancing automatically at his satchel on the ground next to him. "It doesn't make any sense." He shook his head, still refusing to believe Nick's accusations.

"He didn't specify, and I didn't pry. I should have asked to see his proof. If I had known..." Father Terpstra said softly, unable to finish his thought.

Albert stood up from his kneeling position, stretching out his back until it cracked. "Well, I've found nothing suspicious. He must have been bluffing. There's nothing written in the margins of that survival guide, either. I've also skimmed through the last few entries in his journal and found no lists of artifacts or village names." Albert stopped talking and snapped his fingers. He leaned over, grabbed Nick's camera and pulled out the roll of film inside, purposefully exposing it to light. "In case he somehow managed to take incriminating pictures," Albert said in answer to Kees's questioning stare.

"He seemed so sure of himself," the priest said, puzzled. Terpstra wanted to cry out in frustration, his sins weighing heavily on his mind. He'd always been a good, God-fearing man and never imaged he would ever take a life. Was this God's way of punishing him for trying to save the Asmat's artifacts? He hoped and prayed Albert found some sort of proof of their deceit in his possessions. Otherwise, he had killed a man for nothing. Perhaps he didn't pull a trigger, but he still felt responsible for Nick's accidental demise.

A few more shipments and they would have been finished, Kees ruminated with a heavy heart. There were fewer and fewer ritual objects to be traded for steel utensils. Most villages in the region had converted to Christianity and ceased creating ritual objects, as the missionaries demanded in return for medical help, supplies, and food. In his mind, the Church's requirement the Asmat give up their intricate artistic form of expression justified his actions. Though he knew deep in his heart he was wrong to go about it this way.

He should have pushed harder to create a mission museum. Why didn't he store the best pieces in Agats until one was realized, instead of succumbing to Albert's temptations? Perhaps the sheer quantity of exquisite Asmat art would have motivated the Church to take his proposal more seriously.

Although the monies earned through their smuggling operation did allow him to build up the largest and best-equipped mission on the island. Without those sales, he would not have been able to build as many schools and hospitals as he had or extend the Church's reach as far. He had convinced himself the good he was doing outweighed the moral ambiguity of it all. But now that Nick had discovered their secret, Father Terpstra didn't dare continue.

Simply thinking of the young man brought a tear to his eye. He'd comforted the American as best he could, knowing his lifeblood was seeping out too fast to save him. Only after he'd performed the last rites had he raced back to the village to find Albert.

Once they'd returned to his hut, it had taken hours to decide what to do with Nick's body. After much discussion, they determined their only option was to place Nick's bones in crates destined for the Netherlands. They didn't dare bury him in the forest, despite its density. The chance was too great an animal would dig him up and his corpse found by hunters scouring the forest for food in the morning before it could rot enough to become unrecognizable. Burning his body was not a realistic option because it was raining too hard to get a large enough fire going. Besides, the discovery of a tall man's skeletal remains, unrecognizable or not, would raise too many questions once it was known Nicholas was missing.

Any investigation into his death would become an international event, of that he and Albert were certain, and the island would be picked over with a fine-toothed comb. His family was rich and powerful, meaning the colonial government would utilize all of their resources to find any trace of him. It was better for both of them that Nick disappeared—at least for now. Together, they had carried Nick's body and bag to the closest hut used by several physical anthropologists. Their crates would be sent back to Dutch institutions once the bone collectors had enough to fill a container ship. That could take months.

As a sort of penance, Terpstra volunteered to prepare Nick's remains. If only I could have talked him out of going to the authorities without resorting to violence, he cried inwardly. Why didn't I demand to see the evidence Nick claimed to have? If the American was bluffing, as he and Albert now suspected, Terpstra would have let him leave.

While Kees donned his gloves again, Albert skimmed the journal, wishing he could take it back to his hut and read it in its entirety. But he resisted the impulse, knowing as soon as he sounded the alarm and announced Nick had disappeared, the village would be torn apart and all huts searched by the colonial authorities.

They couldn't crate his possessions up with the bones, Albert realized. The belt buckle and journal would stand out and be noticed as soon as it was opened. Someone was bound to connect them to the unusually tall Westerner found in the same batch of crates.

They finally agreed to burn the survival guide, crush his glasses, and sell his Nikon at a pawnshop in Hollandia. The journal and buckle would be packed in with Albert's next shipment heading to the Netherlands. Though Kees wanted to destroy the journal as well, Albert refused to burn it, citing his need to read Nick's final observations and make certain the American hadn't found any real evidence of their illegal activities.

Once the crates were safely in the Netherlands, Albert could retrieve

Nick's possessions before they were moved to the Wereldmuseum's storage facility. The belt buckle was too distinctive to be left behind or even buried. If the hard rains exposed it and a local took to wearing it, any Westerner in the region would recognize its odd design immediately, especially once Nick's photo was distributed across the island. The Mayfields were bound to involve themselves in the search, as well. Albert glanced over at Kees, hoping he could keep their secret in the coming weeks.

Kees stirred the tub, relieved to see the body tissue was already coming loose. He closed his eyes, praying for Nick's family and wishing them strength during their upcoming ordeal.

MS Bali III

October 9, 1962

Albert stared out at the rolling waves, praying the sea would calm down once they'd rounded the tip of India. He hated sailing but knew his presence on board would keep curious sailors from looting his crates of spears, masks, headdresses, shields, and bis poles. He'd lost a few pieces on each trip so far but didn't mind terribly. The sailors' need for a memento was a small price to pay.

However, this time, he couldn't afford to have prying eyes open and pillage the wrong crate. No one could know about Nick's possessions. He'd put the journal and belt buckle in the largest bis pole crate, knowing it would be nearly impossible for looters to gain access to the artifacts on the bottom of the pile.

He just wished he could have gotten to the crate before it was loaded into his reserved container. The long boat trip back would have been the perfect opportunity to read Nicholas's journal and find out more about his suspicions or any proof he'd found of Albert's treachery. He was not entirely convinced Nicholas was bluffing, though he still didn't know how the American could have seen his inventory list—that notebook was always in his satchel. But by the time they had reached Hollandia, the colonial authorities were scouring every village and town, searching for anything connected to Nicholas that could lead them to his current whereabouts. The last thing he wanted to do was draw attention to the crate he'd placed the American's possessions in by requesting access to it.

He toyed with the idea of extracting it during the boat trip back but knew if he did, he would have to order the freighter's hold clear of all personnel while he removed the journal. The sailors were sure to assume his load contained undeclared valuables and would raid it as soon as his back was turned, whether he was on board or not. Besides, the crates were too large to move without help, and he didn't know which of the ship's personnel could be discreet.

No, he would have to wait a few more weeks until the crates were moved to his warehouse in Rotterdam. Because he collected for several cultural institutions, his standard routine was to transport everything to his private storage facility and then divide the objects up by museum. What his employers didn't know was that he first removed the extra, undeclared pieces before sending the rest to their final destination. Those undocumented objects were repacked into smaller boxes for his partner, ones that could easily fit into the trunk of a car. Once this shipment was in his storage space, he would have all the time in the world to extract Nicholas's objects and read his journal.

Albert grabbed at his stomach as the MS *Bali III* crested another wave, dropping the freighter hard onto the ocean's surface. He watched through his window as the boat rose again, bracing for the slap as it fell. His hut at the bow of the ship seemed to skip along the surface. The storms had intensified since they'd passed through the Bay of Bengal and reached the Indian Ocean. Although Albert knew he had to be here, he deeply regretted not flying back. A few days on planes would have been vastly preferable. His stomach didn't respond well to seasickness, and he'd never sailed across the open ocean before. It was harder on his body than he'd expected, though he was beginning to wonder if his symptoms were indicative of something more.

Albert looked over at his plate, full of uneaten bread and apple slices. He hadn't been able to hold anything down since they'd left Singapore almost two weeks ago. He only hoped the seas would be smoother once they'd passed through the Suez Canal.

Knowing he needed to visit his crates, Albert forced himself to rise. The sailors knew by now how fragile his objects were or so Albert repeatedly claimed. It was the easiest way to justify his frequent visits to the holds, under the ruse of checking that the ropes were holding.

Sweat rolled down his face. His pulse raced as he stood. He grabbed his bed for support as dizziness overtook him. He fell back onto the bed. This was more than seasickness, Albert realized. He needed medical attention. He'd had trouble with night sweats and a growing fever for weeks but attributed his symptoms to stress. Now that he was so close to getting rid of the source of his irritation he should be feeling better—or so he reckoned. Nicholas's bones were spread across three crates stored in the middle of the New Guinean jungle. True, his journal and belt buckle were in one of the bis pole crates here on board, and even if someone found his possessions during this trip, it didn't mean Albert was involved with Nick's disappearance. He could easily explain their presence away.

Albert forced himself to push Nicholas Mayfield out of his mind and focus on his own health. First, he needed the room to stop spinning. He closed his eyes tight, sucking air in through his nostrils. Once his dizziness subsided, he dragged himself up, this time, moving toward the medical officer's hut a few doors down.

Pepijn calls the police

June 1, 2017

Zelda didn't know what to do or think. Her meeting with Renee Meerman was distressing, to say the least. Despite the mounting evidence, she had trouble believing the director of one of Rotterdam's most prestigious cultural institutions and a preeminent gallery owner were dealing in illegal artifacts. Why would Albert risk his budding career and Gerrit Visser his stellar reputation? Even in the face of Renee Meerman's accusations, would Albert Schenk try to dismiss her story as lies? Was he powerful enough to make this problem go away?

And how would the museum's board of directors react? They'd just given him a royal send-off, praising his inclusive collection and exhibition policies to any news organization that would listen. Would they also try to sweep this under the proverbial rug?

Zelda jumped on her bike and pedaled aimless away from Renee's, knowing she needed to give herself time to digest all that she had learned. She stopped when she reached the Magere Brug, a thin slip of a bridge rising over the Amstel River. Local legend claims two rich sisters built it in 1691 because they wanted to visit each other daily. Why they couldn't walk a few hundred feet to the nearest existing one was beyond her. Now it was a bike- and pedestrian-only bridge and a popular place for tourists to visit. It was particularly gorgeous at night when the twelve hundred light bulbs outlining its form twinkled in the river's dark water.

Zelda liked to come here and take in the fabulous views of the Hermitage, Carré Theater, shipping locks, and many glorious canal houses lining the river's wide banks. Beneath her, canal tour boats, sailing yachts, transport barges, and rent-a-boats vied for space. She leaned her bike against the wrought-iron railing and soaked up the skyline while she played her conversations with Renee Meerman and Pepijn Visser back in her head. So much was going through her mind. She could use a sounding board.

She started to dial Jacob's number before pausing to check her watch first. It was only four o'clock. He was probably still meeting with his university adviser. Luckily, his adviser was sympathetic, well connected, and promised to do his utmost to help her boyfriend find a solution to his PhD problem. Jacob figured their meeting would take up most of the day. She didn't want to come across as the emotionally unstable girlfriend their first week of living together by interrupting him. He had enough to deal with and would be home soon enough. But she was hankering to discuss it all with someone now while it was still fresh in her mind. Instead of Jacob, she dialed another frequently called number.

"Hey, Friedrich. I was hoping to catch you this afternoon," she said with a sigh, disappointed his phone had gone straight to voicemail. "It's far worse than I had expected. I have proof Albert Schenk was smuggling artifacts out of Dutch New Guinea and selling them to private collectors. I don't know what to do with the information yet. I'm going to head back to Jacob's apartment to try to process it all. Could you stop by later?"

Zelda pocketed her phone as another idea took hold. Before her resolve lessened, she jumped back on her bike and pedaled over the Magere Brug then down the Kerkstraat before turning onto the Prinsengracht. If she couldn't discuss this afternoon's events with Jacob or Friedrich, she could talk it through with the art dealer. Pepijn Visser would certainly want to hear her conversation with Renee.

Zelda wondered again how he was going to react to Renee's

accusations. Pepijn seemed so sure of his father's integrity. The idea that Gerrit Visser was involved with Albert's smuggling operation still didn't sit right with her, but she couldn't think up another logical explanation. *Yet there must be*, she assured herself. And Pepijn deserved to hear this recording before the police or anyone else did. It was thanks to him that she'd found Renee in the first place. He was clearly as motivated to find out the truth as she was.

The art gallery was already closed, but she figured he lived in the apartment above. Zelda wrapped her bike chain around a light pole and then checked the name next to the bell before buzzing it. It was indeed Pepijn Visser.

A few minutes later, she heard his voice through the intercom. "Yes?"

"Hi, Pepijn. This is Zelda Richardson. I hope I'm not disturbing you, but I met with Meerman's daughter and would like to talk."

He buzzed her in without further ado. Mounted on the walls of the narrow staircase were Peruvian masks, an Inuit sleigh, and a carved paddle Zelda thought was Asmat. When Pepijn opened his front door, the crystal chandelier hanging in the hallway lit his body in silhouette.

"Thanks for meeting with me," Zelda said as she approached the landing.

"Not at all. Please, come in." His home was as lavishly decorated as his gallery below. Zelda wasn't sure if she would enjoy living among the death masks, sharp spears, and creepy ritual dolls filling his cabinets and walls. They would probably give her too many nightmares. Though these pieces somehow seemed even more exquisite than those in his gallery. Zelda smiled, figuring getting first dibs on any incoming artwork was one of the perks of running a gallery.

"You already met with Renee? I can't wait to hear what she had to say." Pepijn pointed toward a chaise lounge covered in purple suede. He sat down in a burgundy chair opposite her.

"We ended up having quite a long conversation. She asked me to record it. I think it's better you listen to it, rather than me trying to recap it for you."

Pepijn raised an eyebrow but, otherwise, remained silent. Only a slight nod made clear he'd understood her request. Zelda pushed play and jacked up the volume before handing him her phone. He took it gingerly, as if he wasn't comfortable with modern technology, leaned back in his chair, and listened intently. Once it finished playing, he shook his head in disgust.

"I cannot believe it. My own father. All these years I defended him, refusing to believe he could have been involved in something illegal. No wonder the rumors persisted—they were true."

"You really didn't know?" Zelda asked gently.

"No." Pepijn shook his head violently. "My father spent most of his adult life denying any association to stolen artifacts. I know he was upset when I asked him about Nick's letter and accusations, but I had no idea he was involved." Pepijn's shoulders slumped in defeat. "I never understood how he could afford his house in Nice. I know the sixties were a difficult time for the gallery, for all ethnic art galleries really. I just can't believe he succumbed to temptation."

"Do you think Nick figured out your father was involved?" Zelda asked carefully. "Perhaps that was why he wrote what he did in his last letter."

Pepijn's brow furrowed before he shook his head. "No. If he thought my father was involved, he would have asked me straight out. Nick was never one to pussyfoot around. Oh, God," he called out, looking stricken. "Nick was bullheaded enough to have confronted Albert, even without enough evidence. Would Albert have hurt him?" he wondered aloud.

"He doesn't seem violent, though I'd never suspected he was involved in smuggling, either," Zelda responded, the same thoughts weighing heavily on her mind.

"You need to let the police hear this recording, Zelda. They will want to question Albert about Renee Meerman's accusations. Though after all these years, I'm sure he's thought up a logical explanation already. Still, it is important to get his version of events on record. I hope Renee will be willing to talk to the police about her recollections."

"I don't know. She was shaking when she spoke of him. That's why she wanted me to record our conversation so she wouldn't have to repeat it. But she does blame Albert for her father's death." *As well your father*, Zelda added in her mind. She didn't want to inflict any more pain on Pepijn by saying it aloud.

"If Albert is dangerous, she may not have a choice."

Pepijn picked up his phone and dialed, asking for a police investigator by name. "Jan, how are you, old friend?" He paused to listen before adding, "I have an official request." Pepijn explained what they'd learned and what he hoped the police would do. "Yes, I know perfectly well who he is. I am not asking you to arrest Albert, simply question him. Zelda has paperwork and an audio recording to support her accusations," he spoke passionately, clearly having to convince his friend to honor his request.

"Let me ask." Pepijn covered the receiver with his hand. "Zelda, do you have everything with you?"

"No, my laptop is at Jacob's. My transcription of Nick's journal is on it. I can pick it up on the way to the police station."

Pepijn looked surprised, letting his hand drop away from the receiver. "You transcribed Nick's journal? I had no idea." He recovered quickly, adding, "And your friend Jacob lives in Amsterdam?"

"Yeah, fairly close. He's on the Noorderstraat."

Pepijn raised his eyebrows in expectation.

"Noorderstraat 53, it's a side street off the Vijzelgracht."

"Did you hear that, Jan? He lives close by. It won't take her long to pick up her laptop."

Zelda's phone beeped. She whipped it out to see a new message from Friedrich. "Will stop by after work." He didn't say when, but she knew the media lab closed soon. She should be at Jacob's place before he arrived. Maybe he could come to the police station with her. She typed in "Great."

Pepijn said, "Of course, I will see you shortly. Zelda will meet us at the station."

Zelda nodded vigorously when Pepijn looked to her for confirmation. "Excellent. She'll be there."

Pepijn disconnected the call with a satisfied smile. "Jan Roels and I went to primary school together. He's as honest as they come. I don't know how seriously he's going to take this case, but at least he's willing to listen. Albert Schenk is a powerful man. He will have to tread lightly." Pepijn rose. "Let me get my jacket. We can walk downstairs together. I'll head over to the station now." He took two steps then stopped and turned suddenly towards Zelda. "Why don't you email me the audio file? That way I can explain to Jan what we've discovered and let him hear the recording while we're waiting for you. I know he won't issue an arrest warrant or even bring Albert in for questioning until he has heard it."

What a good idea, Zelda thought. The sooner Albert was off the streets, the better. She pulled out her phone and then hesitated. "Why don't I come with you to the station now and pick up the laptop later? I don't know how useful Nicholas Mayfield's journal will be. He did write about his interactions with Albert, though most of his entries are rather vague. He never specifically mentions his suspicions about illegal smuggling in his journal, so far as I can remember, only in his letter to you."

Pepijn shook his head in disagreement. "The more evidence the police have, the stronger the case. They may be able to use information in Nick's journal when questioning Albert. After all these years, I need to know if he had anything to do with Nick's disappearance."

Zelda nodded silently, understanding his frustration. His friend may have been murdered by a man he'd known for decades. But would Albert really have killed Nick—or anyone else for that matter—to prevent the colonial authorities or museum directors from finding out about his smuggling operation? It seemed so far-fetched.

Though she knew the police would be doing the interrogating, she had so many questions for Albert. Who was his supplier? How many customs officers were involved? How did he manage to move so many artifacts so quickly? Was Gerrit Visser really his partner here in the Netherlands? Or was Albert able to sell them all during his brief trips back home? Even with all of the evidence at her disposal, she was still unable to answer any of these questions with certainty.

She emailed Pepijn the audio file then helped him download it to his laptop. As an afterthought, she forwarded it to Friedrich and herself, just in case. Smartphones were so unreliable. It was always good to have a backup.

They walked downstairs together. Pepijn waved goodbye as she biked away. On her way back to Jacob's, Zelda tried to imagine how Albert would react when the police asked him to come with them, even if only for an informal interview.

A welcome opportunity

Albert gradually opened his eyes, letting them adjust to the bright sunlight streaming in through the hospital window. After propping himself up on his elbows, he managed to kick his legs onto the floor. He rose slowly, holding onto his drip line as he did. A week of vitamin C and atovaquone-proguanil were finally having an effect. He was now strong enough to walk from one end of his room to the other without falling down.

A knock on the door made him turn. Marc Kline, director of the Ethnology Museum of Rotterdam, popped his head in. It was his second visit this week.

"Albert! Seeing you stand makes my heart sing." He clapped Albert softly on the shoulder, afraid to topple his newly regained balance. Marc's visits were motivated by guilt, Albert was certain. He would have felt like an ass if it didn't work to his advantage.

Since being rushed to Wilhelmina Hospital after the MS *Bali III* docked at the city's harbor, Albert had feared the worst. As soon as any curator opened his crates, he would have a catastrophe to deal with. Though he'd been here for a week, he'd been disoriented for most of it. Now that the fog in his brain was finally lifting, he was struggling to figure out the best approach to take once Nick's possessions or the extra artifacts were found. Should he pretend he didn't know they were in the bis pole crate or how they could have gotten there? Playing dumb seemed to be his only choice. He couldn't think of any other plausible option.

The American's disappearance had dominated international and national news since their freighter docked at the Oostelijke Handelskade in Amsterdam. Mayfield's father was still on the island, organizing searches by plane, boat, and land. Luckily, they'd yet to find any trace of Nick.

Marc patted Albert's bed before sitting in the chair next to it, a rather serious expression on his face. "Have a seat. There's something we need to discuss."

Here it is, the moment of truth, Albert thought. He lay back on the bed gingerly, letting his breathing go ragged, playing up his sickly state.

"I'm not sure how much of our political news made its way to New Guinea," Marc said.

"Not much, I'm afraid." Albert chuckled nervously, suddenly unsure where this conversation was going.

"These past few months, we've had protesters camping out in front of our entrance. They represent several indigenous groups who demand we change our displays, asserting the way we present their cultures are racist."

Albert nodded. He knew about the independence movements in the Dutch Indies and Suriname and how most groups believed their representation in museum displays exuded an air of white superiority. He wasn't surprised protesters had targeted Rotterdam's anthropological museum, only by the speed of social change.

"The board of directors has decided to adapt our museum displays to reflect this new paradigm. The pieces we display publicly cannot emphasize the otherness of these indigenous cultures but should focus on our common bonds as children of man. They have also decided to change our name to the World Museum to better reflect this new vision."

Albert couldn't tell from Marc's neutral tone if he was gladdened or saddened by these developments, but he did have his speech down pat.

"The objects and artifacts you have collected for us in the past are topnotch, each and every one. But the rub of it is that we can't use any of them in our new displays because they accentuate the Asmat's exotic nature."

A wave of panic rolled over Albert. He sat up suddenly and grabbed Marc's arm. "What are you trying to say? Did you destroy my artifacts?"

"No, not at all," Marc reassured as he patted Albert's arm. "The seven crates marked 'Rotterdam' are now in our storage facility. The others were transported to your warehouse. We know you'll get us the rest of our acquisitions once you're strong enough to sort through the remaining crates."

Albert breathed a sigh of relief and released his grip. He'd written 'Museum for Geography and Ethnology Rotterdam' on the sides of the seven largest bis pole crates in the hopes their reputation would reinforce the unnecessity of opening them. He was glad he hadn't marked more of the crates. This was probably the last shipment he would be making. Considering how Kees reacted to Nick's death, he doubted the priest would be willing to assist him in the future.

With trepidation, he asked, "And have your curators already checked the bis poles?" Albert held his breath, his mind already racing to invent a reason for the presence of extra objects.

"No, they haven't. Right now, our priority lies in selecting pieces for the new displays. We did debate destroying or selling some of our Oceania collection in order to free up storage space, but we don't know when the next paradigm shift will occur," Marc continued. "For all I know, the bis poles, paddles, and ancestor statues you've collected will be valuable to future generations. It is clear they will soon be a rare commodity, considering how tightly the colonial authorities and Catholic Church has clamped down on the Asmat's production of religious sculptures and their ritual carving traditions."

Albert nodded along, shocked at this turn of events. The timing was incredible. Thanks to a shift in political thought, his secrets were safe. Though it was unfortunate that he wouldn't be able to access the crates containing Nicholas's possessions, at least not right away. And if the museum wasn't interested in buying more Asmat art, where did that leave him?

"Our new exhibitions should educate visitors about the geography, landscape, and daily life of the ethnic groups populating developing countries."

Albert's forehead creased in concern.

Marc noticed and hurriedly added, "Instead of returning to Kopi, we would like you to consider staying on in Rotterdam to head up the Oceania exhibition project team. With your intimate knowledge of the area and people, you are a natural choice."

"As head curator?" Albert asked, surprised yet pleased.

"Yes." Marc smiled. "There's no point in you returning to collect more artifacts we cannot display. But your anthropological research and photographs can help us create compelling and accurate descriptions of the area as it currently is. You have a knack for presenting the Asmat culture in a way that interests amateurs. I've seen it during your speeches at fundraiser dinners. I've also read all of your articles. Your objective presentation of the Asmat culture and of their daily life is exactly what these new exhibitions need to reflect."

"That's kind of you," Albert preened. He was pleased his long nights spent writing were finally paying off. This turn of events was also the answer to his prayers. Nick's possessions were safe from prying eyes, and he wouldn't have to go back to New Guinea and pretend he didn't know what had happened to the American. He thought briefly on Father Terpstra, hoping he was holding up under the scrutiny. This was the answer to his prayers, too. Their sins were buried—at least for now. Bis poles were desired by collectors and museums because of their connection to headhunting. They were the ultimate symbol of 'the other.' As the head curator, he could easily ensure the objects never saw the light of day, no matter how they may be viewed by future generations.

The land, people, and symbols of progress—he had plenty of information and photos to use as the basis for new displays. If maps and technological advancements were what the people wanted, he could deliver in spades.

He would have liked to have read Nick's journal, but he didn't see that happening in the nearby future. However, his new position made it possible to find a way to get to it, one day. But for now, Nicholas Mayfield's possessions were literally buried under crates of Asmat art. And he would do everything in his power to keep it that way.

"I am deeply honored, Marc. And yes, I gratefully accept your generous offer."

At your service

June 1, 2017

When Jacob's front doorbell rang, Zelda's mouth was full of salami and cheese. She buzzed it open, glad Friedrich made it over before she went to the police station. As soon as she'd arrived at Jacob's apartment, she'd packed up her laptop and a few stray documents she had about Nick Mayfield and Albert Schenk before stopping to make a sandwich. It had already been a long day, and she knew from past experience how much time police interviews could take. She figured officer Roels could wait ten minutes longer.

She opened Jacob's apartment door and returned to the kitchen to finish her lunch. As soon her visitor reached the first-floor landing, Zelda knew something was wrong. The footsteps in the hallway were too heavy to be Friedrich. She threw down her sandwich and ran to the open door. Before she could latch it shut, Albert Schenk burst inside. Zelda flew back, hitting her head on the tiled floor and bruising her shoulder in the process.

"Where is it?" he screamed, his eyes wild as he took in the tiny apartment. He pulled Zelda up by her t-shirt and grabbed her shoulders, shaking her violently. "Where is your proof of my treachery?"

He was strong and so motivated. Despite his age, Zelda didn't stand a chance. "On my smartphone," she cried.

"Show me."

Too scared to lie, Zelda pulled her phone from her back pocket and navigated to the audio file. Before she could delete it, Albert grabbed the phone out of her hands and shoved her away. She let herself fall to the ground, hoping he would get distracted by the recording so she could make a break for the door. Unfortunately, Albert had the same thought. He positioned his body in front of her only exit before pressing play. As he listened to Renee Meerman's accusations, his demeanor became more and more despondent. By the time the recording ended, Albert had looked as if he could weep.

"If only Meerman had kept his promise," he said softly.

"How many pieces did you sell?" Zelda asked from her crouched position on the floor.

"More than you'd believe possible," he said with a flush of pride as he pocketed Zelda's phone.

"Wait, how did you know I would be here, at Jacob's place? Or that I'd found evidence of your smuggling operation? Have you been following me?" Zelda didn't know what he was planning to do to her but figured it was best to keep him talking. Besides, she really didn't understand how Albert had found her so easily.

"Officer Jan Roels at your service." Albert bowed deeply, laughing heartily.

Zelda's face went ashen. "Pepijn is your partner?" she said aloud as the realization hit. How could she be so stupid? It wasn't Gerrit Visser but his son Pepijn who had helped Albert find buyers for his illegally gained artifacts. They must have been working together this whole time. They broke into the Tropenmuseum, stole the journal, killed Janna and her housemate—simply to ensure their sins of the past stay buried. No wonder Pepijn insisted she pick up her laptop. It gave Albert a chance to get rid of her and the transcription. Zelda trembled as she realized, in light of all they'd done, her life was worthless in their eyes.

Albert leaned down, his face close to hers. His breath smelled of coffee. "Never mind that. Where's your copy of the journal?"

"On my laptop in the kitchen."

"No, your printed copy."

"How did you know about that?"

"From your text message to Friedrich."

"I texted him about that two days ago!" Zelda did her best to scowl. "How long have you been following me?"

"Where is it?" Albert demanded.

"In the Tropenmuseum," she responded, surprised he didn't know.

"No, that's not possible. I talked to Marijke Torenbouwer yesterday. If she had it, she would have told me." He sank back against the door.

"I gave it to Marijke two days ago. She swore me to secrecy until they could contact Mayfield's family."

Albert covered his face with his hands. "Have you read it?" he asked, his voice muffled.

"Yes, you don't come off well. Nick knew you were stealing artifacts and smuggling them into the Netherlands," Zelda taunted, enjoying his distress. "Pepijn was helping you sell them, wasn't he? Nick's own friend and confidante. Nick wrote to Pepijn about you—did you know that? Did Pepijn tell you to kill Nick because he was getting too close to discovering your dirty secret?" Pepijn's concern for Nick seemed genuine. Yet, if he was working with Albert, he must know what happened to his friend.

"No! I didn't hurt Nicholas. That wasn't me," Albert cried. "They would have all been destroyed. That's what Nick didn't understand. Pepijn was helping me to preserve the Asmat's artwork for future generations."

"By smuggling them out of the country and selling them to private collectors? It's as if they vanished. You weren't saving them but filling your pockets. Otherwise, you should have given all of the pieces you stole to the museums you collected for!" Zelda argued, allowing her anger to creep back into her voice.

Albert frowned as he shook his head. "Without the proper paper-work, we couldn't sell them legitimately."

"Who was helping you collect the artifacts? A colonial administrator? Maybe a customs official?"

Albert cocked his head, surprised by her questions, before a smug sneer formed on his face. "You're as stubborn as Nicholas was. So he didn't figure out who my supplier was? Thanks for saving me the trouble of reading his journal. Though, after all I've done to destroy every copy of his blasted book, I almost wish he had figured out how I acquired all those artifacts."

Without warning, Albert grabbed a clump of Zelda's long hair and pulled her toward the kitchen. Zelda screamed as she slid across the tiled floor. Once inside, he ripped her backpack open and pulled out her laptop. "Is your transcription on this?"

Zelda nodded.

Albert took her smartphone out of his pocket, threw both devices into her backpack, and then zipped it closed. Smiling down at her, he said, "It won't take much effort to destroy these later."

Zelda's body started to shake. Albert was far too calm.

"If Nicholas couldn't prove his claim, I have nothing to worry about. Except what to do with you." He pulled a pistol out of his coat pocket.

"I emailed the recording I made at Renee's to Marijke Torenbouwer. I'm sure she's shared it with Karin Bakker by now," Zelda lied, hoping it was enough to make Albert pause before acting.

His gun drooped. "What? You are bluffing."

"No, I'm not. I wouldn't be surprised if most of the Dutch museum world has heard that recording by now. You know how fast news travels. It doesn't matter what Nick's letters prove," she stretched the truth, emphasizing the futility of killing her. Her voice sounded more authoritative than she felt.

Albert went white. "No! My reputation, everything I've worked for—my legacy will be destroyed!" A tear rolled down his cheek. "After all I have done to keep our secret safe..." His voice trailed off. She thought he would curl up into a ball and cry, but instead, he straightened up and pointed his gun at her again. "The sins of the past never stay buried, do they?"

Zelda was sure this was it. Her life was about to end. She closed her eyes and whispered her love for her parents as a soft mantra, wanting her head to be filled with thoughts of happiness before it was blown off. He cocked the gun the same second the front doorbell rang.

The noise startled them both. Before either could react, Friedrich's voice wafted up from the story below, barely audible. "Zelda? Are you home?"

Albert blinked away a tear. "I should have left the country straight-away."

As he took aim, Zelda squeezed her eyelids shut. She shrieked as Albert pulled the trigger, yet she felt no pain. When she heard a thud, she opened her eyes to see her captor on the floor, a piece of his jaw and his right eye missing. Once her mind registered the macabre scene, Zelda began screaming hysterically. Only after Friedrich broke down the front door, raced inside, and held her tight, did her anguished sobs lessen.

A DNA match

June 5, 2017

"Are they certain it's Nick Mayfield?" Zelda asked.

"One hundred percent," Bert Reiger said.

Unbeknownst to her, Bert had sent the skull they suspected to be Nick Mayfield's to the Federal Bureau of Investigation in Washington D.C. Luckily, he'd mailed the gruesome package right away, before the Anti-Colonial Brigade—a.k.a. Albert Schenk and Pepijn Visser—broke into the Tropenmuseum's storage unit. Being such a high profile case, the FBI was at first suspicious of his request, but once they heard Bert's reasons for wanting to test the bones for a DNA match, they readily agreed.

Zelda could hardly believe it. Albert Schenk must have killed Nick Mayfield then hidden his body in crates filled by physical anthropologists working in the region. They would probably never know the truth, she realized, unless Albert also kept a journal about his time in Papua. The police had interrogated Pepijn for hours, but he maintained he didn't know what happened to Nick. Though he had admitted that he'd always suspected Albert's involvement in his disappearance.

In the end, it didn't really matter. Though the Mayfields would never know why, at least they had the peace of knowing Nick's remains had finally been found.

Zelda's phone rang, breaking her train of thought. "Hi, are you still in the building?" Marijke Torenbouwer asked, her voice strained.

"Yes."

"We need to drive down to Steyl. Did you have any plans tonight?"

"We?"

"Yes, your presence was specifically requested by Father Terpstra."

"I don't understand."

"Nor do I—not entirely. I'll fill you in during our drive down south."

Sins of the past

June 5, 2017

Though Marijke explained the complex situation to her in the car, Zelda was having trouble coming to terms with the truth. Only once they'd arrived at Steyl, entered the director's office, and she saw Father Terpstra and Viktor Nalong already sitting inside, did Zelda believe all that Marijke had told her.

Both men nodded their greetings as she and Marijke took the two empty seats. Victor glowed with joy, but the priest seemed uncomfortable. Covering most of the director's desk was a large Asmat shield ringed with boars' tusks—the same one she'd fawned over during her last trip—and next to it was a stack of documents.

"We've been waiting for you to arrive," the director of Steyl said as he shook both women's hands. "I've just signed documents which effectively return our Asmat collection to the government of Papua. Considering your role in all of this, we thought you deserved to know why, Ms. Richardson."

Zelda was caught off guard, certain the director was addressing her mentor. "That's kind of you to include me."

"I will allow Father Terpstra to explain everything." The director nodded at the priest before taking a seat behind his desk.

"When local villagers converted to Christianity, part of the process was trading stone implements and religious objects for metal ones," Father Terpstra explained in a strong voice, which seemed to defy his body's age. "It was Church policy to only keep those pieces that were given as gifts and get rid of the rest. After that first bonfire, I wept for days. I couldn't bear to destroy such beauty, yet I couldn't keep the objects, either. There were too many." The priest's voice cracked as he spoke. Zelda understood his dilemma. She didn't think she would be able to purposely destroy so much artwork either, especially when she knew it might never be created again.

"I sometimes went against my orders and helped anthropologists acquire objects for Dutch museums, but I couldn't save them all without raising suspicion."

"Did you help Nicholas Mayfield acquire any pieces? He wrote about several shields and spears you'd helped him negotiate for, but I couldn't find any of them in Harvard's online collection."

"I did," Terpstra replied solemnly. "Peabody Museum deserved to have a few authentic pieces. The carvings and decorations are usually better because they were created to honor someone, not turn a profit. Though we only negotiated for a handful—perhaps twenty in total? Nick wasn't in Kopi long enough for me to set up any more meetings with local carvers. Frankly, it was rather difficult to arrange those sales. By then, most villagers preferred to trade with me."

"Do you know where they ended up? If they aren't in Harvard's collection, where could they have gone?"

"Everything Nick commissioned was collected and shipped back to the Netherlands in one container three months after he disappeared. I know most were destined for Gallery Visser and Harvard's Peabody Museum, yet he did acquire a number of pieces for his personal collection. At least, I remember him saying he was going to keep some of the shields and paddles I helped negotiate for."

"I know Pepijn and Gerrit Visser sorted through the crates and sent the objects Nick collected for Harvard on to America," Zelda said, looking to the priest for confirmation.

"Yes," Terpstra responded slowly, hanging his head as if he knew what she was going to ask next.

"Could they have taken Nick's personal collection and sold them to their clients?"

"I don't know. I only found out Pepijn and Albert were working together after Nick had disappeared." Kees shifted uncomfortably in his chair.

The priest must have confused Zelda's expression of disgust for misunderstanding. "I was Albert's supplier, but I never asked how he got them out of the country or who his clients were. I didn't want to know. My focus was saving the objects from destruction, nothing more. Nick often spoke of his friend Pepijn. I knew he was collecting objects for Gallery Visser, but I never guessed Albert knew Pepijn, as well. In retrospect, I think that's why Albert was so cruel to Nick. He didn't want him getting too close. Though it backfired because his horrid behavior made Nick suspect him of wrongdoing. If he'd been kinder, Nick might not have figured out he was smuggling artifacts."

"I thought you created a museum in Kopi. Why didn't you display the objects there?"

"I tried establishing a museum in the early 1950s, but security proved an insurmountable obstacle. I was away from Kopi too often to be responsible for the artifacts, and without proper security, their presence would have put our village in danger of being raided. I couldn't allow that to happen, either."

Zelda's eyes narrowed. She wondered how hard he tried.

"Albert was a good friend and listener. He understood my position. After returning from a trip to Rotterdam, he told me he'd met several collectors who wanted Asmat artifacts and didn't care how they were acquired. Albert had already worked out how to smuggle them back. I burned the lesser pieces and saved the better ones for Albert. He sold them to his network of private collectors, and we split the profits. Thanks to the monies earned, my mission was one of the best funded on the island," he said, his pride momentarily outweighing his shame.

"When Nick returned to New Guinea in 1962, I was finally getting through to my superiors and making them understand the need for a museum to protect these artworks for future generations. As more villages converted, there were fewer objects to trade for. However, Albert refused to stop. It was too lucrative. Their increasing scarcity drove the prices up to ridiculously high levels. He told me if I didn't forget about the museum in Kopi, he would tell my superiors I was smuggling artifacts with the help of a customs officer he knew. Albert had signed one of his shipping manifests with my name, so it appeared I was transporting extra pieces back to the Netherlands."

"I cannot believe it—Albert Schenk? The man I know could never have done these things." Marijke Torenbouwer looked as if she was about to cry. Zelda knew they had worked together on many projects over the years, and Marijke respected him greatly.

How difficult it must be for her to learn about his dark past, Zelda thought.

The priest was less empathetic. "My reputation would have been ruined, all of my work for naught. So I continued to help him. Nick found Albert's inventory list and figured out what he was doing but not who was helping him acquire the artifacts. When he found me in my meditation hut packing up this shield, he figured out that I was Albert's supplier. I pleaded with him to forget what he had seen, but he was determined to tell his father everything. He figured by embarrassing the Church and colonial authorities, he could somehow force the Dutch government into awarding his family's company a mining contract."

"Blackmail," Zelda said, astonished.

"Yes." He sighed. "I pleaded with Nick, begged him to reconsider. He refused. When he tried to leave, I pushed him back into the room. I never meant to kill him, but he fell onto this shield and bled to death. There was nothing I could do to save him."

Zelda's eyes widened in horror as she stared at the sharp tusks lining the body-length shield. *What a horrible way to die*, she thought. Visions of Janna, Elisabeth, and Albert's bodies immediately filled her thoughts. There was no good way to die.

A sudden realization cleared the horrific images flooding her mind.

"Wait, you killed Nick Mayfield? Not Albert Schenk?" She was certain Albert was the murderer. She'd convinced herself Nick had confronted him in Kopi and things got out of hand. She'd never suspected the priest of being involved in his death.

"Albert helped me prepare the body for transport and hide his journal, but he did not kill him."

Zelda was flabbergasted. She was sure Albert chose to end his life because he was responsible for Nick's death. Yet it was his spotless reputation he feared losing the most.

"I saw Nick's death as punishment for stealing from my brethren. To my shame, I was too weak to tell the truth about his disappearance. I allowed his family to suffer for so long. I even stood by his father when he was in Kopi and accompanied him on several search parties. But my conscience still plagued me. That's why I left New Guinea soon after. I couldn't stay, knowing what I'd done."

She nodded at him tight-lipped, hoping he would finish soon so she could leave this place—and this priest—behind her. All of this deceit, treachery, and ultimately, murder—and for what? A few artifacts? It seemed too absurd for words.

Nick was so young and full of life. He had the wealth, upbringing, and education to accomplish whatever he set his mind to, Zelda thought bitterly. She wanted to howl in frustration. His death was so senseless. All of Kees' and Albert's good deeds were nothing in comparison to the wrong they had done. It all came down to greed, pure and simple.

"I always thought Nick was lying about having proof of our deceit. If only Albert or I had found the photographs inside the journal's cover. All these years, I thought he'd died for nothing. I had no idea he was so close to discovering the truth."

As soon as they were back in the car, Zelda told Marijke everything she knew about Pepijn Visser being Albert's accomplice and about Nick's missing collection.

"I know the police already have Pepijn in custody. Do you know if he admitted to keeping some of Nick's artifacts?" Zelda asked.

After Albert's death, the police found evidence in his house linking him and the art dealer to the Anti-Colonial Brigade and the Human Remains lab robbery. Pepijn Visser was still in jail awaiting a trial date. While sorting through his business papers, the police investigators found proof that Pepijn had been selling illegally acquired antiquities from around the globe for years. Judging from his bank accounts, smuggling seemed to be more lucrative than his gallery. Did working with Albert turn him on to the field? Or was his father already involved and shared his secrets when Pepijn came to work for Gallery Visser?

"From what I've heard, Nick's missing collection hasn't been discussed yet. We'll call the police together when we get back to Amsterdam and let the investigators know what you suspect," Marijke said. "I have a feeling Pepijn wouldn't have sold them all if he did indeed keep Nick's artifacts. Wouldn't that be a kick to find his missing collection, as well?"

Zelda grinned conspiratorially. That would be pretty incredible, she thought.

Sculptures from the Rainforest

September 29, 2017

Zelda stood in a forest of bis poles. Spotlights projected their menacing shadows onto the green cloth enclosing the Tropenmuseum's
Light Hall. The music of Asmat drummers played on a loop. Their
monotonous yet melodious rhythm transported her to another world.
Jungle birds hooted and cawed, interspersed with the sounds of
lapping water and soft chanting. All that was missing was the smell
of burning fires.

It was magnificent.

Zelda sat on a bench and soaked up the sights and sounds, imagining
she was in Papua. When a tour group entered the enclosed space, the
spell was broken. She exited the green forest and walked through
the displays built around the Light Hall. The photographs and films
she'd found in archives spread across the Netherlands filled the cases
before her. Her first real contribution to a museum exhibition was
now a fact.

She stopped at the glass-enclosed case housing Nick Mayfield's
journal and belt buckle. Enlarged on one wall was the photograph
of Nick, Kees, and Albert that she'd found in his journal. It had been
cropped to exclude the two men who'd effectively robbed him of his
life. It was strange to see him so full of energy, knowing he would be
dead weeks later.

The police found Nick's journal on Albert's nightstand next to his
bed. On his computer were the digital photographs Zelda had taken.

They'd been stolen for him by a hacker he'd paid royally to corrupt the Tropenmuseum's servers and spy electronically on everyone involved with the Bis Poles exhibition.

Zelda started to tear up as she read the text inside Nick's display, describing his life, passion for anthropology, and his once-missing Asmat collection. She turned away, refusing to let the tragedy of his death mar the pride she felt. Instead, she admired his artifacts. Pepijn did indeed keep several for himself. The Mayfields allowed Nick's collection to be displayed in the exhibition. The paddle Zelda admired in Pepijn's stairwell now hung from fishing line, suspended in the air so visitors could walk around it and view both sides of the intricate carving. The rest of his collection was as exquisite. *There was no question that Nick Mayfield had excellent taste*, Zelda thought.

The early reviews of the exhibition were extraordinary. It was wonderful to see young and old wandering through the forest of poles while learning more about physical anthropology, Catholic missionaries, the Dutch colonial government, and Nicholas Mayfield.

Albert Schenk and Kees Terpstra were not mentioned by name. It was a condition of the Mayfields that his killers not be a part of the exhibition. Not that it mattered what the museums did. Kees and Albert's roles as smugglers and sellers of illegally acquired artifacts had been covered extensively in both the Dutch and international press for months.

In a misguided way, they were trying to save Asmat art for future generations, Zelda thought. If only Kees Terpstra had founded his museum earlier or convinced the Church that their policy was wrong. Nick Mayfield would probably still be alive, and both Albert and Kees would, instead, be remembered for their positive contributions to New Guinea.

She slowly wound her way to the end of the exhibition, glancing at the credits as she walked past. Twelve exhibition collection researchers were listed, though her eye caught on her own. Zelda stopped in her tracks, a swell of pride growing as she realized what this meant. Interns were never mentioned in an exhibition's credits. Marijke warned her of that long ago. She fumbled for her phone, quickly snapping a flash-less photo before any of the museum's security guards saw her.

Footsteps closing in fast from behind caused her to snap her phone shut and to shove it in her pocket before turning around.

"Zelda, here you are," Marijke said, out of breath. "Did you forget our appointment?"

"What? Oh no. Is it four already?" Zelda blushed as she checked her watch and saw it was already fifteen minutes after four. "I'm so sorry. I didn't have a chance to see the whole exhibition last night. The opening was so busy."

Marijke chuckled. "Did you see it?" She jerked her head toward the credits.

Zelda nodded, blushing.

"It was Karin Bakker's idea. We figured after all you've been through, you deserve official credit."

Zelda's own role had been kept from the press, thankfully. Only a few reporters had been by Jacob's house, the address police reports listed as the location of Albert Schenk's death. It had been easy enough to pretend she didn't know why they were there.

"The opening went well last night. Even the Mayfields seemed to enjoy themselves."

All eight of Nick's brothers and several cousins had attended. Theodore Mayfield had even unveiled the display dedicated to his older brother for the press.

"Now, are you ready for your exit interview? I have to leave in thirty minutes. That should be enough time to fill out the official paperwork."

"Sure, no problem." Today was the last day of her internship. Technically, this marked the end of her museum studies program, as well. All that was left to do was to write her master's thesis. Six months was more than enough time to figure that project out.

Zelda gazed up at the forest of bis poles, smiling as she followed Marijke up to her office.

One adventure was about to end, she thought, though another would soon begin.

Zelda was sure of it.

THE END

Thank you for reading my novel!
Reviews really do help readers decide whether they want to take a chance on a new author. If you enjoyed this story, please do leave a review on BookBub, Goodreads, Facebook, or with your favorite retailer.
I really appreciate it! Jennifer S. Alderson

Reading Group Questions

The author switches between two distinct periods of time when telling this story. How did this affect your reading and appreciation of the book? Could the present-day portion of this story have taken place in another European city or is it unique to the Netherlands? And the historical part—could it have taken place in another country?

Were you drawn into the mystery aspect of this novel? Did you figure it out before Zelda did? If so, at what point did you begin to piece together what really happened? If not, which of the many red herrings spread throughout the novel tripped you up?

What do you think of Nicholas Mayfield? Can you understand his desire to impress his father? Does his deaf ear and his inability to serve in the military justify his often horrid behavior?

Can you understand why Albert Schenk was involved in illegal activities? Or do you think he was a fool for risking his career? If you had the opportunity to do something similar, knowing there would be little to no risk, would you consider doing it?

Do you sympathize with Father Terpstra's dilemma concerning the burning of artifacts? Would you have done the same to save them? Or would you have tried to find another solution? What might that be?

Mission Museum Steyl has a fascinating collection. However, I shared

Zelda's discomfort when viewing the human skulls. This museum is not unique. Many anthropology and ethnography museums exhibit human remains. Do you agree that they may be displayed? Or do you think they should be removed from public displays out of respect for the dead? Why or why not?

Acknowledgments

I am deeply indebted to my husband and my mother for their support and encouragement while writing, researching, and editing this novel. My son also deserves a big kiss for putting up with me writing another book.

I am forever grateful to my beta readers Philip, Cherie, and Janice for their constructive criticism. My editors, Rogena Mitchell-Jones and Colleen Snibson, also deserve a huge round of applause for helping make this novel shine.

This story was directly inspired by collection research I conducted in 2008 for the Tropenmuseum, an anthropological museum in Amsterdam. Just as Zelda in this novel, I was tasked with finding audiovisual material suitable for the upcoming *Bisj Poles: Sculptures from the Rain Forest* exhibition, though, technically, I was no longer an intern but a temporary collection researcher.

Journals, travel diaries, and administrative reports written by anthropologists, surveyors, colonial officers, and missionaries working in the region between 1930 and 1963 informed my descriptions of Dutch New Guinea in the 1960s. It is perhaps important to note that I cannot find the names of several villages referred to in these journals on modern maps.

The village of Kopi is my own creation, based on films and journal descriptions of the villages and settlements located on the Lorentz River in the 1940s through 1960s.

Both restitution cases mentioned in this novel—of human remains and the Asmat artifacts housed in Steyl—were created by me. At the time of writing, no claims have been made on any Asmat artifacts in publicly held Dutch collections. Though Steyl does have a fine Asmat collection—which I accurately describe in this novel—Hendrik Groosman is a figment of my imagination. I've not had the pleasure of meeting any of the curatorial staff of the Mission Museum in Steyl. The Human Remains lab, its working methods, and Jacob's database are all my creations, as are the curators and staff of the actual Dutch museums mentioned in this novel.

For more information about bis poles, Asmat culture, missionaries active in Dutch New Guinea, and Dutch museums' collection policies, I highly recommend the book, *Bisj Poles: Sculptures from the Rain Forest* by Pauline van der Zee, for both the collection of essays and extensive literary sources listed in the bibliography. I am not impartial. During my internship and time as collection researcher for the Tropenmuseum, I helped edit and research sections of this book, which also served as the official Bisj Poles exhibition guide. In the Netherlands, the English spelling of the Asmat's headhunting ritual is *bisj*. However, in most other countries, it is spelled *bis*, which is why I chose to use this version in my novel.

The literary sources and archival documents I relied on while writing this book can be found in these amazing libraries, archives, cultural organizations, museums, and websites: Tropenmuseum Photography Collection and Library, University of Amsterdam Library and Special Collections, National Museum of Ethnology in Leiden, Rotterdam Wereldmuseum, Royal National Library in Den Haag, National Audiovisual Archives (Beeld en Geluid) in Hilversum, Mission Museum Steyl, Museum Bronbeek, Erfgoed Papua Nederland, Smithsonian Museum in Washington D.C., Harvard's Peabody Museum of Archeology and Ethnology, and the Amsterdam City Archives.

The complex problems inherent to restitution, missionaries' roles in developing countries, and cultural inequalities in museums had to be simplified in order to move the story forward. One of those instances is the Church's policies regarding Asmat art. Though my archival research shows their objective to wipe out headhunting is crystal clear, it seems missionaries working in the region were split about the artwork. Some gladly destroyed stone implements and ritual artifacts associated with the bis ceremony. Others pleaded for its survival, going as far as documenting in scientific journals the traditional carvings and techniques used, as well as founding mini-museums in the region to help preserve the finer examples for future generations.

The renown Dutch missionary Gerard Zegwaard was most definitely the latter. Zegwaard is well known for his appreciation of Asmat art and his role as its protector. In 1953, he established the first mission post in Agats, New Guinea. His work and ability to connect with the Asmat helped pave the way for other churches to establish missions in the area. I've used several articles he'd written as source material for this book. The most enlightening is a Dutch-language piece entitled 'Missionarissen en menseneters' (translated: 'Missionaries and Cannibals'), which is comprised of journal entries he wrote while working in the Asmat region. In them, he describes his work as a priest, the social structures within a village, daily life in Asmat, and many details regarding local customs. The intricacies of headhunting raids are also described, including a gruesome passage describing how their victims were beheaded by the women—yes, the women—then dismembered by the men. [Zegwaard, G.A. en G. Offenberg, 'Missionarissen menseneters', in: Spiegel Historiael, 31(1996), nr. 7-8, p. 286-291]

In many ways, his early successes and passion for Asmat culture served as the model for my fictitious Kees Terpstra. However, I have found absolutely no documentation suggesting Zegwaard stole a single feather from the Asmat, people he clearly admired and respected.

And now, the elephant in the room. Nicholas Mayfield is NOT a fictionalized version of Michael Rockefeller. Yes, Rockefeller really did disappear in 1961 while on a collecting trip in Dutch New Guinea, as did several other explorers and anthropologists throughout the 1930s to the present day. However, this book is not my theory about his death—far from it! My intention was to explore the world of artifact smuggling through fiction. My research for the Bis Poles exhibition solidified my choice of Dutch New Guinea as the setting.

With that said, I have found several documents written at the time stating Rockefeller did offer too much for artifacts. There are instances recorded in the colonial documentation of Asmat villagers asking permission to go on one headhunting raid so they could make a fortune by selling the skulls to Rockefeller. He was by no means unique. Anthropologists, colonial government officials, surveyors, missionary workers, and adventurers from several nations have all been accused of or admitted to having stolen ritual or culturally significant objects from Asmat villages. Many of these thefts resulted in tribal wars and headhunting raids.

One example is Carel Groenevelt, a professional collector who acquired thousands of Asmat artifacts for Dutch museums, including fifty of the seventy-five poles in the Netherlands. Father Zegwaard sometimes acted as a middleman, helping him make contact with the Asmat in order to barter for their artwork. Groenevelt later admitted to finding poles on the ground in 1953 and taking them—without asking permission from or paying the locals who carved them. All of the artifacts he collected are still part of these museums' collections. As far as I know, none have been returned to Papua, nor have requests for restitution been submitted.

At the same time, when we were preparing the Bis Poles exhibition, the Tropenmuseum was wrestling with an extensive collection of human remains, many of which were collected in the 1930s through the 1960s in Dutch New Guinea. As described in my book, crates of unidentified bones were found in the Academic Medical Center's basement after a series of water leaks flooded their atomic bomb shelter. They were moved to the hospital in 1973 when anatomical museum Vrolik was being remodeled and forgotten about.

After they were rediscovered, the Tropenmuseum agreed to sort through them. The museum's staff worked for six years sorting and documenting this collection of human remains. Yet once they'd determined where they came from, the museum ran into an unexpected problem. In contrast to my book, there were no claims laid on any of these remains—in fact, no one wanted them. The question became how to dispose of the bones ethically.

The only remains that may one day be claimed are a collection of 1,225 bones taken from a single gravesite in New Guinea. They were collected by a government doctor named Van der Hoeven. He was an SS'er found guilty by a Dutch court of collaborating with the Nazis. Given a choice between jail time and working as a doctor in Dutch New Guinea, he chose the latter. He also sent back the remains of Japanese prisoners of war he'd dug up on the island, labeled as 'Asmat.' Though the documentation Van der Hoeven kept proves they were taken from the island of Biak, no official claim has been submitted for their restitution.

These facts provided the context; the rest of the story and specific characters involved are pure fiction.

The debate around the aesthetic value of an ethnic artifact versus its cultural or ritual significance, as well the context in which these objects should be displayed, is as old as the ethnographic and anthropological museums themselves. For the purposes of this fast-paced novel, I've simplified many of the subtler points and arguments. I hope, dear readers, that you'll forgive my artistic license. This is, after all, a work of fiction.

I'm sorry to see the Tropenmuseum succumbed to subsidy cuts in 2011. Several of their exhibitions have been gutted, and their vast and wonderful collections of books and objects are now spread among cultural institutions across the country. Luckily, the Oceania and Colonial History exhibitions still stand. Though the museum remains open, it is now part of a larger network of ethnographic museums in the Netherlands and no longer has its own staff of dedicated curators and collection researchers.

Because the Tropenmuseum and its exhibitions are still in transition, I chose to describe their collections as they were in 2008 when I briefly worked for this incredible institution. Whatever displays are currently filling their massive exhibition halls, it is certainly worth a visit when in Amsterdam—if only to see the monumental building.

My thanks to the Bis Poles exhibition project group—made up of many wonderful staff members of the Tropenmuseum in Amsterdam, Rotterdam's Wereldmuseum and the National Museum of Ethnology in Leiden—for making me feel like part of the team.

Although I have done my utmost to ensure all of the historical facts, events, policies, and attitudes described within this book are accurate, any factual errors that remain are solely my responsibility.

My deepest apologies to all those named Petunia. It is a lovely name, but I had to make a choice.

Happy reading!

About the Author

Jennifer S. Alderson was born in San Francisco, raised in Seattle, and currently lives in Amsterdam. After traveling extensively around Asia, Oceania, and Central America, she moved to Darwin, Australia, before finally settling in the Netherlands. Her background in journalism, multimedia development, and art history enriches her novels. When not writing, she can be found in a museum, biking around Amsterdam, or enjoying a coffee along the canal while planning her next research trip.

Jennifer's love of travel, art, and culture inspires her award-winning, internationally oriented mystery series—the Zelda Richardson Mystery Series—and standalone stories.

The Lover's Portrait (Book One) is a suspenseful whodunit about Nazi-looted artwork that transports readers to WWII and present-day Amsterdam. Art, religion, and anthropology collide in *Rituals of the Dead* (Book Two), a thrilling artifact mystery set in Papua and the Netherlands. Her pulse-pounding adventure set in the Netherlands, Croatia, Italy, and Turkey—*Marked for Revenge* (Book Three)—is a story about stolen art, the mafia, and a father's vengeance.

She is also the author of two adventure thrillers: *Down and Out in Kathmandu* and *Holiday Gone Wrong*. Her travelogue, *Notes of a Naive Traveler*, is a must read for those interested in traveling to Nepal and Thailand.

Visit Jennifer's website now to sign up for her newsletter, follow her on social media, and learn more about her novels: www.JenniferSAlderson.com

The Lover's Portrait: An Art Mystery

A portrait holds the key to recovering a cache of looted artwork, secreted away during World War II, in this captivating historical art thriller set in the 1940s and present-day Amsterdam.

When a Dutch art dealer hides the stock from his gallery—rather than turn it over to his Nazi blackmailer—he pays with his life, leaving a treasure trove of modern masterpieces buried somewhere in Amsterdam, presumably lost forever. That is until American art history student Zelda Richardson sticks her nose in.

After studying for a year in the Netherlands, Zelda scores an internship at the prestigious Amsterdam Historical Museum where she works on an exhibition of paintings and sculptures once stolen by the Nazis, lying unclaimed in Dutch museum depots almost seventy years later.

When two women claim the same painting, the portrait of a young girl titled *Irises*, Zelda is tasked with investigating the painting's history and soon finds evidence that one of the two women must be lying about her past. Before she can figure out which one and why, Zelda learns about the Dutch art dealer's concealed collection—and that *Irises* is the key to finding it.

Her discoveries make her a target of someone willing to steal—and even kill—to find the missing paintings. As the list of suspects grows, Zelda realizes she has to track down the lost collection and unmask a killer if she wants to survive.

The Lover's Portrait: Chapter One

June 26, 1942

Just two more crates, then our work is finally done, Arjan reminded himself as he bent down to grasp the thick twine handles, his back muscles already yelping in protest. Drops of sweat were burning his eyes, blurring his vision. "You can do this," he said softly, heaving the heavy oak box upward with an audible grunt.

Philip nodded once, then did the same. Together, they lugged their loads across the moonlit room, down the metal stairs, and into the cool subterranean space below. After hoisting the last two crates onto a stack close to the ladder, Arjan smiled in satisfaction, slapping Philip on the back as he regarded their work. One hundred and fifty-two crates holding his most treasured objects and those of so many of his friends were finally safe. Relief briefly overcame the panic and dread he'd been feeling for longer than he could remember. Preparing the space and artwork had taken more time than he'd hoped it would, but they'd done it. Now he could leave Amsterdam knowing he'd stayed true to his word. Arjan glanced over at Philip, glad that he'd trusted him.

He stretched out a hand toward the older man. "They fit perfectly."

Philip answered with a hasty handshake and a tight smile before nodding toward the ladder. "Shall we?"

He is right, Arjan thought, *there is still so much to do.*

They climbed back up into the small shed and closed the heavy metal lid, careful to cushion its fall. They didn't want to give the neighbors an excuse to call the Gestapo. Not when they were so close

269

to being finished.

Philip picked up a shovel and scooped sand onto the floor, letting Arjan rake it out evenly before adding more. When the sand was an inch thick, they shifted the first layer of heavy cement tiles into place, careful to fit them snug up against each other.

As they heaved and pushed, Arjan allowed himself to think about the future for the first time in weeks. Hiding the artwork was only the first step; he still had a long road to go before he could stop looking over his shoulder. First, back to his place to collect their suitcases. Then a short walk to Central Station where second-class train tickets to Venlo were waiting. Finally, a taxi ride to the Belgian border where his contact would provide him with falsified travel documents and a chauffeur-driven Mercedes-Benz. The five Rembrandt etchings in his suitcase would guarantee safe passage to Switzerland. From Geneva, he should be able to make his way through the demilitarized zone to Lyon, then down to Marseilles. All he had to do was keep a few steps ahead of Oswald Drechsler.

Just thinking about the hawk-nosed Nazi made him work faster. So far, he'd been able to clear out his house and storage spaces without Drechsler noticing. Their last load, the canvases stowed in his gallery, was the riskiest, but he'd had no choice. His friends trusted him—no, counted on him to keep their treasures safe. He couldn't let them down now, not after all he'd done wrong.

* * *

Marked for Revenge: An Art Heist Thriller

An adrenaline-fueled adventure set in the Netherlands, Croatia, Italy, and Turkey about stolen art, the mafia, and a father's vengeance.

When researcher Zelda Richardson begins working at a local museum, she doesn't expect to get entangled with an art theft, knocked unconscious by a forger, threatened by the mob, or stalked by drug dealers.

To make matters worse, a Croatian gangster is convinced Zelda knows where a cache of recently pilfered paintings is. She must track down an international gang of art thieves and recover the stolen artwork in order to save those she loves most.

The trouble is, Zelda doesn't know where to look. Teaming up with art detective Vincent de Graaf may be her only hope at salvation.

The trail of clues leads Zelda and Vincent on a pulse-pounding race across Europe to a dramatic showdown in Turkey that may cost them their lives.

Available as paperback, audiobook, and eBook.

Marked for Revenge: Chapter One

Marko Antic softly hummed the Dutch national anthem as he cut another watercolor from Vianden Castle's cold stone wall. As the gilded frame dropped into his free hand, he automatically looked to the life-sized portrait of William II hanging at the opposite end of the narrow room, almost sensing the Dutch king's disapproval.

"Will you stop already," his partner-in-crime whispered.

Marko ceased mid-chorus, the last bar of 'Het Wilhelmus' hanging eerily in the air. He opened his mouth to reprehend Rikard for being such a killjoy when he realized his friend was right. Although the Turret Room was at the back of an unoccupied medieval castle—and the sole security guard had already completed his rounds—they'd do better to be prudent.

Marko slipped the painting into a padded canvas bag, careful not to put unnecessary pressure on the other two watercolors he'd already plundered from the castle's walls. He looked to his friend and saw Rikard was placing the tenth and final painting into his bag. As soon as all of the watercolors were secure, it was time to complete this job. Marko sucked in his breath, excited yet nervous about their exit, inspired by the castle's extraordinary location.

Vianden Castle seemed to grow out of a rocky promontory jutting out into the Our Valley. It was the jewel crowning the tiny village of Vianden—literally. The town's homes, businesses, and church were carved into the steep ridge, covered in a thick blanket of tall trees. A single road led up to the castle at the top.

At first, Marko and Rikard were overwhelmed by the castle's position and the seemingly insurmountably high stone wall built around it. Once inside, they were pleasantly surprised by how easily looks could deceive. The castle itself was the main tourist attraction, and that was impossible to steal. Cameras were trained on the main entrances and exits but were not hung up in each room. During their tour, Marko realized why. Only a few inexpensive pieces of art were permanently displayed, and none appeared to be hooked up to an alarm. But then, his trained eye told him, they weren't worth more than a few thousand euros, thus probably not worth insuring. The only additional measure taken to secure the temporary exhibition of watercolors they'd just stolen from, was a single camera pointed at the entrance to the Turret Room. One that Marko had covered up with tape before they'd entered the space.

Breaking in had been incredibly easy. Because the castle's entrance was literally at the end of the road, there was little chance of a random passerby seeing them return at two in the morning. Marko and Rikard used rappelling hooks to climb over the wide stone wall surrounding the castle and were inside in a matter of seconds. Thanks to the waning moon, they didn't have to look hard to find shadows to climb up in. Getting out would entail a different route entirely.

Marko triple-checked his canvas bags before glancing over to see Rikard doing the same. The burglars locked eyes and nodded, then rose and crossed the darkened stone floor.

A door on the left side of the Turret Room led to a wide balcony extending far out over the valley below. As soon as Rikard opened it, a strong wind blew inside, chilling Marko to the bone.

Both men dragged the bags of artwork out onto the balcony then closed the door firmly behind them. Marko knew from their previous visit that the views from here were breathtaking. Because the balcony extended a few feet out over the abyss, visitors could see for miles up and down the valley. Now, a swath of blacks and grays met their eye. The Our river was invisible. A handful of lights—presumably from homes—sparkled through the dense foliage of this sparsely populated region.

Before looting the Turret Room, they had placed two large tote bags onto the balcony. Marko opened one and took out a harness shaped like a padded chair. He slipped it over his back and quickly strapped himself in, then using a series of bungee cords and carabiners, he secured a crate of artwork to each side. The extra-thick padding should cushion any jarring, and both Marko and Rikard were skilled enough to land softly. Their job depended on it. Once satisfied, he slipped on night-vision goggles, buckled on his helmet, then picked up a small nylon sack with two lines hanging out of it. Marko hooked them into the specially-built loops hanging from his chest. He yanked on each, ensuring they were secure before unfurling the nylon wing. The soft fabric billowed up and out above him. Marko turned on a flashing red beacon attached to his chest and stepped out onto the wide stone railing. The strong winds tugged on the nylon, pulling him forward.

The balcony wasn't large enough for both to jump simultaneously, but Marko could see that Rikard was almost ready. Pulling tight on the controls, Marko waited until his friend had his own wing clipped in properly. As soon as Rikard gave him the thumbs up, Marco released the hand brakes and stepped off the ledge, giving in to the wind's desire. Marko's heart raced as his stomach dropped away. For a brief moment, he was plunging toward the earth. Seconds later, his chute grabbed an upward draft and raced up the ridge, jerking him high above the treetops. A smile split his face; he loved the rush. He used his hand grips and weight to control his lateral movements, slowly maneuvering himself away from the tree-covered ridge and back above the river, his night-vision goggles helping him orient.

A minute later, he heard the whooshing sound of another chute catching the wind. He turned his head back toward the castle and searched until he could see his friend's red beacon flashing. Marko's grin intensified when he noticed there were no lights visible inside the castle. The robbery probably wouldn't be detected until the morning.

Marko relaxed the tension on his hand grips, allowing his wing to race down the valley, relishing the brief moment of freedom. He couldn't believe his luck. Marko had always loved his work, but since he began working for his uncle a year ago, his job satisfaction had increased significantly. Thanks to years of stealing paintings and antiques from private homes, Marko had developed a real eye for quality. The mental thrill of creating a devious plan and seeing it through was a real adrenaline kick, but getting rid of these illicitly gained goods was always such a pain. There was so much risk involved. More and more of his associates had been tripped up by selling them to undercover cops. And when Marko did find a trustworthy buyer, they offered very little payout.

He always knew he could count on his family if he ever got into real trouble, but he had enjoyed following his own path. That is until several of his friends were arrested during a recent sting operation. When his uncle Luka offered to take care of all of that hassle, Marko couldn't refuse. And his uncle did pay top dollar, more than he'd been able to organize on his own. From time to time, Luka even supplied him with an interesting theft, to boot. There was no shortage of greedy people willing to pay anything to acquire what they wanted, especially when the object of their desire was completely out of reach even to people of their financial stature.

He kicked his legs around, reveling in the liberating feeling of flying. Too soon, he made out a set of headlights blinking in the distance. Marko adjusted his direction and relaxed into the harness, determined to enjoy the rest of his short flight.

He looked up to the moon and turned his face into the wind, letting it whip across his face. God, how he loved his job.

* * *